Kicker

Kicker

A Novel

Matt Brown

Copyright © 2010 by Matt Brown.

ISBN: Softcover   978-1-4568-0389-6
           Ebook   978-1-4568-0390-2

All rights reserved. No part of this book may be reproduced or transmitted in any form or by any means, electronic or mechanical, including photocopying, recording, or by any information storage and retrieval system, without permission in writing from the copyright owner.

This is a work of fiction. Names, characters, places and incidents either are the product of the author's imagination or are used fictitiously, and any resemblance to any actual persons, living or dead, events, or locales is entirely coincidental.

This book was printed in the United States of America.

To order additional copies of this book, contact:
Xlibris Corporation
1-888-795-4274
www.Xlibris.com
Orders@Xlibris.com
82964

1

*All men should strive to learn before they die
what they are running from, and to, and why.
~ James Thurber*

Some blokes just can't run that fast. It's not our fault; it's just our makeup. What they ought to do is line all the lads up in the gymnasium and run them forty yards. Then take all but the top one or two aside and tell them, "Look fellas, by all means, keep playing football. It'll make you better fans. But you're not going to be major league footballers. So forget all the bloody underdog stories. They're only setting you up for heartache. You're not bloody fast enough and that's final. Now bugger off so we can work with the lads with some potential." Then they could take their whittled down group a few years later and line them up on a wall, telling them, "Alright lads, all of you shorter than the red line, bugger off. You're too bloody short. And any of you shorter than the black line can stay, but with the understanding that at some point you'll likely be cut from a team just because you're too bloody short too. But stick around for now because we need bodies to run a decent practice with the real players."

Perhaps I'm a bit jaded. But I'm also a realist. I've seen what happens to the castoffs who believe for too long that they'll be the exception. They forsake their schooling, scoffing at the authorities who, at the end of the day, were just trying to save them.

I was an exception. When it was clear that I was too slow, I was relegated to keeper. And I was good. Very good. I could sense where shooters would go, read their movements, anticipate where the shot would come from, when, how hard, and then I'd time my movements perfectly to get in the way. I was, as they say, a natural. But alas nature had the last laugh. At fourteen, I stopped growing, cursed to remain 5'9 for the rest of my natural life . . . until I get old enough to start shrinking of course. And if you've watched professional soccer, you *know that the keepers are all about six and a half feet tall, with wingspans like pterodactyls. The ones who aren't are still six feet with arms like orangutans, or like those dolls that you can stretch. Only you've stretched them so far they won't regain their original shape. I forget what they're called.*

At any rate, the one thing I could do better than anyone else was kick the ball.

February in Liverpool is gray, damp, and cold. Although the city has evolved and become more metropolitan, it remains, at its heart, blue collar and tough. To Mickey Doyle, it was simply home. Baptized Michael Shannon Doyle, he was a proud Liverpudlian, or 'Scouser' to the locals. The weather, the smell down by the docks, the narrow streets, and the crowded pubs were like comfort food to Mickey.

Mickey's father had come from Ireland at fifteen, proud and feisty. For all that Liverpool had become, 'Ole Shannon Doyle' or 'Shanty' as he was known, wore its history on his face. Weathered, scarred, and graced with a charmingly crooked smile. He worked the shipyards, and he was the shipyards. He sought nothing that he couldn't receive from his work, his wife, his children, and of course, the Muddy Anchor Pub. Both father and son were lean and strong, hair as wild and dark as the winter sea.

But for all the physical similarities with his father, Mickey was, in mind, very much his mother's boy. Elizabeth Wells was a local girl who had fallen for Shanty's smile, his honesty, and perhaps most of all, his simplicity. The daughter of a University professor and a nurse, she was sharp as a blade. Despite her acceptance to Cambridge University, she opted for the University of Liverpool to stay close to her Shanty. After five years and the arrival of two young daughters, she completed her degree and began teaching at a local primary school. The folks in their neighbourhood respected Elizabeth the same way they adored Ole Shanty, as evidenced by the fact that in over fifty years, she had not become Liz, Lizzie, Beth, or Betty. She was to all, and would always be Elizabeth, or the beloved Mrs. Doyle.

Mickey had inherited the best of both. Like his mother, he valued knowledge, not as a stepping stone to better things, but rather as a virtue by its own right. To live well was to understand the world around you. And by this criterion, Mickey lived *very* well. He was inquisitive and well read: in philosophy, psychology, science, and literature. But to everyone's surprise, save perhaps his parents, Mickey spurned his many opportunities in formal education to pursue his greatest passion: football.

To Mickey, the principles of physics, biology, and mathematics informed the sciences of training, kicking technique, goaltending and injury rehabilitation. The fields of philosophy, psychology, sociology, and history could be applied directly to game preparation, motivation, player development, how best to help his teammates, how to outsmart opponents, and how to approach the game tactically.

But for all his knowledge, Mickey's common touch was as prominent as his father's. He liked people almost as much as he liked soccer. And his quick wit and playfulness disarmed and delighted the people around him, save those who found themselves on the receiving end of his sarcasm if he was frustrated, tired, or too full of alcohol (not an infrequent occurrence). But even then, most would agree that the target of his jabs had usually done something to deserve it.

One would have expected someone as blessed as Mickey to be very much at peace. But alas, the one thing he couldn't have consumed his thoughts daily. And the ache was fueled by the observation that the most deserving only occasionally inherited the ultimate gifts.

I don't dislike Rodney Banks because he's talented or occupies a roster spot that I or any of my mates would kill for; I dislike him because he's a wanker. Plain and simple. He's lazy, stupid, arrogant, and, worst of all, spoiled bloody rotten. How can you chalk up to jealousy my contempt for a man who asked if Tony Blair was a midfielder for Chelsey? Or who claims that the bubbles in his cola make him run fast? Or that, this is classic, thought that our first division club would benefit greatly from a trade for Al Qaeda! In fairness, Allen Clyde is a brilliant defender for the Celtics, but you get my point.

Alright . . . I admit, I'm jealous of the gifts that Rodney possesses, but the real aggravation is the fact that he's never done anything to deserve them, and most certainly has never demonstrated that he respects or appreciates them. And he is bloody gifted. He can run like a cheetah, and with an ounce of hard work, could become one of the greatest natural goal-scorers the game has ever seen. But that potential will go untapped because he has no inclination to work hard or really learn the game, and he uses his consistent top-15 scoring rank as a reason to change nothing and listen to no one.

Truth be told, it bothers me that it was Rodney who was so instrumental in the event that would alter the course of my life dramatically. Wanker.

It was meant as a joke. It was two days after Superbowl Sunday, and Sergio Mendes, the Liverpool Premier Division defender, brought an

American football to practice. A field full of world-class athletes looked uncharacteristically awkward flinging the 'pigskin' around their practice field, and even more so trying to catch it. By the time Mickey and the third division team were making their way onto the field, the premier players had abandoned their game of catch for a more comfortable, but still comical, competition of kicking the odd-shaped ball over the net. A Eurosport cameraman, setting up for a post-practice interview with head coach, Jurgen Jannsens, turned the camera on the spectacle. Players laughed as each other would shank the football to the left or right, and they celebrated with every successful stroke of the ball. Ever the antagonist, Rodney Banks honed in on the third division keeper.

"Hey, Doyle! Have a lash. You're still looking for a sport, aren't you?" Banks poked.

"Piss off," Mickey mumbled. Then in a face-saving recovery, "Has anyone explained to Banks that the Superbowl is not the same as a wok?"

The players of both teams chuckled at the cut, then awaited an inevitable retaliation from Banks.

"Right then, tosser, let's see you have a go? Fifty pounds says you can't put it over from here," Banks replied, pinning the ball about forty yards from the net.

Mickey had never seen an American football up close, much less kicked one. But the chance to stick it to Banks was irresistible, regardless of the potential cost. The cheers and laughter swelled again as Mickey lined up to attempt the kick. Harold Sheffield, who had found the feel for kicking the ball as well as any of the others, whispered from nearby.

"Almost in the middle, Mick. Under it a little. Otherwise pretty much the same."

Even with a couple extra stutter steps, Mickey contacted the ball almost perfectly, sending it safely over the net, almost dead center. The players teased and patted their irate striker, rustling his hair and, clearly, his feathers.

"Shit luck!" Banks protested, "double or nothing!"

"Sure, Rodney, and move it back 10," Mickey added, in spite of himself.

Slightly to the right, but still comfortably over.

By the time the players relented, Banks was down 200 pounds, and Mickey had gone 5 for 8, including a complete shank, and a spectacular near-miss of almost seventy yards (wide but not short). The first-division team made their way off the field, still buzzing, while the third division squad went about their warm-up. A delighted Eurosport camera man forgot his Jannsens interview, and headed back to the studio with his prize.

I like being around the lads on the Premier Division team. Not because they're so good, but rather because most of them view the game with the same reverence that I do. The Rodney Banks-type is really an exception. Most of his teammates are nearly as gifted as he is, but also exhibit equal amounts of character in the way they prepare for and play the game.

Second division is a mix of the young lions and the veteran 'almost's, even the oldest of which cling to the possibility of a call-up, should they get on a roll at the same time as an injury. It's a bit like the slots, I reckon; it hardly ever happens, but happens just enough to keep them playing, and believing the next lucky one will be them.

The third division is quite an interesting stew. You've got the talented-but-mental-weaklings, the under-talented-mental-ironmen, and virtually everything else in between. But for most, the writing has been on the wall for some time, and their spirits are either broken or bent on why their place with the club is someone else's fault. So in many cases, they're just going through the motions, plugging through the daily task of accepting that they may be as far up the mountain as their legs or wills will carry them.

The talented underachievers are viewed as the most tragic. For some reason, the talented that fail to develop drive, intelligence, or resilience are declared the poorest souls of all. "What a terrible waste of talent" they say. Whereas the physically mediocre who have gotten to that level through hard work, determination, ironclad focus, and courage are meant to be "proud of what we've accomplished", "lucky to have the opportunity" or simply "too bloody stubborn to know when to give up". We're meant to find solace in the fact that we're "men of character". Bullocks. A 7-million quid salary, a vintage Jaguar, and a 4000 square foot flat overlooking the ocean are a smart trade-in for character. Damn, I hate that Rodney Banks!

Across the Atlantic, a man sat uncomfortably in traffic. He inched along, almost claustrophobic in the exhaust-filled Fort Pitt Tunnel. But the slow traffic was not the source of his discomfort. In truth, he'd have preferred to sit in the tunnel all day if it spared him the task that he had ahead of him. Moments earlier he'd received a call from the Pittsburgh Steeler's All-Pro kicker, Justin Merritt. The message would have to be delivered in person to team owner, Joe Kenney. Mr. Kenney's 'manhood code' precluded the delivery of bad news over the phone. "Look me in the eyes and say it or don't say it at all." Although he was only the messenger, the young assistant general manager began to sweat as he fidgeted for the unsympathetically fast elevator ride up the Kenney building.

"Good morning, Ross," the receptionist chimed. "Looks like you took the stairs," she poked, noticing the shine on his forehead. Then her face changed as she detected something else. "What's wrong?"

Ross Killackey overadjusted his tie, now crooked on the other side, and spoke softly, "Justin hurt his knee."

"Training?" she whispered back, now understanding the gravity of Killackey's mood.

"Waterskiing, . . . in Hawaii," he winced, still barely able to believe it.

"He was on the phone a minute ago. Hold on," she said as she picked up her phone and tapped a button. "Mr. Kenney, Mr. Killackey is here to see you." A pause as she listened. "No, but I think it's something important." She looked up at Ross, "He'll see you now . . . good luck."

"Rosco!" Mr. Kenney boomed affectionately. "Think you can barge in whenever you want?" he joked. He quickly read his employee's face and then spoke softly, "What is it?"

On the other side of the usually soundproof door, the receptionist jumped at Kenney's exclamation.

"Waterskiing?!!"

Ross stood uncomfortably beside the chair opposite Mr. Kenney's desk, unsure whether he should sit. Instead he stood awkwardly, his hand alternating between his hip and the chair (steadying himself), occasionally and discretely wiping his interminably leaky forehead.

"Jesus Christ, Killackey! Don't we have something in his contract about crap like that?"

Ross nodded, relieved that the rage couldn't be turned in any meaningful way on him. "Yes, sir. It's a clause in all of their contracts," he answered softly.

"Well we could string him up for breach! Does he know that?" Kenney ranted, never really entertaining the idea.

"Yes, sir. He knows we have that option."

Ross then stood and listened to a prolonged monologue about 'kids these days' and 'spoiled millionaire athletes' before Kenney finally focused on the problem at hand.

"Siddan before you fall dan, Killackey", Kenney finally insisted in his native Pittsburgher tongue, never more pronounced than when he was upset. "Why are you sweating anyway? It's freakin' February! . . . Well what the hell are we gonna do?!"

"I'll get on this right away, sir."

"And having Carle do the punting *and* the kicking is not a solution. *I placekick better than him!*" Kenney went on, referring to a failed experiment four years earlier.

"I know, Mr. Kenney."

"Do you, Ross?" Kenney challenged sincerely. "This team is right there. We're in striking distance to win it all again, just four years after our last title. That's no small feat in the cap era! Ah shit, you know all that. You had a hand in building this team," he added, momentarily revealing his soft spot for the young executive. "You and Ray put your heads together on this. First priority! We're six weeks . . . not even . . . five weeks, four days from mini-camp," he corrected, glancing at his calendar. "We can't have any chinks in the armor. This year, Ross, . . . is our Goddam year! Anything else will be a failure."

"Yes, Mr. Kenney. I understand completely. We'll . . . I'll fix this."

Ross sat slumped over the bar at 'Hightops', down the street from Heinz Field, still picking at his fries after he was full.

"Why do you have soccer on the big screen, Steph?" he pouted to the waitress.

She gestured to the table nearest the screen with her head as she refilled his IC Light. "Brits here on business."

Then Ross's body shot up straight as he watched a replay of a sixty yard field goal by a curly-haired soccer goalie.

American football has a decent following in the U.K., actually, but I think it will always be something of a novelty. Most of us grow up conditioned to the flow and continuity of football, or I suppose 'soccer' in America. And the closest cousin of American football is rugby, but it too is fairly continuous. And its players don't look horribly out of place in the cue at the store. American football brings to the screen all of the stereotypes that we hold about America. It's about being the biggest, strongest, fastest, meanest, loudest, and most willing to step on another bloke's throat to win. To most Brits, begging your pardon, it's something of a freak show, featuring characters that would fit nicely into a video game or professional wrestling, or perhaps one of those cartoons that parents let their children watch only because it's a cartoon and they haven't stopped to watch the thirty seconds it would take to find it offensive.

Mickey sat at the Muddy Anchor with Abbey, his friend-since-primary-school-soulmate-without-ever-actually-hooking-up-but-acting-suspiciously-like-a-married-couple...type...other. But to avoid an unwieldy acronym, we'll just say they were each other's best mate. Abbey knew Mickey better than anyone, including his parents, and even, at times, better than he knew himself. She was his match intellectually and every bit as sarcastic, which he loved.

"Enough about Rodney-shagging-Banks, Mickey! God, when you go on about him like this, you sound like a worse wanker than he is!" she chastised as she tipped her pint.

Mickey was momentarily stunned by the cut, then managed a smirk and a shrug when he realized she was right.

"Just felt good to stick it to him is all," he muttered.

"Noted. Now can we move on to something less pathetic please?" she teased, punching him in the shoulder across the table. "Tell me about the lass your mum introduced you to. Carol was it? Are you going to see her again?" she pressed on.

Mickey shrugged, "Don't think so. Nice and all, but not much of a spark, I'm afraid."

"Pity. I thought she was quite pretty. And she seemed very sweet, Mickey. Why don't you take her out again before rushing to judgment on the poor girl? It's not always a lightning bolt."

"Because *you* fancy her? That's my ticket to love, isn't it? 'Really not feeling it, love, but Abbey thinks you're the bomb so . . . what the fuck . . . will you marry me'?"

Abbey nearly choked on her beer laughing, then shook her head, "You're such a wanker."

"Besides, I think I might have a go with Jennifer again," he added sheepishly, not unnoticed by Abbey.

"Oh FUCK! Please be fucking kidding! She's bloody awful! God Mickey, sometimes I wish I wasn't married so I could shag you when you're that desperate. That way you wouldn't make such God awful decisions with women," she teased.

"Bullocks. You never shagged me before you were married and I made even worse decisions back then," Mickey poked at himself. "Besides, you don't know her. Why do you have to break her down?"

"Miss tanning salon silicon? Oh, I know her. Besides, she's not a girl you get to know; she's a metaphor for how shallow men are . . ."

"That you resent, I know," Mickey countered.

"You tosser," Abbey jabbed, conceding his point with her reply.

"That's right. Between times, I am a tosser. And I'd like to shrink those 'between intervals' if that's alright with you." Mickey carried on as he reached into his pocket for his phone, "You and Mr. British Airways get to bonk bi-weekly and I get to endure those tender early stages of budding relationships. Translation: right-hand Mary, week after week?"

Mickey's phone vibrated on the table.

"That's the little tart now, isn't it?" Abbey jabbed.

Mickey glanced at his phone curiously. "It says *Pennsylvania*."

"Hello?"

Abbey sat quietly, trying to read Mickey's face that eventually registered dismissive disbelief. She shrugged and mouthed 'who is it?'

Then Mickey finally spoke, "Mr. Killackey, is it? Right, could you hold on for just one moment?" Mickey covered his phone and leaned across the table. "You're a techno-nerd; is there a way of changing the call display to something else?"

Abbey smiled, "I'm sure there is, but not by anyone you know," she snickered.

Mickey finally dared to entertain the call as legitimate and listened intently, looking increasingly stunned. Finally he blinked, with something dawning on him.

"Well, I'm currently under contract with my club here, Mr. Killackey . . . well . . . I suppose you could ask . . . sorry, Mr. Killa . . . fine, Ross, this is all very sudden. Perhaps you could call the manager of our club in the morning, then call me back. That way I'll have time to digest it." Mickey glanced up at Abbey, his eyes wide. She again probed with her expression.

"Okay. I'll talk to you tomorrow then. Thank you, Ross."

Mickey hung up the phone and stared at the table.

"Who the bloody hell was that?" Abbey asked impatiently.

Mickey muttered as he sat in his trance, "Got to be someone shamming, someone who knows someone in Pennsylvania," he rationalized.

"Who was it, Mickey?" again from Abbey, this time more curious than impatient.

"Well, . . . if it's real . . ." he paused, almost unable to say it out loud, "that was the assistant general manager of an American football team called the Pittsburgh Steelers. He wants me to come for some sort of trial."

They looked at each other for a long moment, both of their heads dizzy with the idea.

"Someone's having you on, Mickey. This can't be real," Abbey finally concluded.

Mickey shrugged, "well, if it's a joke, it'll take real stones to call my general manager and attempt to negotiate a release," he laughed.

Another long pause.

"But what if, Mickey?" Abbey wondered out loud. "Would you go?"

"I'd be mad not to, wouldn't I?" he replied surely.

"I guess," Abbey answered, less convinced. "But think of all the other doors you closed because you wanted to play football, Mickey."

"Come on, Abbey! Those guys are rock stars in America, and the money's got to be fantastic," Mickey argued, "eight bloody years I've toiled in this organization for a shot to play at the top . . . and for what?"

"That's rubbish, Mickey. And you should be fucking ashamed for boiling it down that way," Abbey chastised. "You made that choice because it's what you love . . . and I've always had the utmost respect for that decision," she pressed, her tone dead serious. Then with a melancholy smile she added, "Besides, who will I go to the pub with?"

Then to escape the heaviness of the idea, Mickey finally dismissed it, "Come on, it's got to be a joke. And we've both fallen. Look at us. I'm not going to give it a second thought," he concluded, downing the last of his beer.

"Bullocks. You won't sleep a wink tonight," Abbey insisted.

"Yeah, you're probably right," he admitted. "Buggers. Someone's going to get a good laugh about this one." Mickey tapped the table with both hands and stood up. "Well, I've got early physio on my hand. Best call it an evening. Talk to you tomorrow . . . after the punch line," he smiled and kissed his friend on the cheek. More about you next time."

Abbey smiled, "Call me tomorrow."

Mickey shot her a two finger salute on his way out. She slumped down in her seat and sighed as he disappeared out the door.

"Be careful what you wish for, Mickey."

It's difficult to describe the cocktail of emotions that coursed through me as I sat in Mr. Murdoch's office listening to the details of my contract buyout. Ordinarily I'm very tuned in to all things legal, as I'm a firm believer in self-advocacy. But as he spoke, a voice inside my head drowned his out, like that of a narrator. But thinking back, it must have been my voice, but divided into three different characters. When I read about Freud in school, I found it to be funny stuff. Oedipus and penis envy. It's all pretty classic. But as I sat in the office of my club's general manager, the voices of my superego, id, and ego rang unmistakably in my head. My superego, bloody annoying at the time, went on about my responsibility to myself. About the fact that I'd forsaken much to indulge my love of football, but that 'love' is a justifiable reason for such sacrifice. That running off to America to be a kicker for an American football team truly made me a sellout, an adolescent starving for attention and material gain. And nodding along with this voice were my parents and Abbey. Dad because he loved football as much as me. Mum out of principle. And Abbey . . . well, I guess in the end because she understands that where the heart and mind converge lies the soul. And she knew mine as well as she knew her own. And of course they nodded; my superego is, after all, an internalized construction of them.

'Bullocks!' said my id, the voice of self-indulgence, pleasure and pain. Disappointment, resignation, regret, guilt; that's what my clinging to football had brought. I'd worked as hard as anyone I knew. I lived the life of the elite athlete, good clean living, despite the fact that I'd never really be elite. I deserved a day in the sun, a roaring crowd, and maybe even a shagging sports car.

And then the mediating of the ego. Perhaps American football would be a suitable extension of my football career. Perhaps I would develop a new love, a new sense of belonging. Perhaps the experience would challenge me and stretch me in healthy ways. As he spoke, my id looked on smugly, certain that he was about to get his way. And as Dr. Freud looked down at me, stretched on his couch, he too smiled, tying my whole predicament neatly back to my castration anxiety. Oh, it is funny stuff, isn't it?

But then the narration faded and all that remained was the shrill and unsettling silence of the surreal. I felt like I was falling. But was I just afraid of leaving my comfort zone, despite its modest landscape? Or was I falling from myself? It was difficult to tell. Not even Freud could tell. He still thinks I want to shag me mum.

Pittsburgh Steelers Training Facility.

Three of the Steelers players were working out in the weight room, discussing the fresh news of their kicker's injury and Killackey's 'plan A' for a replacement. Emanuel Bunch, their All-Pro safety fished for a spotter.

"Yo, DC. Can I get a lift-off?" His call was ignored.

"Why England? Ain't no kickers anywhere in North America we could sign? No veterans that missed one important kick and got axed? No Div

II standouts that went undrafted? I mean, come on," Dillon Carmichael marveled from his power clean platform.

"Dillon," Bunch tried again, "quick spot, my brother?"

"Is he a brother at least?" the gargantuan Vaughn Sellers queried between arm curls.

"Is he a brother?" Carmichael laughed, "Ain't no brothers in England, 'V'."

"There are millions of brothers in England, fool. Now will you please give me a spot?" Bunch repeated impatiently.

"Oh, yeah? Name one," Carmichael queried playfully.

"How many brothers are there in Africa, Dillon?" Bunch trumped.

"None . . . that *I* know," Carmichael replied triumphantly.

"See the sad thing is you actually think you just won the argument," Bunch muttered in disgust.

"A'ight, Triple A, I give! I know you the smart one; spare me the knockout blow," Carmichael submitted mockingly.

"Yeah, just give him the 'blow', Triple A!" Sellers teased as he replaced his weights, shaking the whole rack.

Bunch shook his head and smiled, conceding that the dig was a little clever. Then his face grew serious again.

"But it's a good question, DC. It sounds like a distraction we don't need, to me. What we need is a vanilla kicker. One that just shuts up and kicks. Does his little stretches and drills in the corner of the field," Bunch gestured with his hand, "then comes in and quietly does the job. This team has enough 'personality'."

"Vanilla?" Sellers protested, "What we need is a black kicker, dog! A little soul power! Know what I'm sayin', baby?"

Bunch resisted the temptation to quiz Sellers on the colour of a vanilla bean.

Carmichael challenged, "Ain't no self-respectin' brother gonna be a kicker, y'all!" Besides, we gotta throw those white boys a bone now that all the best quarterbacks and coaches is brothers!" he celebrated his point with a high-five/finger snap with Bunch.

Bunch tried one more time. "A'ight, DC. I'm goin' for six here. Gimme a spot."

"Hey, hold on, y'all! What about ma' man, Reggie Roby?" Sellers recalled.

"Reggie who?" from Carmichael.

"Reggie Roby was a punter for 'the Fish'. Now that boy could punt the ball! Brother had like 10-second hang time."

Bunch snickered quietly to himself.

"What up, Bunch? You don't know! I watched the Fish every Sunday, baby! Boy put the ball in the air for 'bout 10 seconds! Don't be laughin' punk!" Sellers challenged, growing irritated.

"V, if the ball was in the air for 10 seconds, his punts would have been like . . . one hundred and fifty yards, dog," Bunch countered.

"Did you watch the Fish every Sunday? Did you see my boy kick?" Sellers bobbed.

"No."

"Then you don't know," Sellers pressed.

"I didn't have to, V. It's physics. It's impossible," Bunch corrected.

"Oh now you Isaac Newton, mother fucker? I'm tellin' you the boy put the ball in the air for like seven, eight seconds!"

"Oh now you're at seven? You sure, V?" Bunch continued to challenge. "You know, if you paid a little bit of attention in school, I wouldn't have to explain this shit to you." The playfulness in Bunch's voice faded.

"Explain it to me? You don't know shit, Bunch. Shut the fuck up!" Sellers advanced slowly towards Bunch, playing his physical trump card, "I'll show you physics, motherfucker! Like what happens when a large object hits a narrow, mouthy motherfuckin' object like your ass!"

Bunch backed away from his bench, his tone pleading, "Hey, easy, V. All I'm saying is, what you're saying is impossible. If he was the best punter of all time, and maybe he was, V, then his hang time would have been about five seconds at the most. . . . That's all I'm sayin', dog. Relax."

Sellers relented. Bunch shook his head, annoyed that their would-be adult conversation would go the way of the school yard so easily.

"Now will someone give me a damn spot? It's my last set; I wanna get outta here."

Carmichael piped back in, "Damn?!" he started, covering his mouth, then carrying on in his best 'Mr. White' voice, "Hey, Emanuel, there's no need for profanity here. We're just trying to have a discussion. Take it easy, man," he gestured downward with his hands. Sellers laughed rambunctiously along.

"Yeah, besides, Galileo, you don't need a spot; you just need a new equation, baby! E=MC Hammer or some shit. Haha." More high fives.

Bunch finally lost his patience and walked out the door, shaking his head, mumbling something about 'encouraging him'.

"Hey, Manny! Come on, dog! We just playin' wit you. Hey, come on! One more set, baby! You only cheatin' yourself!"

The plane ride was a bloody nightmare. For a week, after the buyout, I'd been training lightly and resting, trying to make sure I was fresh for the trial. Then I got sick. Murphy's Law in action. I squirmed in my seat for six hours wondering if the pressure in my head was a combination of a head cold and the pressure of flight or if, in actual fact, I had a brain aneurysm the size of a tennis ball that was ready to burst. That's one of my weak spots, I guess. I generally have the discipline to catch myself when I'm being overly pessimistic and right the ship more or less. But when I'm sick, my mind becomes a runaway train of despair, and my cabin mates are Eor (that horrid ass from Winnie the Pooh), Chicken Little, and me hypocondriacal Uncle Ted, who literally willed himself into the ground. But in the end it was a heart attack that got him, not the cocktail of cancer, pneumonia, syphilis, and bubonic plague that he had forecast. In any case, when I'm under the weather, I can make any one of them sound like Pollyanna. And the timing was unfortunate, as the content of my reflections happened to be the significance of my life and my place in the world. Not a portrait you ought to ponder with shit-coloured glasses.

Abbey had thrown me a bit of a send-off at the pub. Dad was bloody shit-faced. He had worked hard to warm to the idea of my going. He really had, bless his heart. But the more he drank, the more he oscillated between how proud he was of me and what a complete tosser he thought I was for leaving the club. By about midnight his oscillations were fast and furious, even occurring within the same sentence. Mum took him home when, in her words, he had "leaped over the boundary of appropriate public parenting", which I think means he wanted to fight me.

Abbey brought her hubby, who I actually get on quite well with, but she was uncharacteristically reserved. I understand why; when we're both drunk, we do tend to get flirty. Raymond (the bartender) puts it a bit stronger; "fixin' to shag" is how he puts it. No real intent or danger there, but point taken. In any case, not seeing things that clearly myself, I had twisted her demeanour into a protest against my decision to leave, and a sign that she'd lost all respect for me. That was about the same time Mum and Dad left, so by then I was feeling quite alone despite a fair number of mates that stayed right until close.

If I'm honest with myself, I'd have to say that it would have been much easier if Mum and Abbey had been angry about my leaving. Instead, Mum's reservation came in a much more potent form. She said the morning after the pub (of which there are many, but specifically my send-off) that although she understood my decision, the whole thing made her feel very sad. Ouch! There was no blame or accusation in her voice, in fact she was almost apologetic, which made it even worse. She wasn't lamenting my leaving, I don't think, but rather what she thought I had lost. Abbey never said so explicitly, but she became much more quiet, and her eyes seemed to convey me Mum's sentiments. It was pity. That's the name I'd put to it. And that made me angry, though I fought hard not to impugn the two people that knew me best.

After four hours of a throbbing head and interminable bumper car turbulence, my anger had been turned inward. I was a sell-out; I was shallow; I was juvenile; I was disloyal; I was weak; and barring a miraculous physical recovery, I would return very soon, tail between my legs, a complete failure, without the comforts I'd had all my life about 'at least having my principles'. And the tiny Tiramisu in my meal had no flavour whatsoever. At least none that I could detect.

What rescued me was a conversation that I had with Harold Sheffield at the send-off. Thankfully it came to me before I flung my Tiramisu at the crying baby across the aisle and dove out the emergency exit door to my merciful death. You see, Harold had been an inspiration of mine for many years. To say I idolized him would be incorrect. He carries himself with such genuineness and humility that it precludes his being placed on a pedestal. He's talented, hard-working, charismatic, patient, and his discipline in all aspects of the game leaves him nearly beyond reproach with coaches. And he's always been particularly nice to me, though I didn't know why.

In any case, Abbey had called three or four of the premier team players. Harold was the only one that came. It was enough of a thrill to me that he had come at all. 'He had me at hello' if you will. But he stayed for two hours and patiently waited for an opportunity to chat with me alone.

"Well, Mick," Sheffield chimed warmly, tapping Mickey's glass with his own as he slid into a chair across the table, "we're sure going to miss you around here, mate."

Mickey shrugged, "I might be back in a week, Shef. Could end up being a bloody disaster".

Sheffield wasn't biting; he was shaking his head before Mickey could finish, quiet only because of his mouthful of lager. "No, Mick. You won't be back. Not any time soon," Sheffield asserted confidently. Mickey suddenly felt astonishingly sober as he listened.

"It's a fluke that it came about, but in the end this is a perfect fit," Sheffield began, "Way I see it, being a kicker in American football requires three things: a strong leg, a good, consistent stroke, and mental toughness. You're three for three, Mick. You're a bloody lock. And you deserve it. That's what's brilliant about it. Finally, the most deserving guy gets the spoils," he said, winking and tussling Mickey's hair. "The shit end is that you've been such a stalwart in this club. So steady, so hard working. So professional. Setting the best example. And we all lose a little with your departure. We lose our beacon." Sheffield paused. "Come on, Mick. Don't look so surprised. It's a long bloody season. A steady flow of inspiration is as important as a good striker."

Mickey sat quietly, unsure how to respond. Finally, Sheffield smiled, drained the last of his pint, and stood up, assuming that the beer may have deflected his message.

"I'm gonna call it a night, Mickey. Good luck, mate. Let us know how it goes."

I was so moved by Shef's words that I was left speechless. I was actually trying to formulate a response that conveyed how much I appreciated his comments, how much I admired him, and how kind it was for him to turn up for my send off. But I was, in fact, well on my way to 'inebriated' and when my brain very nearly spit out "I love you, Shef", my mouth instinctively clamped shut, thank bloody God. Freud would have a field day with that one.

But there it was. A beacon? Inspiration? Complete sodding validation of my whole athletic career in a two minute conversation. But I hadn't dared to believe that my contribution had been of that scale. Who would? Banks perhaps. His pathologically high self-esteem inspires humility in the rest of us, I suppose. But now I was walking away from it, cruising at about 850 kilometers per hour. But perhaps it was because I deserved the opportunity. Perhaps it was karma, if you believe in that sort of thing. My own introspection had turned up very little, least of all any sort of peace of mind. I hadn't truly convinced myself that this was the right thing. But thankfully Harold Sheffield had given me something I could not give myself: satisfaction about how I'd spent the last several years of my life, and license to enjoy the next chapter.

When my mind finally settled on the recollection of my chat with Harold, it was the perfect elixir for the bolus of fear and doubt that sat uncomfortably in my stomach, and the pounding in my head mysteriously subsided. Around that time, I also dislodged a record setting plug of mucous in an inspired blow, the overflow of which I discretely cleaned from my shirt without being detected. That also helped, I reckon.

Abbey had given me a little book to scribble any thoughts, ideas, or quotes that I came across. She was careful not to call it a diary or a journal. She knew me better than that. I accepted it politely, not really expecting that I would use it. I've actually filled it and half of another since. I opened it, wrote the word, 'beacon' on the first page, with Harold's name beside it, then closed it and finally drifted off to sleep.

2

I hope that people will finally come to realize that there is only one 'race' —the human race—and that we are all members of it.
~ Margaret Atwood

When Mickey emerged from the gates, he spotted Ross Killackey immediately. He was dressed in a shirt and tie, top button undone, and his belly poking slightly over his belt. His gelled back hair was starting to lose its form but was still relatively tidy for late afternoon. Mickey had pictured a 'stereotypical American businessman' and Ross' appearance matched for the most part.

Ross had brought no sign for Mickey to spot him as he remembered Mickey very well from the video. He'd viewed that video a dozen times or so on YouTube to show off his recruiting fluke, and probably another dozen times at home to reassure himself that his solution would work out. He smiled widely when he spotted Mickey and stepped towards him.

"Mickey," he exclaimed warmly, holding out his hand. Mickey shook his hand firmly, one of the habits his father had drilled into him as a boy. "Great shake," Ross added, already feeling a little better. "Welcome to Pittsburgh."

Then Ross turned and gestured for another man to come over. The man was leaning forward on his crutches, talking on his Blackberry. He acknowledged Ross and the newcomer with a smile and a head nod, then wrapped up his call quickly and hurried over. It dawned on Mickey that he was about to meet his predecessor.

Justin Merritt was, by all accounts, a 'pretty boy'. He was lean and tanned, and looked only a fraction of his thirty-one years. It pained many in the locker room that he might be the best natural athlete of the lot, considering the 'non-athlete' status that usually tags football kickers. But the look about him preserved, for the time being, Mickey's feeling that he would be an athlete of equal standing with the other players. That bubble would not burst for at least a day or so. But it did bother Mickey a little that he ran his fingers through his wavy blond locks right before offering his hand to shake.

"Mickey, this is Justin Merritt, our *damaged* All-Pro kicker", Ross introduced, simultaneously acknowledging his status and inserting a gentle dig for getting hurt in the off-season. But it came with a smirk and a sort of benevolence that revealed the affection that Ross felt for all of the players. Justin wasn't bothered.

"Looks like I'll be your personal coach, bro," Justin added, in an accent that matched his look perfectly. The phrase 'California surfer dude' flashed in Mickey's consciousness. Just as well that he didn't find out for weeks that Justin was actually from Minnesota.

"Brilliant. I'll need all the help I can get, I'm sure", Mickey replied humbly.

"Dude, I'm gonna love listening to that accent," Justin laughed. Funny, Mickey was thinking exactly the same thing, substituting 'dude' for 'mate', of course.

Fortunately for Mickey, Justin had embraced the idea of mentoring him. And with good reason. Any success that Mickey had would help to relieve him of the guilt that he felt towards his team and Mr. Kenney. Justin was the kind of free spirit that wasn't typically burdened by emotions like shame and guilt, a fact that no doubt helped to explain his success as a kicker. But as Mickey would come to experience for himself, the Kenney family, the Steelers organization, and the community inspired a unique sense of loyalty and commitment from the players. The word 'institution' would not be too strong, as 'Steeler Fever' was woven into the very fabric of life in Pittsburgh, quite literally in fact, as the most common household items often bore the insignia (coffee cups, trash cans, blankets, scarves, lamps, you name it). Players who did not adopt this sense of obligation to the cause were either converted quickly from within or were alienated and eventually cast off, either by management or at their request. It fit Mickey's personality to a 'T'. Yes, if Mickey was going to give professional football a whirl, this was the right place for him.

One might have expected Justin to demonstrate some degree of insecurity under the circumstances. He too had seen Mickey's '60-yarder' on YouTube after all. But Justin understood that mechanics and leg strength are secondary to the most precious resource of a successful kicker: performance under pressure. The same way that every player who can throw a tight spiral thinks he could be a quarterback, many soccer players have scoffed at the football kicker without really understanding the magnitude of pressure inherent in his task. You may stand on the sideline for three hours before being called upon. And when you are, you get one shot, and thousands of pounds of ferocious athletes are bearing down on you. Not a walk in the park.

Really Justin had good reason to be confident that his position was 'on loan', not up for grabs. His 91% success rate in the previous season was second only to the 94% posted by his rival in Denver, and the difference was more attributable to the Pittsburgh coach's willingness to let him try from further out. And he delivered on those gambles, striking six times from midfield or further.

Justin was also something of an anomaly. Place kickers were generally of two types in this league. The 'robokicker' had nerves of steel. They were generally very flat emotionally, affected by very little. As such, they were affected less by the pressure and could go about the task of simply stroking the ball, free from distraction.

The 'neurotic kicker' was so nervous by nature that he had developed a routine so repetitive and consistent that his body had no choice but to refine the skill. These kickers were the obsessive compulsives of the sport. Absolute basket cases. Poster boys for Alka Selzer and Pepto Bismol. And they stressed out everyone around them but kept their jobs out of proficiency.

Justin was neither. He was demonstrative emotionally which removed him from category 1, but not the least bit nervous by nature, expelling him categorically from the second group. In fact, his off-season waterskiing was the tip of an iceberg that Mr. Kenney had no knowledge of. Heli-skiing in Argentina, cliff jumping in Venezuela, bungy-jumping, white water rafting, downhill mountain biking, and so on. His multimillion dollar salary had funded an extreme sport checklist that covered the offseason no-no's identified in every player's contract and then some. But he wasn't flaunting it; he just wanted to play. And treating placekicking as 'play' had given him a profound advantage.

As they drove from the airport, Mickey's attention piqued when Justin stated that a successful few months with the Steelers would open "all kinds of doors around the league". He studied Justin's face carefully after he said it, deciding in the end that he was saying so earnestly, not marking his territory. Unlike most of his placekicking peers, it just wouldn't have occurred to him.

In less than twenty minutes, Mickey had decided that he was going to enjoy Justin's company very much. With a simplicity and spontaneity reminiscent of 'Ole Shanty', Justin was like a slice of home, despite the cultural contrast. Then he settled in and enjoyed Ross' introduction to the city itself.

For all the amazing experiences that would endear me to the city of Pittsburgh, the one that may top the list was my first glimpse of it. The drive from the airport is hilly and green, already an unexpected surprise considering the 'Steel Town' image I had in my head. But then you go through Fort Pitt Tunnel and when you emerge from the other side, the city appears like the center-piece of a pop-up book. They call it 'the gateway to the city' and I can't overstate its impact. The downtown buildings shoot up where the Ohio River splits in two. As you peer down the Monongahela River (the southern offshoot), bridges cross it as far as you can see. In fact, there are over 600 bridges in Pittsburgh, second only to Venice, believe it or not. I was so taken by the view that when the giant ketchup bottle featured at Heinz Field was pointed out to me, it actually looked kind of charming. A shagging ketchup bottle! God bless America!

Abbey emerged from the ensuite in her robe, still drying her hair. Her husband, Jeffrey, flicked through the channels with the remote, settling on nothing, then gave up and tossed it to Abbey's side in deferral.

"Mickey off to America soon?" he asked.

"Left this morning," she answered, pursing her lips to resist reopening a previous discussion. A short pause and Jeffrey gave in.

"Why can't you be excited for him?"

"Because he's invested his whole life in something and he was seduced away from it in an instant," Abbey charged. She disappeared into her closet for cover, her pajamas already laid out on the bed. Jeffrey poked his head in.

"I'm not trying to upset you, love. I just wish you could see the good in this," he offered softly, wrapping his arms around her and nestling in. "He's your best mate, Abbey. And he's really excited about this. Or he was . . . before you sent him off second guessing himself," he challenged, his tone still gentle.

"He *is* my best mate, Jeffrey. And my gut keeps telling me this is a mistake. Isn't it my job to protect him?" she pleaded.

"It's your job to *support* him, Abbey. You caution him, then you let him decide. What's *his* gut telling him? Doesn't that have some bearing here?"

Abbey relaxed into his arms, relenting slightly, so he continued in a whisper. "He's a smart bloke, Abbey. One of the smartest. Trust him with *his* life. If it's a mistake, he'll figure it out." Abbey nodded slowly, still staring straight forward. "Maybe his whole life has prepared him for this opportunity," he carried on, sensing some progress. "He deserves good things, Abbey. Maybe this is just a build-up of Karma. Men aspire," he stated slowly. "We need to achieve; we're weak that way," he conceded with a smile. "This just might be the break he needs to find that contentment that he's never been able to find."

"Maybe," Abbey whispered, finally opening to the idea. "Now stop telling me how to feel. That drives me mad," she asserted, elbowing him playfully.

"Done," he assured. "Telly's all yours. I'm going to sleep. Early flight tomorrow."

They kissed delicately on the lips and crawled into bed. Abbey breathed a heavy sigh then finally settled.

Steelers Training Facility, Pittsburgh's Southside.

Mickey had to work not to stare at his would-be teammates in the locker room. He quickly realized that the dimensions he joked about over the internet now appeared *not* to be overblown, that the players listed at 300 pounds were every bit of that, and much leaner than he had imagined. The smooth, chiseled torsos, particularly of the black players, dwarfed his, which he quickly covered with his new Steelers T-shirt. He felt very small, and less like an athlete than he ever had. The 340-lb offensive tackle, Blake Hollweg simultaneously welcomed . . . and terrified the diminutive Doyle with a slap on the back.

"Welcome to the 'Burg', . . . Nick is it?"

"Mick . . . actually. Or Mickey if you like," he sputtered.

"Well Mick, hopefully you can save Sunshine's ass for his dumb-ass injury," he said, as much for Justin's ears as for Mickey's. Before Mickey could word a humble reply about 'giving it his best shot', Hollweg wandered away to the conversation already in progress between the offensive linemen. Mickey recognized immediately that even on the first day of mini-camp there was a palpable tension about the doubt that had been cast on the team's season. For some reason, it hadn't yet registered that he was stepping into a world where people were *deeply* invested in the outcomes he was to contribute to. He glanced up at Justin who gave him a face-saving wink and a pat on the shoulder. But Justin's eyes had changed, if only slightly, revealing something that Mickey hadn't anticipated. Although Justin was an All-Pro kicker, he was still a kicker. Mickey had just been dealt his first lesson about the peripheral nature of his role, as witnessed by Hollweg's tone and Justin's submission to it. The culture shock would take a few more weeks to truly set in, but the loneliness started right then.

The session started out very well. After a team warm-up, Mickey and Justin retreated to a corner of the practice facility for some extra stretching. Justin then had Mickey kick a series of balls into a kicking net (taking the kicks themselves off of any immediate display) so that Mickey could get used to the added weight of a helmet and shoulder pads. He adjusted quickly, and Justin was immediately impressed by the refined stroke that Mickey had already honed on the soccer pitch. Mickey too settled once he started to kick. That at least was comfort zone for him, different shaped ball or otherwise. Mickey smiled to himself at the encouragement that Justin offered, tickled by the colloquial.

"Nice stroke, bro."

"Oh, yeah; that's money."

"That's three."

"Yep, that's three more."

"Money."

"That's cash, Mickey."

Then it was time for his kicks to be seen by all. The two long snappers in camp set up in the middle of the field with a bag of balls. The punter substituted as pinner as was customary until special teams practice when the backup quarterback would step in. From Mickey's perspective, it was going famously, each kick splitting the uprights easily, with only one misfire in the set. But Justin's feedback shifted.

"Don't wait for it Mick."

"Don't wait."

"Mick, you've gotta step as it hits his hands, bro; he'll get it down."

Although he remained calm, Justin's prodding took on a real urgency, as he knew that failure to correct this timing aspect of the kick would be detected quickly by the special teams coach, and would invariably fall on Justin's shoulders for now.

This was new. Stepping in to kick a ball that wasn't there yet, and wasn't even coming in on the same plain (like a moving soccer ball) was certainly foreign. He had adjusted to the ball and even to kicking a ball from under someone else's finger fairly quickly, but for some reason, this rush to get it away was throwing him, and his kicks started to pull as he got more anxious about it. Although no more eyes had turned his way than before, he felt them on him. And he could feel his chest tighten with every rushed stroke that didn't feel just right. Thankfully, Justin knew what he needed.

"Hold on, bro," he said to the long snapper and pulled Mickey away gently by his new face mask. Then, lowering his voice, he addressed his protégé.

"Your body can do this, dude. You've shown it all day until now." He paused, waiting for Mickey to acknowledge. Mickey nodded. Then Justin smiled and continued.

"Just get out of your own way, bro. Look where the ball is going to be. Imagine there's one there and you're looking right at that point of contact. When you see the snap, just . . . corner of your eye, you see it. Don't fuckin' look at it, cause it's just a cue. Stop trying to follow it."

Mickey snickered, knowing he'd been caught, and finally starting to relax.

"Just let that cue release you, bro. Then stroke through that point. Don't think it. Just stroke it, dude . . . like you have all day," he finished with a pat.

Justin's guidance paid off, and Mickey went to work putting on a relaxed display of his talent that drew more eyes the further back they moved. Thirty, forty, and finally fifty yards, a set which coincided with the water break horn when the other players could stop and watch the show. Mickey felt good. And Justin felt relieved. Justin had observed that Mickey would have to get under the ball more to get it over the line consistently, but preferred to let Mickey get some momentum before tinkering. He didn't know defensive tackle Vaughn Sellers would go to work so early as the antagonist. He probably should have.

"Blocked!" Sellers called from a distance.

"Blocked again, dog," after another, gaining Mickey's attention.

"That ain't clearing the line, dog! Come on now! Gotta git it up, K!"

Mickey carried on, relatively unphased, but irritated that he was being targeted so early in his trial.

"Blocked for a TD, dog! Come on, *Kicka*!"

Sellers walked right up to Mickey, his helmet in both hands, his glistening bald head bobbing.

"Don't waste the drive with a block, dog! Get that shit up! That ain't clearing the line!" he carried on.

Justin said nothing, submitting to Sellers' daunting presence.

But Mickey's wit and fuse got the better of him and he countered.

"You'd need a crane to get *that* body up that high, mate," he chirped, in spite of all the instincts shushing him.

Most of the players heard the cut, and Sellers knew it. Justin's eyes closed as a retaliation was now inevitable.

"Oh you funny now, mofo? That shit will hit me in the *chest* when I get up, bitch!" Seller's countered stepping into Mickey with a shove that sent him easily to the turf.

"Easy, V," Dillon Carmichael pleaded, daring to step in between. Sellers relented slightly, but his challenge continued verbally.

"You got some more funny shit to say, Ringo? I'm listening," he said gesturing to his ear, "but I can put yo narrow ass in from 'fitty' flingin' you by your nostrils, bitch! Got somethin' to say, dog? I'm listening."

To everyone's relief, Mickey shook his head. Eyes down. Frightened. Justin breathed a sigh of relief that the moment had passed, and everyone went back to work.

It's not that I believed that he could actually throw me through the uprights by my nostrils. Of course he couldn't. But I'd done my research. The man was 6'2, 295lbs. When he was drafted, he bench pressed 100 kilos 48 times in a minute. He couldn't have tossed me through . . . but it surely would have been a spectacular attempt.

So there it was. At the end of an imperfect but encouraging initial trial, I somehow managed to provoke one of the most fearsome players in the National Football League. I already knew the name, Vaughn Sellers, from poking about the internet before my arrival. He'd been to the Pro-Bowl (the NFL all-star game) five of his eight years as a pro, including two defensive player of the year nominations. I should have recognized his face, as it is featured on the cover of Madden 2007, a videogame that one of my teammates from Liverpool had shown me. He took great joy in thrashing me using the lowly Oakland Raiders. It astounds me how much time some of the lads spend playing videogames. In any case, I didn't have to be a 'gamer' to realize that Sellers was an impact player. The irony that I'd knocked several of my mates' players over with the video version of Sellers struck me only seconds after I hit the turf following a shove from the real one.

Justin seemed quite pleased that it had ended as quickly as it did. What I hadn't found on the internet were the three assault charges of which he'd been acquitted. None had occurred during his four years in Pittsburgh, but one had to assume that the potential was still there. It was painfully clear that standing up for myself like I did with Rodney Banks was not the wise approach to dealing with Vaughn Sellers. He was the giant 'silverback' of the group if you will (no racial reference intended whatsoever, I learned the sensitivity of primate references quite uncomfortably later on). Anything other than submission carries significant risk.

*What also struck me was the curious lack of involvement from the coaching staff. Presumably they all saw the incident; it was center stage at that point. Not a word was said to Sellers, except by Dillon Carmichael, a teammate. I still owe DC a pint for intervening, now that I think of it. It wasn't without some personal risk. In dramatic fashion, I had learned the lesson **not** to assume that pro football . . . I mean soccer, and American football were parallel worlds. A different set of rules and 'non-rules' governed this environment. And I would have to be much more careful about the assumptions I made . . . lest I become famous for a YouTube video of a more painful sort.*

The football portion of the next few weeks passed uneventfully. The team spent some time on individual drills but the emphasis was on conditioning. In truth, the 'team synergy' that the camp was intended to enhance was really a cover for the desire to ensure that all of the players completed a minimum volume of training. For his part, Mickey started to accumulate some social currency through his hard work. That at least would never be questioned. He was immaculately fit, so he showed very well in any session that required endurance and general fitness.

He did, however, dread their trips into the weight room where his weak upper body was most on display. But despite the occasional jab from another player, most often by Sellers, there was little pressure or shame exerted by his new teammates. They really had no expectations about his closing this deficit as it was irrelevant to his role. Instead it was largely a construction of Mickey's mind. Standing beside any of the other players, even Justin, his upper body looked small. The comparison was so visible that he took to spending extra time in the gym (alone) to address it.

Everyday that he refined his kicking form, visible to all those in the training facility, the players accepted him as a legitimate new feature of their landscape. As their questions about his ability faded (except for the lingering question of whether he could do it under pressure), the fear that they would be a great team with a vulnerable Achilles dissolved as well. So the other players *slowly* granted him limited access to their social world (he was still a 'kicker' after all). They had fun with his accent and Mickey learned whom he could poke back at, never with much of an edge, mind you (once bitten, twice shy). But as he settled into his role, one irrefutable pattern nagged him.

Once his fear of being excluded by all had diminished, he started to recognize his place in a very polar dynamic. He was on the white side. The idea of it bothered him profoundly, as he had always prided himself on his equitable treatment of all of his soccer teammates, regardless of nationality, race, or religion. And he found himself working extra hard to connect with his black teammates, a personal attempt to bridge the gap. But it was largely in vain. If anything, he was enough of a novelty that some of the black players took a bit of a liking to him. But he felt more like a pet or a retarded cousin, treated nicely out of pity or a diminutive fondness. The shine that third-year runningback Dillon Carmichael had taken to him seemed to serve him very well, as Dillon or 'DC' was generally liked by everyone.

Regardless, Mickey's nature kept him searching for resolution, if only between him and his black teammates. One day, after practice, he found himself in the weight room with Emanuel Bunch. Bunch had impressed Mickey on multiple levels. It was clear that his remarkable training habits were a product both of determined focus and a firm understanding of training principles. His preparation for training sessions was airtight, regardless of how minor the workout. Mickey couldn't wait to watch him on game day. He was also the intellectual superior of his teammates and probably most of the coaches. A graduate of Colgate University, Bunch was the go-to source on just about everything, most notably history, politics, religion, and anything relating to the players association. Finally, he was a family man. He had married his high school sweetheart and they had three young daughters, aged 18 months to five years, whose faces graced the inside of his stall. Bunch was much of what Mickey valued the most rolled into one person. Surely, if a meaningful connection could be made, it was with him.

"You'll let me know if I can spot you or anything, eh?" Mickey offered.

"I'm good. Nothing heavy, just maintenance stuff today," Bunch responded without looking over.

Mickey abandoned his chin-ups for some dumbbell work, feeling conspicuous with his sets of five, particularly having watched Bunch effortlessly rattle off at least a dozen during his warm up.

"So why do the lads call you Triple-A?" Mickey inquired, pushing for some sort of exchange.

"The lads," Bunch echoed with a smile, still not looking over. "Triple-A stands for Academic All-American," he replied.

"Oh, brilliant. Sounds impressive," Mickey chimed.

"Not really," Bunch shook his head dismissively as he lined up against the wall and swung his leg fluidly parallel with it. "Maintain a three-five while you play a sport," he explained glancing at Mickey long enough to see that he wasn't familiar with the GPA reference.

"Basically between a B+ and A—average for four years. More than attainable with half decent habits and half a brain," he added.

"Modest to the end, eh? Well, good on you anyway," Mickey praised.

Bunch fought off a smile, then switched legs to face the other way.

"DC's quite an athlete, isn't he?" Mickey carried on to fill the quiet. "Amazing to watch someone over 100 kilos move like he does."

"Yeah, some nice genetics there," Bunch responded, implying that they may not be fully utilized. "Could be Canton-bound if he ever takes anything seriously," he added. He glanced back at Mickey who again missed the reference. "Hall of Fame," he tacked on to clarify.

Mickey nodded to acknowledge, simultaneously thinking that, while DC could do more to take care of his magnificent frame, the pure joy that he brought to the game, and virtually everything else, was probably a performance enhancer for all of them.

Another few minutes passed quietly and uncomfortably for Mickey. But not one to give up, he continued to initiate.

"Vaughn was a bit on the warpath today, eh?" Mickey prompted with a snicker, "went at Hollweg pretty hard."

Bunch rolled his eyes and replaced his weights, then finally looked directly at Mickey.

"Look, Mickey. You're a smart man, and I think a good man, so let me level with you," Bunch began.

Mickey tried fruitlessly to swallow, nervous about whatever was coming.

"You will never be 'one of us'. So you should stop trying to be." Bunch's tone was eerily calm and even. Mickey didn't and perhaps couldn't respond, so Bunch continued.

"You read a lot of history, don't you?" Emanuel asked, already knowing the answer.

Mickey nodded, his eyes lowered, and sheepishly understated, "a bit."

"Know much about American history? Specifically with respect to African-Americans?" he led Mickey along. Mickey shrugged.

"Well, let me boil it down for you; this country will never fully recover from its history. Never. It's come almost as far as it can: two separate worlds coexisting in the same space, peacefully most of the time. But that's it. Great men have been trying for centuries to repair the damage . . . but the A-bomb was dropped, Mickey," Bunch explained, softening slightly, "and the pieces are too damaged to fit back together."

Mickey looked down and shrank like a scolded child, and Bunch's harsh tone faltered as he sensed the blow he had delivered.

"It's not your fault, dog," he carried on, surprising Mickey with a softer address, "but it's what it is. Don't upset the equilibrium. Know what I'm saying? Respect the sensitivities of your new home." Mickey finally looked up, shaken by the word 'home'. Bunch smiled sincerely, yielding to his empathy.

"That's right, Mickey," he continued, almost laughing, "You're not a visitor here. If you're on this team, pulling that helmet on come September, then you *live* here. This is home. Your community. America. And there are some rules of engagement, though they're not written on a sign at the borders and airports. But they're real. I'm just saying . . . respect that. It's best for everyone." Bunch patted Mickey on the shoulder, stood up and walked towards the exit. He stopped in the doorway, looking sideways but not turning all the way around, and spoke once more to Mickey.

"And don't underestimate Vaughn. He's impulsive and sometimes a bit of a fool, but most of what he does is calculated. He pushes to toughen people up, to get them to man up, to be better. Lots of times he goes too far, gets too hot . . . but it works *a lot* of the time. And it's done deliberately. When you see him on game day you'll understand."

Bunch walked quietly to the locker room while Mickey sat silently, digesting.

What a kick in the shagging stomach. I was utterly deflated. In my insecurity, I had felt that Emanuel might not like me. But then I had reassured myself that I was being overly sensitive, that he probably just needed some time to warm up. Then he informs me, unambiguously, that I would never really belong in his social world, never really be his friend. At first, I was personally offended that he would exclude me categorically based on skin colour. It seemed so misplaced from a bloke of his intelligence. But was it?

In truth, I had taken an interest in American history long before my opportunity in the US. To be certain, the manner in which Africans had found themselves in the Americas would surely have fractured the potential for trust and true integration. And the aggression and conviction with which 'White America' had oppressed African-Americans socially and economically long after the abolition of slavery could surely have broken even the most patient and hopeful. One can't help but appreciate the anger, the hurt, the mistrust. But now here I was, a default member of the other side, with no opportunity for appeal. And it was a dreadful feeling. My illusion that I might enjoy some exemption, not being American, burst like a bubble.

As Bunch had put it, "You're not a visitor here." I could no longer sustain my self-righteousness about the bruised social dynamic of the American people. Because I was, at least until the end of my sporting quest, an active participant in it. It struck me how difficult it would be for anyone, black or white, to believe that these two worlds would ever converge in a place where both sides were so resigned to status quo.

But let me explain what was so remarkable about my experience of race in America. From the outside, you hear about the conflict, the occasional unrest and violence, the sensational. But from day to day, my experience was not that way at all. The two sides were curiously invisible to each other. They work in and frequent the same public space, though they live separately. And in that space, it is as if the other does not exist, except for the occasional glance of fear or suspicion. A silent but intensely palpable divide.

To me it was surreal, because I could see both, plain as day, something of a twilight zone episode, if you will. And I seemed to have been granted limited interactive access to both, until now. So where did I belong? To accept default status on one side felt like passive compliance. But to seek status to both seemed to have offended at least some, most notably the man who had impressed me the most, ironically the man who I fancied myself most like. On reflection, the better question seemed to be 'Do I belong?' with a nagging feeling that the answer was 'no'.

I was instantly sobered by my place in this world. I was alone, and would be until I returned to the U.K. No, that's not it. Right up until that point, I had felt alone. And that was ok; the excitement of my new adventure took much of the sting out of it. But now in an instant, I felt lonely.

"Hello?"

"Hi, Abbey. It's Mickey."

"Mickey, you splendid bugger! You finally called! Oh, I miss your voice. How are you?" Abbey began excitedly.

"I'm good . . . mostly," Mickey began.

"How's the gridiron going? Getting the hang of that odd shaped ball?"

"That part's good actually. Not much to it so far. Their regular kicker's been fantastic help," he went on, soothed by the sound of his friend's voice.

"That's the Justin bloke, is it?" Abbey clarified.

"Yeah, that's him. Bloody God-send."

"That's terrific, Mick. And you're getting on well with the other lads? Oh God, I sound like your mother," she added apologetically.

"Um, yeah, I suppose . . . a bit mixed on that front, I guess," Mickey admitted.

"Well that's always going to be the case on a new team, isn't it?" Abbey surmised.

"Sure, yeah, yeah . . . bit of a different experience here though, I reckon," Mickey said, revealing in his tone a measure of discomfort. Abbey was on another pitch however, and failed to pick up on his subtle cry for help.

"Well, Jeffrey and I have some rather exciting news," she began, bubbling.

"Brilliant! Let's hear it," Mickey willingly shifted gears.

"Well, about the time we wondered if there was something wrong . . . we're pregnant!" Abbey blurted exuberantly.

"Oh, Abbey, that's fantastic! Magnificent news, mate," Mickey reveled earnestly in the announcement.

"Thanks, Mick. We're absolutely thrilled. Jeffrey's giddy as a school girl; it's bloody adorable," she added.

"Well, that's absolutely brilliant, Abbey. Smashing news. I told you it was just a matter of time, didn't I?"

"Yes, and you were right again, as usual. Thanks for putting up with my going on like a loony about it. Must have been a lot to take," she offered apologetically.

"Yeah, you were, actually," Mickey teased, "seeing as how I wasn't getting laid at all, while you two were shagging your brains out with this little project. Something of a relief now, I reckon; now Jeffrey and I can commiserate while you get round and moody," he added.

"Oh, bullocks! You're probably neck-deep in cheerleaders by now, you filthy bugger," Abbey played along. "Oh Mickey, I'm so glad you called. We only just started telling people today. Twelve weeks to the day, if the dates are right."

"That's lovely," Mickey offered, in only slightly more than a whisper.

Abbey paused, detecting something, then asked, "Is everything alright, Mick?"

Mickey was truly thrilled for his friend, but curiously he now felt the same ache in his stomach that Emanuel Bunch had delivered. Perhaps he was never entirely kidding when he and Abbey had played at their ongoing joke about shacking up if she and Jeffrey hadn't worked out. But he was fairly sure that wasn't it. For whatever reason, he could feel every drop of the ocean that separated them. Agonizing distance, despite the comforts of her laugh. The poignant realization that 'home' would go right on living without him. Whatever the issue, he wasn't going to spoil her moment.

"With me? No, brilliant, everything's good. Everything's fine."

I know what you're thinking. I thought it myself for a moment. I was jealous of Jeffrey. And I am, I suppose, for a lot of reasons; he's an amazing bloke. But that's not what hit me on that day. Not the hardest at least. I guess I imagined that if things didn't work out, I could return seamlessly to Liverpool and slide easily back into my life. But here I was, just a few weeks away, suddenly stricken by the idea that the longer I was gone, the less I'd belong back home. Unsettling to say the least, considering the social limbo of my place in the U.S. But of course that would have to be true, wouldn't it? It still caught me off guard. Not sure why it hadn't occurred to me. Like the "holy fuck, it's cold" I felt every time we dipped in the ocean as lads, along with the "of course it's cold, you daft bugger" from another place in your mind. But in my own defense, these were unchartered waters. I had no previous experience to help forecast what I'd feel. But in the early going, it was clear: choppy and bloody freezing.

Well now, that's not fair. Uncle Ted acting up in me again. Because I had already experienced considerable warmth in my short stay. We in the Commonwealth like to look down at the Americans for their worship of the almighty dollar. We sustain this condescension despite the fact that Americans have achieved excellence in virtually everything they've tried to by appealing to the idea that it's all been accomplished in a climate of moral bankruptcy. Where a 'bottom line' replaces principle, or where their principles, at the very least, are governed by that bottom line. It's easy and comfortable to think that way when you don't live among them, when the only Americans you encounter are tourists asking for directions to the nearest McDonalds. But despite the complicated history of their social dynamic, and the sharp disparities between their economic classes, most of them retain a curious optimism.

Dillon Carmichael was the youngest of eight children that grew up in a three-bedroom home in rural Georgia. The youngest of five boys. Talk about a tough spot in the pecking order. But when I asked what that was like, he replied "It was good; brothers toughened me up; big sisters patched me up; and Mama kept sayin' "Ma lil' Dill Pickle, big things is comin' fo' ya, baby". And she was right." And he looked at me with this enormous smile that wrapped me like a hug from his mum.

That's it, I guess. Despite good reasons to believe otherwise, Americans seem to maintain a belief that something better is always coming, provided you work hard, stay strong, and have faith. Statistics dispute them. But in the end, perhaps the outcomes are immaterial. People that live with hope are happier and more resilient. They are healthier, more patient, more community-minded, and simply find more meaning in their lives, including their suffering. It's a profound form of wealth, whether its origin is illusory or not. 'Better false hope than no hope at all', someone once said.

And Dillon had been absolutely wonderful. I wasn't thrilled when my 'Ringo' tag stuck. Vaughn threw it out in anger, and I'm fairly sure he had no idea that I came from the same city as the Beatles. He meant it derogatorily, like I hadn't earned the right to be called by name, and he might just as easily have blurted 'Prince Charles' or 'Tony Blair' or even 'Lady Di' . . . or more likely 'Austin Powers' now that I think of it. So thank goodness for 'Ringo' on reflection. But when Dillon said it, there was an unmistakable affection in his tone. A sort of unabashed acceptance of someone different. But again, I think it's his sense of optimism that guides his response to things. Chance didn't bring me into his life; God did. So I must be alright. Or 'A'ight' as the black lads say it.

And thank heaven for Justin Merritt. He was just the right medicine for my fears. He modeled the voice that I would need to internalize to be good here. He starts and finishes with what's great about life and himself and the people around him, gently nudging the negatives in the right direction with the patience of a granny. "Just focus on the stroke, bro", he kept telling me. "You know what it's supposed to feel like; just go there in your head and your leg'll follow." Brilliant stuff really. So many thoughts can go through your head before a kick. But none of them even fit in your head when you're focused on the feel of the kick.

But the most striking example of Americana has to be the Killackey family. In the first month of my stay, I dined at their home a half dozen times. And nearly half of my meals had been prepared at their home, as Ross' wife, Kathleen, kept stocking the freezer of my flat with home cooking. Both Ross and Kathleen were children of Polish-American steelworkers, so they appreciated every single luxury they had acquired. Their children less so, which fed a daily monologue about gratitude and appreciation that one would leave off and the other would pick up seamlessly. The kind of hilarious stuff that made me feel very much at home. 'Ole Shanty' used to go on about working the yard and how easy my sisters and I had it. His stories became more and more hyperbolic with each pint he ingested.

And since he never had fewer than three or four, it was pretty steady. But there was something very comfortable about the universality of that dynamic.

And in the end, their kids were really great. Stephanie was the oldest and the quietest, typically called to dinner three or four times away from whatever teen novel she was digesting. Clayton was a 'B' student who had to scrap for every grade he received. But he had the work ethic of an ant which he also carried onto the gridiron pitch where he was an undersized linebacker with supersized (part of the American fast food vernacular) courage. His room was a shrine to Pittsburgh Steelers past and present. Steeler lamps, Steeler sheets, Steeler alarm clock, rubbish bin, and rug. Probably thousands of dollars worth of Steeler memorabilia passed down from his father. And although he poked fun at his dad fairly regularly at the dining table, it was clear that he was intensely proud of him and his dream job within a Pittsburgh 'institution'. The affinity made perfect sense, considering Clayton was really just a miniature version of Ross, both physically and in personality.

Their youngest, Kyle, was something of an enigma, as he appeared to have been granted twice the ability that his older siblings had, but consequently worked half as hard, making him conspicuous relative to the others. But he was only eight, so he had lots of time to assimilate the habits that were being modeled for him. And he had a charm and humour not unlike Dillon's that disarmed the others.

But more to the point, they were simply warm, hard-working, perfectly imperfect, normal folk. The habits of the two older kids seemed not to be economically driven, but rather an attempt to make mum and dad happy. Ross and Kathleen ran on about hard work, not as a ticket to accumulating wealth, but rather to obtain a sense of pride and a feeling that one is making a valuable contribution.

'American' was fading as an idea in my head. It was becoming the faces of people that I knew and liked. People like me, or people that I wanted to be like. People. Just good people. Families like mine. I shamed myself for viewing them so cynically, then began drawing from the comforts of being around them. But alas, the 'talking to' that I received from Emanuel drew my focus back to the ways that I was different. Back to a foreignness that chilled me.

3

Language... has created the word "loneliness" to express the pain of being alone. And it has created the word "solitude" to express the glory of being alone.
~ Paul Tillich

"Where de party at, y'all?" Dillon queried giddily from his stall. Team training had wrapped up and the remainder of the off-season preparation would be done individually before training camp opened on August 1st.

"Where—de—paaaaarty—at—y'aaaaaaaaaall," he repeated in song, gyrating his hips to his own rhythm.

"Southside, my brother," from linebacker, Percy Dawkins, "at 'the Max' to start, then we'll see."

"Nah, fool," Sellers protested, "Gentlemen's club, then the Max. Ringo need a lapdance to get it started," Sellers tussled Mickey's hair, "whadaya say, dog?"

Mickey was a bit confused, wondering if he was being set up by Sellers.

"I'd go for a pint," he offered cautiously.

Vaughn shot up straight, clenching his glutes, "I'd go for a pint, lads", he mimicked, in his best British accent. "Hell yeah, y'all! Ringo's ready to get it started."

"Let's get it started—let's get it started in here," Dillon filled in the soundtrack.

Emanuel glanced over uneasily. Mickey caught his eye, as did Dillon.

"What about you, Triple-A? Come for a pint?" Dillon added, carrying on the joke.

"Nah, dog," Emanuel smiled, loosening up, "get the kids down early, bottle of wine, maybe a little Pendergrass, . . . and see if the missus will get a little freaky."

"Aaaaaahhhh yeeeeaaaahhh, boyyyyy!" Sellers laughed then finger-snapped with Bunch.

"Pendergrass, huh?" Dillon queried mischieviously, "well, uh, if it don't work on yo lady, it's bound to work on V's mama!"

Before he finished the dig, Dillon was over the row of benches and out the exit in only his shorts, displaying superhuman agility in the process. But it was out of necessity, as Sellers nearly snagged him at the door and continued his pursuit out onto the field. The only thing more impressive than Dillon's agility was 300 lbs. moving almost as quickly. The players could hear the trail off of Dillon's pleas from outside.

"Come on, V! You know I's just kiddin'. Come on, dog. Yo mama love Pendergrass; you even said! You bought her that box set & shit; you was all excited."

Sellers finally walked back into the room, out of breath. Then shouted back out the door, "You can run . . . but you can't hide, motherfucker! You know I'm a' get yo ass!"

Faintly from somewhere out in the field, "Come on, V! You know I love you, dog! *Looks like another love TKO.*"

The players were escorted quickly to a private back room of the gentlemen's club by a hostess who would see to their requests throughout their stay. Mickey wasn't unaccustomed to the celebrity treatment, having spent enough time with the premier division players back home. Membership certainly has its privileges.

About a dozen players had arrived together. A few more would trickle in about the same time that the group lost a few of the married players who had come for a few drinks but knew not to settle in for the full swing of 'bachelor activities'. The group had a distinct 'team feel' as it included about even numbers of black and white players who wouldn't ordinarily mix outside of a team function.

Mickey would not have had much of a buzz, sipping his IC Lights (local light beer that he playfully equated with club soda relative to his native suds), but he'd lost count of the shots of 'Jack' that he, Dillon, and the gargantuan Blake Hollweg had consumed. Within an hour or so, the evening had faded into a fuzzy blend of the surreal.

He remembered looking over at Sellers who had Dillon in a headlock and delivered blows to his thighs until he had recited with adequate volume, "I will never dis V's mama again." He made him try several times, and it was good that they wouldn't be training for a couple of days, as the bruises on Dillon's legs would surely take that long to heal. "I told you I'd get yo ass," Sellers added to close.

The image of Blake Hollweg receiving two lap dances at once, one girl on each massive thigh would stay in his head for a long time. Blake had forsaken his shot glass in favour of a full bottle of Jack Daniels in one hand, alternating gropes of the two dancers with the other.

The free flow of cash made the bills look like play money as different dancers popped in and out over the course of the evening, eager to earn their share of the windfall. A few of the players, including Vaughn, ducked out with girls, retreating discretely to small private rooms further in the back. Dillon sat patiently, sipping his drinks, as if the money that others were spending would not be necessary for him to have female company at the end of the evening. His confidence was well-founded.

The hostess, who was lean and slight in frame, had a chest that was dwarfed by the dancers, but whose short dark hair and haunting green eyes continuously caught the eye of the teetering Mickey. They flirted intermittently as she came back and forth with drinks. Their exchanges felt more normal to him and cut through the overt sexuality that was all around him.

"How about a lap dance for Ringo?" Sellers bellowed from his spot in a booth. His booming voice startled both Mickey and the girl. Mickey felt immediately uneasy, as if their very comfortable ongoing exchange had been contaminated.

"I'm sure he'd prefer one of the dancers," the girl answered awkwardly, breaking her eye contact with Mickey. Mickey suddenly felt more sober than he wanted to.

"Come on, Chantale," Sellers pleaded as he rose from the booth, "*Kick*'s only got eyes for you, anyone can see that." Mickey's blushing cheeks were detectable, even in the dimly lit room. Sellers slapped a $100 bill on her empty tray. Chantale looked like a child next to him.

"I'm pretty sure he'd be happier w . . . ," *slap*. Another hundred on the tray. Chantale gave in to an impish smile, appealing to Mickey, "Is that what you'd like?"

Mickey swallowed hard and muttered breathlessly, "that would be lovely," sending Vaughn into another fit of laughter.

"Aaaaaahh, yeah!" he exclaimed, plopping back down in his seat to watch the show.

Somehow this had become the main event, even though scenes like it had been going on for a couple of hours. Chantale started to move seductively to the music, slowly removing her white blouse and then her short black skirt. The other players laughed, whistled, and 'whooped' as they watched their new kicker sitting uncomfortably on display. The diminutive Chantale shyly covered and uncovered her modest bosom as she danced, swaying hypnotically in just a thong and heels. As she danced, she moved so fluidly on and off of Mickey's lap that he forgot that she wasn't one of the dancers. Eventually, she settled onto his lap, straddling him, pressing herself against him, and rubbing intimately with him. She smiled at the feel of him, his stiffness affirming her movements. Her tiny hands ran through his curly dark hair, taking his breath away. She giggled when her teeth grazed his ear and his chest inhaled spastically from the oxygen debt (he hadn't taken a full breath for over a minute). When the song ended, all too quickly, his entire body tingled. She kissed him on the cheek, quickly dressed, then returned to the bar to get more drinks.

"Mm mm, that's what I'm talkin' about," Dillon called, smiling widely. "That girl's got it goin' on, Ringo! You gotta get wit that!"

"Let him go wash up first," Hollweg teased, setting off the whole room.

"She's fine, but she need some titties," Percy Dawkins slurred from his seat.

"Ah, dog, . . . that shit's not cool," Dillon murmured, shaking his head.

"Hey y'all, let's tho' in fo' some implants fo' that lil' girl," Dawkins chuckled, flicking a few bills onto the table, completely missing the vibe of disapproval that his teammates were giving off. Mickey sat quietly, relieved that she wasn't in the room to hear him. Sellers spoke up.

"That ain't ok, Dawk. That shit's not ok," he stated firmly, his tone serious and imposing.

"Ah, whassup, V? Now you siding with yo' new boy? Sidin' wit *kicka*?" Dawkins protested sarcastically, staring Mickey down.

"It ain't about that, Dawk," Sellers replied surely, his eyes widening, "You know that shit's not ok! You know. You can see he likes her, dog. Show a little respect," Sellers boomed, now standing and facing Dawkins. Mickey was frozen, wishing the moment to end.

"She's a freak, V! This is bullshit! We all bin wit dat! You bin wit dat! Don't act like she ain't trickin'! She ain't no player's wife!"

"Ain't about that, Dawk," Dillon reinforced.

"Hey, fuck you, DC!" Dawkins objected.

"Go home, Dawk! Just go, fo' I bust you up!" Sellers finally threatened, looking away from Dawkins to keep his composure, pointing to the exit. The few dancers in the room cleared to the corners of the room, fearing a brawl.

"Oh, I'm gone," Dawkins spit out angrily, storming towards the door, stumbling as he went through it.

Hollweg followed him out, pausing at the door, "I'll put him in a cab," he said quietly. No one had any doubts that if it came to it, Hollweg could literally *place* Dawkins in the back of a taxi, especially in his current state.

The mood had been killed. The players slowly trickled out. No one had any more to drink after the altercation. No one felt like it. On their way out, Mickey cautiously approached Sellers to thank him for standing up to Dawkins' indiscretions.

"Hey, Vaughn, I just wanted to,"

"Ain't no thang," Sellers interrupted.

"Beg your pardon?" Mickey prompted, a bit confused.

"Ain't no thang, Ringo. Just tryin' to do the right thang. Know what I'm sayin'?" Sellers explained.

"Of course. Well, thanks all the same," Mickey offered to close. Sellers acknowledged with a nod, never having looked at Mickey.

Dillon patted Mickey on the back as he was walking by and pulled him under his wing affectionately, "Ain't no soccer team, dog," he said with a smile, sensing Mickey's feeling out of place. Mickey smiled back, relieved that someone understood what he was feeling, at least that much.

Chantale met the group at the front door on their way out.

"Thanks for coming, fellas," she offered, having no idea what had transpired in her absence. Certainly none of the dancers were going to tell her.

As Mickey walked by, she nudged him and said, "I hope you come back some time," and smiled at him over her shoulder as strolled back to the bar to carry on with her duties.

Needless to say, I had to hit the shower when I got home from the club to bring closure to my lap dance. Couldn't think about much else after that, to be honest. But after my shower, while I sobered up, the evening reassembled in my head and there was much to think about.

Most notably, for much of my time with the team, Vaughn had busted my balls. I had more or less concluded that he just simply did not like me. And perhaps he still didn't. But that didn't really jibe with the fact that he called out a teammate, on the defensive side of the ball no less, over something that he felt was an affront to me. Or perhaps he was just backing up his mate, Dillon, who was the first to react. In any case, he was quite dismissive of it after the fact, which I took to mean that he wasn't that comfortable with his handling of Percy.

But according to Dillon, there was no real danger of fallout, as he assured me that Percy was drunk enough that he would have little or no recollection of the incident. Bit of a precedent there apparently. I guess Percy has a history of 'wandering off the reservation' as Dillon put it. I wasn't familiar with the reference, but I guessed it had something to do with substance abuse in aboriginal communities, so I decided to file it under 'politically incorrect' until I learned otherwise. At any rate, Percy's had some pretty memorable benders, none of which he remembers.

I thought Chantale was quite stunning, assuming that was her real name (what the hell; the lads had her calling me 'Ringo'). And I'm not exactly hung like a horse, so I wasn't about to cast stones at her chest. Besides, it wasn't that big, but a lovely shape to it, I thought . . . especially up close. Ordinarily, I would have been bothered that the only physical affection I'd received in all that time was in a strip club, but most of my adventure had been decidedly out of the ordinary, so why would this be any different?

Latrobe, Pennsylvania. Steelers' Training Camp.

The surprisingly hot and humid conditions matched the mood of the camp. Killackey and general manager, Ray Tennison, had done good work in the off-season. Their already remarkable depth, virtually across the board, would be challenged by a batch of draft picks and free agents that were nearly as talented as they were hungry. Only a handful of players felt like their spots were guaranteed. And the starters on both sides of the ball took nothing for granted. With leaders like Bunch and Sellers on the defensive side, who pushed themselves daily like their lives depended on it, and veteran quarterback, Ricky Wild, whose stalwart professionalism steered the ship on the offensive side, the environment was simply 'world class'.

Mickey would be pushed by two successful collegiate kickers, the better of which had gone undrafted quite surprisingly. His stats were near the top of the Division 2 rankings in the only position that could be compared fairly across divisions. But in truth, the kicking question had nearly been put to rest. Before training camp had even commenced, Mickey had grooved a kicking stroke that had finally started to make Justin Merritt a little nervous. Not an easy task.

What was even more impressive was how thoroughly he prepared for every day of training. He completed the same physical warm-up that many of the premier Liverpool players had mimicked, trusting in Mickey's understanding of physiology. It was dynamic and fluid, each exercise leading seamlessly into the next, so engaging the athlete that there wasn't time to get nervous as the mind was locked on the movements. Mickey had tailored the preparation to his tasks as kicker, incorporating dynamic stretches and activation exercises which stimulated every link of the physiological chain that would fire during each kick.

Then he would go about his kicking progression which took him from 30 to 60 yards in about eight minutes, carefully painting the middle ground between under and over-preparing. For each kick, regardless of distance, the stroke was identical, having borrowed from the march-off that Justin had shared with him. It seemed to put him in just the right spot, so why reinvent the wheel? Three long steps backward, two side steps to the left, then a comfortable forward lean while awaiting the snap.

For the mental narrative that accompanied the routine, Mickey again trusted in his kicking mentor, Merritt, whose even, confident voice rang in Mickey's head. "Just feel the stroke, babe," "money", "automatic" as Mickey visualized his kicks, then validated his belief during the on-field warm-up. The voice was already starting to sound more like Mickey's, the accent subtly shifting day by day. And all this had taken root before camp had even started, and it would not be long before the agents of both college kickers would begin testing the water elsewhere in the market. The gap between them and Mickey was apparent to even the most amateur observer. For the first time in his life, before a single preseason game had even been played, Mickey was beginning to feel what it was like to be exceptional, perhaps even the best. And he liked it.

I thought I'd be a shagging basket case going into training camp. But it was quite the opposite. I felt magnificent. Absolutely euphoric. Justin's guidance had been brilliant. I felt thoroughly prepared. And one might have expected me to be bothered by the limited scope of my task, but I wasn't. In fact, it would not be an overstatement to say that I was 'reveling' in its simplicity.

For one thing, my dimensions had lost their relevance completely. 5'9, 7-foot, 4 feet tall? Didn't matter a fig. So long as I continued to split the uprights, which I did.

And the addition of a rush to the equation also had surprisingly little impact on my execution. Again, Justin's input was invaluable. "Like a TV on in the background, bro; you know it's on, but it's not what you're paying attention to." Every kick was the same. Same set-up. Same timing. Fixed on a spot where the ball would be, stroking through it like a robot.

And it felt great. There's a curious exhilaration about being the kicker. 99% of the time, you're completely ignored, save for the occasional dig in the weight room or locker room. Then for that 1%, you matter. Every player's hope rests in your hands, or your foot, more to the point. And it's just a moment, but what a wonderful moment.

So, surprisingly, my mind was free to digest the spectacle that was unfolding around me. To be clear, I will go to my end in eternal awe of the footballers that played in the premier league and in the World Cup every four years. I aspired to their athleticism for my entire life. But what I witnessed in my NFL camp left me completely humbled. It was power, speed, size, strength and skill on a scale that was humourously out of reach. It was freakish.

Whether it was wide receiver DeMarco Sands accelerating down the field with the sleekness of a world class sprinter, or cornerback Bo Townsend running with him step for step, a full head shorter, it was absolutely breathtaking. The clash of pads hitting in concert as a play began, opposing forces numbering in the thousands of pounds for each collision. The effortless launch of the starting quarterback's throws, some of them covering 70 meters, with the accuracy of a handoff. The frightening agility of the linebackers, 250 lbs. each, with the unpredictability of a jungle cat. It was astounding.

But my favourites dazzled most of all. Emanuel Bunch, reading plays clairvoyantly, then swooping in to make the play with the stealth of a bird of prey. The fluidity and grace of Dillon Carmichael, whether he was knifing through the defense, all 230 pounds of him, like a border collie cutting sheep, or the brute force with which he impacted the poor souls that could line him up, he was a demigod.

And of course, there was Vaughn Sellers. Per Emanuel's assurance, I understood, well before my first game day, what he meant. Vaughn was the lone silverback. The 'nuke' in our arsenal. If the rage that he unleashed when the ball was snapped in scrimmage was even greater on game day, as promised, then the ball carrier, or anyone between him and Vaughn, would only ever be a single snap away from high risk of injury. Surely a team with him on it would enjoy a valence of supreme confidence. Not a quiet confidence, mind you; he never stopped talking. 'Trash-talking' or 'talking smack' the lads called it. But the constant assurance that you were never more than one play away from a momentum shift in your favour.

And against all odds, I fit curiously into that mix. What would you make of that? Little Mick, the 'kicka', a spoke in the wheel of the Pittsburgh Steelers. Like a dream you wake up from because it's too bizarre to be real. But it was. Yes, the start of training camp marked the quieting of my mind about whether or not I belonged. I was integral to the team's success. And as the substantial group of players was whittled down to the final roster, our collective confidence swelled as each of us fed off the readiness and mastery of all the others. A vibe to which I had contributed. I belonged. I was relevant. I mattered. It was nearly intoxicating. I counted the days to my debut like a five year-old counting down to Christmas.

The Thursday before the first preseason game, Ross Killacky took Mickey to dinner at *Dell's*, a family-owned and run Italian restaurant in Bloomfield (Bloom*filled* to the locals), Pittsburgh's little Italy. Ross was greeted with a hug by the matriarch of the establishment. She shook Mickey's hand with both of hers and welcomed him warmly then retreated to the kitchen to see to a special appetizer in their honour. While one of the daughters seated them, she recalled out loud, in some detail, the story about Mickey she'd seen on television the week before. She too voiced her appreciation for his coming, not simply to the restaurant, but to the city, to *their* team, into their *lives*.

They were there for well over three hours, greeted by countless regulars and other locals. Huge bowls of food were rushed from the kitchen along with two handpicked bottles of wine from the cellar, and lots of water for Mickey (they knew he'd need to stay hydrated for the big game). The restaurant was abuzz with the 'celebrity' in their midst. Mickey sheepishly acknowledged their well-wishes time and again. He hadn't even played a game yet.

The overwhelming warmth and his reflexive modesty shone in Mickey's cheeks, accented by the wine. Ross would occasionally glance at him, surveying his face for signs that he was 'getting it'. He was. But for whatever reason, he wasn't fully getting it until just now. All the signs slid into place in his mind. His thoughts were coloured by the images of folks in Steelers attire, worn by more people than not. He thought about the toothy smile of the old man that worked security at the training facility, a grin that expanded impossibly as opening day approached. He reflected on the omnipresence of the *Stillers* as a topic of discussion everywhere he went: the grocery store, the Starbucks, the pub nearest his furnished condo on the waterfront (that he could no longer frequent inconspicuously since his feature aired). It was everywhere. And he was part of it.

They say the body responds pretty well the day after a poor sleep. Thank God. I rolled about interminably on Saturday night. The novelty of my pursuit was fading, to be replaced by the gravity of my task. These people lived and died by the fate of their beloved footballers. It transcended everything. It was as if this social glow was cast on the entire city. Everyone talking about why this would be another championship year, why the visiting Panthers would be no match, how this team measured up to the great teams of the 70's. The cashier at Giant Eagle (grocer) assuring everyone who would listen that the Steelers would 'kick butt' on Sunday. She wasn't sure who they were playing but was confident that it didn't much matter. Who they were playing? Who we were playing! Me and my team!

How had this snuck up on me? It's the same in the UK. Just a different sport. Perhaps every region assumes that the rest of the world could not understand the fervor that exists for their favourite team. How quickly that fog was lifting. People love their team. Everywhere. Though by most accounts, Steeler fever was exceptional. But regardless, it's very simple. Life is hard, and often draining, and just as often boring. People need their team. Communities, cities, regions, and countries are brought together by them. Across race and religion. Across social boundaries. Across wealth, poverty and status. They infuse passion, hope, and purpose, probably more than any other single thing. It's a good thing. Until it rests on your shagging shoulders.

Now 'calm down, Mick', I instructed myself. I had a strategy for this, though the scale of the expectations had obscured it. When I was fourteen, I played on a pretty elite squad. We represented the city in a huge tournament that drew sides from all over Europe. Going into the final against a German team, I was nearly paralyzed with fear. So my coach boiled it down for me.

"Look, Mickey. You want to play well, right?"

"Of course."

"Well, what's your job?" he asked. Straight away he saw my head was complicating it. "Simplify it, Doyle."

"Keep the ball out," I finally offered.

"Bloody right. Keep the shagging ball out. So just focus on that. Every time something else enters your head, see yourself keeping the ball out and you'll be fine."

Brilliant. Remember it like yesterday. We lost 1-nil, but I was at my absolute best. Maybe the best game I ever played.

So the night before my debut, I fell asleep to 'the stroke'. No, not that stroke. Tried that at 11pm and again at 2am. No, I mean I drifted off to the stroke of the kick, splitting the uprights again and again. The ease and the rhythm of it. The feel. The simplicity. Then I slept beautifully, if only for a few hours.

Heinz Field, Pittsburgh. Pre-game.

Mickey would again rely on the comforts of his well-established preparatory routine that he had tailored to football, or at least his role within it. But despite his well-established ritual, he would be occasionally distracted by the dramatically different atmosphere.

He arrived a full four hours before kick-off and the massive parking lot was already about ¾'s filled with tailgaters. They were already 'aglow' and raucously welcomed him as he walked from the players' parking area to the stadium, escorted by security. It already smelt of brats and beer. He smiled and waved shyly at the throng and thanked them when they offered him good luck. One fan was already completely intoxicated and urged him to "fuckin' kick some Carolina ass". He snickered and assured him, "We'll try".

While Mickey went through his on-field warm-up, his gaze was continually drawn to the steep Heinz field bleachers as they filled. He reckoned it would feel like the 65000 fans were right on top of them, and couldn't wait to hear how loud it would get. He laughed at a banner that someone had managed to put up below the front row of seats. He wondered out loud to the long snapper if the sign would be taken down. The "but Panthers are cats" defense probably wouldn't exempt the sign that read, "Give those Carolina Pussies a Lickin".

Mickey examined the goose bumps on his arm as he sat in the locker room after the on-field warm-up. In contrast to the low rumble outside, the room was astonishingly quiet. Little groups of players conversed in barely more than a whisper about specific plays, players, adjustments, and coverages. Most conspicuously, Vaughn sat alone in his stall silently, his head bobbing to music that wasn't playing, his brow wrinkled with the anger that he had been manufacturing for the whole pre-game. His scowl broke for the briefest of moments when he cracked a smile and winked at Mickey. It relaxed Mickey immediately and he remembered what Bunch had told him about Vaughn on game day, realizing that the wink was probably a calculation in Sellers' head about what his kicker needed from him. He was right on target.

Bunch tapped Mickey on the head on his way by. His expression looked like that of an executive on his way to a board meeting. Businesslike and cerebral. He would be the general of this highly touted defensive unit (Sellers the drill sergeant). He crossed himself, kissed his index and middle finger together and tapped the photo of his wife and children that hung in his stall. Then he spoke aloud to the whole room.

"Showtime, fellas. They're introducing the 'D', then we turn this motherfucker out," he said matter-of-factly.

"Ah, yeah," from Sellers.

"Everybody up," Bunch added as he pulled his helmet on.

Mickey's goosebumps sprung back to attention when they all rose together and made their way down the tunnel. They wouldn't retract until well after kick-off. The ground shook as the players took to the field, led by the defense. The crowd was deafening. Mickey could feel the noise in his stomach and his feet.

After the coin toss, the players crowded around Sellers.

"Whose house, y'all?"

"Our house!"

"I said, whose motherfuckin' house we at?"

"Our house!"

"You Goddam right! Curtain's up my brothers, 1-2-3,"

"Contact!"

As the kicking team took to the field, Mickey smiled in spite of himself at the special team coach's final instructions on his way out.

"Just kick the fuck out of the ball, Doyle. And if it goes out of bounds, I'll kick you in the nuts."

Mickey loved kick-offs. Lots of margin for error, pure gross motor strike. At the whistle, he shook the last bit of tension right out of his finger tips, jogged into it, and crushed the football into the center of the end zone. The speedy Carolina returner hesitated for a moment, then ran the ball out. Mickey's heart pounded in his chest as it occurred to him that 'they were live' and he would be the safety if the runner broke through the cover team. He didn't. He'd barely crossed the 15 yard-line when the first man downfield took his legs out at the thigh, nearly flipping him. The crowd voiced their approval of both the deep kick and the first hit of the preseason. They were under way.

The starting units only played the first half, enough to give the fans a taste of what was bound to be the regular season roster. Thereafter, those players who were fighting for spots on the roster would get their turn to impress. But the second half was anticlimactic after the show that the starters put on.

Dillon Carmichael outpaced the whole Carolina offense with 112 all-purpose yards: 68 on the ground, another 44 in receptions, along with both Steeler touchdowns. The offensive line had served notice that they would give DC lots of room to run. And run he did. The crowd was treated to a spectacular display of athleticism, including a short yardage launch into the end zone that could have cleared a minivan.

But the defense was not outdone. The Panthers managed a paltry 92 yards of total offense in the first half. Near the break, they stood holding their collective breath for two long minutes while their starting quarterback eventually got to his feet on his own after a crushing hit by Sellers. Vaughn had bull-rushed right over the guard, on the blindside, and jolted the sophomore starter right off his feet. A chilling display of brute force. However, what was most impressive was the manner in which the eleven players functioned as a unit, in virtual synchronicity. The 2nd coming of the 'Iron Curtain' appeared to be impenetrable from top to bottom, at least as far as the Panthers had tested them.

For his part, Mickey was two for two, including an impressive 44-yarder in a swirling warm wind. He then watched comfortably for the remainder of the game while the one remaining kicker made his only attempt of the second half. But the 'tryout' had been concluded; the youngster would stay on the development squad while Mickey would assume the placekicking duties.

The final score: Steelers 30—Panthers 10. And Mickey had a first National Football League game under his belt, albeit exhibition. But if today was any indication, his kicking would be the final ingredient to a Pittsburgh squad without a single glaring weakness.

I think it's fascinating that we can lose ourselves so completely in what we're doing sometimes. No, there's a better way of describing it. Perhaps we find ourselves completely in what we do. When we stop thinking about winning and losing, status, what other people think of us, when the past and future stop contaminating the experience of the moment we're in, surely that's when we're best connected to ourselves. To the self. The real self has to be rooted in the present, doesn't it? I mean, as someone once said, "It's never not now." But there's an artificial construction of the self that most people associate with the term. Do people like me? How do I compare to others? To the old me? To the me I seek to be? To the me I'm going to be? To our 'potential'; wow, now there's a tension-loaded construction. And we're taught that this construction is meant to be our beacon, our target. I'm not so sure. Because I've always been at my best when these comparisons quiet for a while. When my self-evaluation shuts off for a time. Intuitively, there has to be some value in that process. It's part of growing and improving. But surely there's equal value in shutting it off at the right time. When our seeking gives way to performing, to simply being. That's when I'm most myself. Least alone. Most free. And there's a purity in those times that I want to protect more aggressively.

The Carolina game felt that way. It wasn't until well after post-game that it occurred to me that I had truly 'made it', so to speak. That I'd lived up to the expectations of management and my new teammates. I was too busy enjoying myself. My self. And ironically, that's when I felt the greatest sense of belonging, when I felt most connected to my teammates. When I stopped wondering if I fit. When I was just being. Being Mick. Playing.

Mickey stood timidly at the entrance of the strip club, waiting for Chantale to be retrieved from the back. She came around the corner, curious to see who had asked for her.

"Ringo!" she greeted warmly when she recognized him, giving him a hug.

"Actually, it's Mickey. The lads just call me that. Uh, anyway, sorry to bother while you're working, but Ross from the team gave me these tickets for the baseball game so I thought I'd check what you were up to later," he pitched nervously, "Fancy a night out? They're right behind the Pirates bench . . . or dugout rather . . . I think he said." Chantale covered her mouth to keep from laughing. Mickey started to retreat, "Oh, sorry . . . I just . . . you're obviously busy."

"No. I . . . um, sure, we could do that," she said, still seemingly amused.

"Oh, brilliant!" he immediately perked up, "I've never been. I'm quite curious to see what all the fuss is about, actually," he added, speaking very quickly.

"Um, I've gotta zip home after work, but why don't I meet you at the main entrance just before game time," she proposed.

"Lovely! Right then, really good. I'll see you then," he concluded excitedly.

"Seven?" Chantale asked.

"Beg your pardon?"

"Seven? . . . Seven o'clock?" she prompted.

"Seven! Yes, seven, sorry. Yes, seven o'clock," Mickey giggled, managing to laugh at himself.

"Fine. Main entrance at five to seven," she confirmed with a wink, thinking he was awfully cute.

They had the full 'ball game experience', complete with beer and a Primanti Brothers sandwich (a local favourite: shaved beef with fries and coleslaw right there in the sandwich). Chantale did her best to explain the rules as the game progressed. Mickey thought there seemed to be an awful lot of them. He delighted in the seventh inning stretch, swaying to a song he'd never heard (*Take me out to the Ball Game*). What pleased him even more was how 'touchy' Chantale seemed to be, which he took as a great sign.

Near the end of the game, the camera spotted him and projected them together on the big screen. Most of the Steeler fans in attendance recognized him and applauded. He acknowledged them shyly with a wave while Chantale shrank down in her seat, seeming to recoil from the attention, making her even more attractive, he thought.

At game's end, she turned to him and rather forwardly suggested, "I live really close. Let's go to my place."

"Uh . . . lovely, sure, we could do that," he agreed, thinking this seemed awfully easy.

The moment they stepped into her condo, she closed the door quickly and pinned him against it, locking her lips with his, unbuttoning his shirt dexterously, sliding it off, and going straight for his belt. Then she suddenly stopped.

"Are you ok?" she asked suspiciously.

"I'd say. Just amazed how well it's going, to be honest," he admitted self-consciously.

Chantale's eyes widened and she let out a silent laugh of uncomfortable revelation.

"The guys did tell you I'm a *pro*, right?" she asked, fearing the obvious.

"Pro?" he asked, oblivious.

"Oh my God," she exclaimed, covering her mouth and turning away.

"Are you? Oh! Oh, Christ," he said, finally getting it. "Oh, God, Chantale, I'm such an idiot," he chastised, putting both his hands on his head, " . . . I don't know how I . . . oh, bugger, piss, shagging, cock-up," he added, his eyes squeezing shut, seeing no obvious escape from his agonizing embarrassment.

"You're not an idiot, Mickey; Oh, God, this is my bad," she consoled him, and snickered, somehow finding the humour in it.

"Look, if I cost you money by taking you to the stupid baseball game," he started, taking his wallet out.

"Put it away, Mickey," she insisted, dropping her shoulders and looking to the ceiling, now quite embarrassed herself.

"I'm really sorry, Chantale, I just thought . . ."

"You thought I'd like to go to a ball game," she finished his sentence, tilting her head in sympathy, moved by the innocence of the gesture. "You are too cute."

"Right, well, I've taken up quite a lot of your time, so I'd best just sod off," he mumbled in resignation, turning to the door.

"Wait," she said. He stopped, awaiting her last word. She looked him in the eyes.

"Fuck it," she said, pressing him up against the door again, and without breaking their kiss offered, "This one's on me."

They quickly undressed each other, although she was much smoother with the process than he was. He tried not to remind himself why. Then she led him by the hand into a bedroom and pushed him gently onto his back. Her hands caressed him from his arms, down his chest, stomach, and then finally took him delicately at the base. He gasped as he felt her mouth around him. Then she took him in an accelerating, perfect rhythm, up and down. He marveled at her proficiency, fighting hard to stave off the images of how her craft had been honed.

Then he glanced down, feeling her eyes on him. She was smiling as she worked. But, he thought, she was working as she smiled. It was a moment of profound sobriety, suddenly feeling the disconnection in the act. She was clearly enjoying the process of turning him on, arousing him towards his climax. But it felt like a show. An intensely engaging show, mind you, but a show all the same.

He shamed himself for allowing it to happen, then gave way to his arousal, and savoured it in spite of himself. Then without looking, she discreetly pulled a condom from the night stand, opening it and applying it to him in a single fluid movement. She mounted him, her feet flat on the bed, holding his lean stomach, then began to move on him, again in perfect rhythm. Each time he marveled at her talent, the moment was again contaminated by the reality.

But she was indeed skilled, and eventually arousal overcame the cascade of thought. She too seemed to get caught in the moment as she rode him, her movements feeling less and less precise. Finally he climaxed and she collapsed on his chest, breathing heavily, taking his hands in hers.

He was astonished by what he felt next. It was sympathy. She had relaxed completely on top of him, and clutched his hands tightly, resting her cheek next to his. He thought for a moment that he might have felt a tear fall on his neck. But as suddenly as it had all begun, she climbed off of him and retreated to the bathroom.

A few minutes later, he was at the door saying goodbye. She had gone from the bathroom to the front hall to get her clothes and quickly redress, which he took as his cue to clean up and do the same.

"Thanks for the ball game," she offered sincerely.

"Oh, not at all, you were my baseball tutor for two hours," he laughed, "Thanks for . . . thanks. That was lovely," he returned.

"It was," she agreed, "but um, please don't take this the wrong way, but . . . it's probably best for me if we keep this to ourselves . . . the freebie and all," she urged, with an embarrassed smile.

"Oh, yeah, of course, . . . who would I tell?"

"You are making this up!" Abbey exclaimed over the phone in disbelief.

"I wish I was. I was completely oblivious," he admitted, able to laugh about it after the fact. "She's got this 'Are you bloody kidding me?' expression painted all over her face, you know, like 'how the fuck did this guy end up in my flat?' So I'm standing there like a prize idiot, looking for the nearest exit.

"Oh, God, Mickey," Abbey laughed aloud, trying to stifle it, "I'm sorry, mate, but this is funny stuff." He was laughing with her.

"So you just slinked out the door?" she went on.

"Hm?" he murmured. A long silence.

"Mickey . . ." she prompted suspiciously. "Tell me you didn't shag her!"

"Well, . . ." Mickey began, wincing, "she shagged me, more like."

"Mickey Shannon Doyle! Are you fucking kidding me?!" Abbey shouted in outrage.

"Look, I didn't plan it out, Abbey; she just sort of took over, . . . and she didn't charge me; we were just caught in the moment."

"Christ, Mickey! Are you actually trying to defend this?" she pressed.

"I don't know, Abbey . . . I . . . I just can barely believe it myself . . . I . . . God, Abbey, I just really need not to be judged right now, especially by you."

"Oh God, Mickey," Abbey relented, suddenly softening, "you're a Seinfeld episode."

"Quite right," he conceded softly. Another lengthy pause. "It was my first shag since Jennifer, you know."

"Mickey, fuck, don't even start," Abbey rose again, although she had yielded to the absurdity of the whole matter and was no longer angry.

"And quite a good shag, in the end," he deliberately provoked, unable to resist.

"In the end?!" she charged. This set them both off.

"No, no. Not what I meant," Mickey snickered, then finally exhaled all the way. He felt relieved that his best friend knew and seemed not to have disowned him. He needed that to let it go himself.

"Baby's good?" Mickey moved along.

"Baby's good. We've got an ultrasound in a couple weeks so we'll . . . No, you know what Mick; I really can't go from this to the baby," she explained.

"Right, of course," Mickey accepted, "Well, I should probably get some sleep anyway; it's getting quite late here. Miss you, mate," Mickey said to close.

"Miss you too, Mickey . . . you daft bugger."

There are certain things that ground you when you're home. 'Home' being wherever you grew up. Proximity to your parents, the scenery of your childhood, your own language, accent, or dialect, the music that played, even the smells of home: for me the ocean, the docks and shipyards, the cobblestone streets that seem to hold so many smells. It's as if we're constantly surrounded by reminders about how we ought to behave, who we are, what's our identity, where the boundaries lie.

I think this is a big part of why people feel so disconnected when they go somewhere else for any length of time. They're not just away; they're set adrift, unanchored. At first it can be liberating, particularly when 'home' felt oppressive or stifling or boring. But it can just as easily trigger a feeling of being lost, without that frame of reference that's rooted in the physical, in our senses. It's probably the same reason that people go to such lengths to reproduce a miniature 'home', complete with the sights, sounds, tastes, and smells.

But away from those sensory cues, our frame of reference is a compendium of ideas tucked away in a corner of the mind, unless accessed directly. And it can be easily obscured in the face of physical forces: our emotions, moods, hunger, lust, fatigue. And we can find ourselves blowing in the wind, falling out of well-established habits, eating like crap, acting more impulsively, . . . or in my case, failing to divert course and sleeping with a prostitute. A prostitute. Bugger. Never wanted to be that guy. Oh, piss it; it was still a magnificent shag.

In any case, I don't think we realize how rooted we are by these physical cues until they're withdrawn. Think of the visceral reaction we have to a photo of home, a familiar smell, a song we grew up with. All rooted in the senses. Could we all be better at preserving a 'virtual' landscape in our heads? One that would save us from this drift? Probably. But it's a hell of a lot easier when our nervous system gets to have a go. And that's a lot easier at home.

4

*I have found the paradox that if I love until it hurts,
then there is no hurt, but only more love.
~ Mother Teresa*

Heinz Field. Regular Season Opening Day.

Mickey looked around the dressing room at the final roster of the Steelers. Gone was the air of anxiety about being cut, about being noticed and acknowledged, about personal aspirations hanging in the balance. The quiet of the preseason remained, but in it was a tone of resolve about what each player needed to do for the team to win. Each of them quietly played the mental images of his job, his contribution, his link in the chain.

They would open the season against their division rivals, the Bengals, whose late surge the previous season had served notice but had come too late for a playoff berth. So they would be hungry. And they would field a defense as heralded as that of the Steelers, with their strong side defensive end and tackle tandem of Winslow and Cage. Even if the Steelers offensive line was at their best, it promised to be a dangerous three hours for quarterback, Ricky Wild. They had numerous quick pass plays in place to exploit the high-risk tendencies of Bengals defensive coordinator, Chuck Little, but many of them would involve the veteran quarterback taking a shot to make the play.

And so it went. They were able to move the ball, 'nickel and diming'. Wild's reads were masterful, picking up in a heartbeat the source of the blitz, then finding the open man. Statistically, he seemed to be having his way, completing 10 of 13 passes in the first half for 120 yards. And with modest success on the ground thanks more to Dillon's strength than his speed (he kept his legs pumping for about four hard-earned yards per carry), they took a 9-3 lead into the locker room.

But the game sheet didn't reflect the cumulative effect of Winslow and Cage, who found their way to Wild on almost every pass play, just in time to deliver a hit after his delivery, but not so late as to take a roughing penalty.

Mickey routinely notched kicks of 21, 33, and 28 yards. It was good news that the offense came away with points all three times, but the bad news was their failure to penetrate the end zone from inside the 20 on three different occasions.

Fortunately the Steeler defense was nearly impenetrable, save for a penalty-extended drive that led to a 46-yard field goal by Mickey's Cincinnati counterpart. Whatever toll the visiting team's defense was taking on Wild and Carmichael was being met in kind by the swarming Pittsburgh unit. The constant double-team that Sellers drew created openings for his teammates, taking their turns teeing off on the Bengal ball carriers and quarterback. Dawkins seemed to be everywhere at once, and Bunch out-leaped a 6'3 wide receiver for his first interception of the year.

The locker room was of two distinct moods. The defense was upbeat and determined, hungry for more Bengal blood, chatty and brimming with confidence; the offense was quiet, with an air of frustration.

"We've got to do a better job of picking up their stunts, boys. Inside out area blocking; it doesn't get much more fuckin' simple than that," Hollweg charged, "Ricky and DC saved our asses in the first, so let's fuckin' pay them back. Just get yer hat on the right guy and move 'em!"

"Word, Hollywood," from another lineman.

"Some of those are just me taking too long to get it away," Wild said quietly as he rubbed his blood shot eyes. "We'll wear 'em down, fellas, just . . . try to get a piece of Cage and . . . that other fuckin' grizzly, so they don't get any clean shots," he pleaded, summoning the courage not to voice his frustration.

Dillon seemed curiously subdued to Mickey. Indeed, the whole offensive unit was affected by his conspicuous silence.

"Brilliant job pounding away at them, mate", Mickey encouraged. Dillon snapped out of his trance and winked at him, then stepped back into his usual persona, as if a switch had been flipped.

"Time to roll now, 'O'. Come on, y'all," he prompted, standing up, "our mufuggin' house, y'all!"

"That's right, DC! Come on, y'all; warriors gotta battle," Sellers added.

In spite of his collision-free role, Mickey could feel the tingle of goose bumps as he listened to the mounting spirit. By the time the team headed back to the field, there was a buzz of optimism more befitting of their lead.

But both offenses sputtered in the third quarter, squelched by the defenses that lived up to their billing series after series. Wild's proficiency faltered under the barrage of pressure. And their running game stalled despite DC's determination to give as good as he was taking. His efforts were valiant but inadequate, and the punters kicked back and forth for the third and most of the fourth. But something was bound to give.

Steeler's punter, Davey Carle, pounded a kick deep into Bengal territory, driving the return man back. The speedy Wesley Rowe caught the ball over his shoulder, near the sideline, almost stepping out, then accelerated up the middle of the field behind the wedge of the return team. His blockers executed beautifully, driving a hole in the Steelers' cover team. In an instant, Rowe was in full flight with only Carle to beat. He accelerated around the lead-footed punter who dove fruitlessly, trying to make the play.

The Heinz field faithful looked on in silence as the Bengals mobbed Rowe in the end zone. No flags. 10-9 Bengals with just under two minutes to play. Making matters worse, Carle hobbled off the field with an as yet undetermined injury.

Head coach, Shawn Baker, strode by Mickey, and spoke without looking right at him.

"Get ready to win this thing, Doyle. We'll get you a shot, guaranteed."
The message was as much for the offense as it was for Mickey. He began kicking into his net on the sideline, already rehearsing the scenario in his head.

But the offense quickly found themselves 3rd down, 8 yards to go from inside their own 25 yard-line. The restless crowd rumbled as the offensive unit lined up.

Wild took the shotgun snap and dropped three more steps. Mickey held his breath as he watched the Bengal pass rush penetrate the line of the Steelers, pinning their ears back en route to a battered Ricky Wild. Then Wild dumped the ball off quickly to Carmichael, just over the fingers of the pass rushers. Dillon bolted upfield, behind the lead blocks of Hollweg and another Pittsburgh lineman. He outran his blockers and made his way for the sideline, either to turn the corner or to at least get out of bounds after picking up the first down. As he neared the sideline, wide receiver, DeMarco Sands threw a shoulder into the chest of the Bengal strong safety, blindsiding him, jolting him right off his feet. The crowd ignited in an instant as they watched Carmichael turn the corner with a full head of steam and the sprinter speed that had been contained for nearly 59 minutes. Two nifty open field moves and some timely downfield blocking (and a hold that was undetected) and Carmichael was trotting into the end zone, out of breath and elated. 15-9 with 1:04 to play.

Mickey strode onto the field to kick the extra point, barely touching the turf in his excitement. They lined up to execute the routine point after. But as Mickey initiated his motion, he watched the ball squirt through the fingers of the pinner, dribbling to his feet. Confused, he picked the ball up and froze for a moment as it registered that the frenzied Bengal rush had their sites set on him. He skittered away towards the sideline, impressively outracing the onslaught behind him. But in a panicked movement that would be the fodder of humiliation for months to come, he tossed the ball out of bounds with both hands and turned away from the rush, turtling onto the ground.

Thank Christ the play didn't really matter. 15-9 was the final, and everyone was happy. But . . . how bloody humiliating. The only thing missing from my panicked response was shrieking like a little girl. Perhaps I did and don't remember. Bugger. The play aired for days on sports center. It was a running joke on the telly. I had been completely emasculated. I was the laughing stock of the American sports world for a full week. I had visions of Rodney Banks laughing his fucking face off while he watched it on YouTube. All of my effort to gain credibility over the preceding months dashed in about five horrifying seconds. Even the Bengal players managed to share in the laugh at game's end. It took an unlikely source to help me put it into perspective at the time.

"Chin up, Ringo. One and 'O', baby!" Sellers started. Mickey glanced up sheepishly, still smarting from the 'point-after debacle'.

"Hey . . . Ringo . . . know what, dog?" Sellers continued. Mickey looked at him and listened, nervous about what ribbing might be coming, but wanting to get it over with.

"Three for three, my brother. All that matters," he stated surely. Mickey was about to speak, about to dismiss the performance in light of the ending. Sellers wouldn't have it. "Ah, ah, ah," he interrupted, waving his hand to silence his teammate, "three for three, dog. Three for three. Convert wasn't no thang. Bad snap; that's all. Ain't no thang!" he insisted, standing up and smacking Mickey on the shoulder pad. Then he put his hand on Mickey's head and his eyes widened.

"That shit *was* funny though," he finally said as he burst into laughter, setting the whole room off. This time, even Mickey was able to laugh. As he did, he was finally able to acknowledge to himself that, in his role, he had remained perfect, though he felt decidedly *im*perfect. But perhaps that was ok.

The moments always come when you least expect, I reckon. When all of your problems are thrown into sharp perspective. Justin had Davey Carle and Glen Wray, the other kicker and me over for a barbecue after the game. My blooper was the favourite topic of discussion. I'd like to think it's because each of them was just relieved it hadn't been them. Regardless, I was licking my wounds in the evening, watching the telly over one last pint, when my phone rang. It wasn't that unusual for Jeffrey to call me back in the UK, so I didn't think much of it.

"Hello, Mick?" Jeffrey began quietly.

"Hey, Jeffrey, what a nice surprise. What's up?" Mickey welcomed the voice from home.

"Not so good, mate," Jeffrey answered, his tone sullen, "We lost the baby, Mick. Abbey's had a miscarriage."

Mickey's heart sank. He sat down, breathless, searching for words to capture his sympathy. He could faintly hear Jeffrey's stifled cry through the tortured silence.

"God, Jeffrey. Mate, I'm so sorry. I know you guys were . . ." Mickey struggled to take a breath, through the tightness of his chest. "I'm so sorry. Is Abbey alright?"

"No Mick, she's really not. She's not herself. I don't feel like I can leave her alone. She's . . . I mean, we had a good cry together at first, but since then . . . well, she's a complete zombie. She just lies there, eyes open and glazed. She won't eat. She hasn't slept. She's just completely non-responsive, Mick," Jeffrey explained desperately. "I don't know what to do, Mick. I was hoping maybe . . . I don't know . . . I thought maybe if I could get her on the phone with you. I . . . I'm sorry, Mick. I know it's late there but I just don't know what else . . . I don't know what she needs. I'm really scared mate, she's . . . it's like she's not even in there anymore," he went on, accelerating.

"Ok, Jeffrey, I . . . just put the phone close to her and tell her it's me," Mickey suggested, clueless as to how he could be of any help.

"Right, thanks, Mick," Jeffrey said, his voice registering an ounce of hope.

"Abbey, Mick's on the phone, love . . . he's on the phone, I'm . . . I'm just going to set it right here where I think you'll be able to hear him." No response that Mickey could hear. He tried in vain to swallow.

"Right then, I'll . . . I'm just going to go downstairs and leave you to it." Nothing more from Jeffrey. The silence was piercing.

"Hi Abbey," was as much as he'd mapped out, he was improvising from here. "I wish I was there, Abbey. Wish I could sit with you . . . be there with you in the quiet. I wouldn't say much, I don't think. Not much I can say, I reckon. Just sit. Just be there with you, mate," he said quietly, deflated by the fruitless search for healing words, underestimating his impact.

"Mickey?" a familiar but eerily vacant voice finally came, a million miles away.

"Yes, Abbey, it's me."

"What's happened to me, Mickey? Why can't I stop falling?" she pleaded, a wave of emotion suddenly infused in her voice, "I've never felt like this before. Nowhere close. I just want to fall asleep and not wake up, Mickey. I can't see my way out, I . . ." she cut herself off giving in to her sobbing. The distance tortured Mickey. He paced about his apartment helplessly.

"It's ok, Abbey. Just . . . just cry. Just . . . that's how this will pass eventually. It has to. You've got to surrender to it, I reckon, just . . . let it take you over, I think." Mickey could hear his friend sobbing loudly now and he questioned whether he was leading her through the tunnel or off the ledge. He had to commit to it.

"That's right, Abbey. That a girl," he encouraged her.

"Why, Mickey? Why is this happening to us? It was my baby!" she carried on weeping, no longer fighting, completely immersed in her grief. Mickey's eyes were clinched tightly, squeezing out his own tears, desperate to hold his dearest friend.

Jeffrey had run back upstairs and was now holding Abbey, rocking her.

"I'm so sorry, Jeffrey! I don't know why this happened! I don't know what I did wrong!" I'm sorry," Abbey apologized unnecessarily to her husband.

"Ok, it's going to be ok, Abbey. You did everything right. It's not your fault love, it's not your fault. Ssshhhh, ok, it's not your fault, love. I don't understand it either, but we'll get through this."

Mickey sat in a ball on his couch, listening helplessly. A couple of minutes passed before Mickey gave up waiting and hung up the phone. A few interminable minutes later, Jeffrey called back.

"So sorry, Mick. I didn't want to let go of her. But whatever you said, thanks mate; you're a magician. She's actually fallen asleep. God . . . she needed this so desperately," he said appreciatively. "I can't thank you enough."

"It's nothing, Jeffrey, just told her to give into it, I think," Mickey said, trying to remember whether anything he said could have been that helpful.

"Well, in any case, thanks so much. I might curl up myself since she's asleep," Jeffrey decided, leveled by exhaustion as he finally let down.

"Oh, yeah, of course, mate. Don't let me keep you. Just . . . give me a call later. Ok?"

"Of course, Mick. Thanks again."

Mickey hung up his phone and finally exhaled all the way. He headed straight to the kitchenette, seeking something much harder than his beer to sedate himself.

He spent a lot of time on the phone with Abbey in the weeks that followed. Mostly she just wanted to hear about his life in America, far away from Liverpool and what she'd just been through. But in her own time, she tackled the loss. Bits at a time. The fruitlessness of wondering why; whether or not there was anything she could have done to stop it; how weak she felt; how sad she was for Jeffrey and for herself. Mostly Mickey just listened, challenging her gently when he needed to. But mostly just listening. That's what she needed from him.

We rolled through September like a tank, with convincing wins over San Francisco, Miami, and Cleveland. For my part, I was quite pleased, going 12 for 14. My first miss came at home, a 38-yarder in a swirling wind (the kind Heinz Field is famous for). But I was much harder on myself than any of the lads or the coaches. The second was more a product of the coaches' confidence that I had earned. Coach Baker let me have a go from 54 yards out. Long enough but I hooked it a good three yards wide. Nonetheless, it was exciting for the moment after it left my foot. Great contact before it started to hook. Lots of helmet pats and smiles from the lads which felt strangely comforting for a miss. I think they liked the idea that we were potentially in range from outside of 50.

The other exciting development was that I started working on punting with Davey and Glen in practice. Davey's hamstring was injured in the Cincinnati game, though he managed to carry on his duties. But it was actually his suggestion that I take some reps. Glen seemed a bit put off at first, but relaxed about it when he saw how erratic I was to start. Now that's a finicky skill. I can bomb a soccer ball with a drop kick. But punting a football (listen to me; already referring to a football as a soccer ball and an American football a football) leaves very little room for error. Three centimeters of variance in where it lands on your foot can be the difference between 60 yards in the air or 30. It took quite a lot of tries to start to find it with any consistency.

But I did start to find it. There was no pressure to. Only a curiosity and the motivation to master something I thought I'd be good at. Funny how quickly we can pick something up under those conditions: patience, curiosity, confidence. It's a much straighter motion than punting a soccer ball. With a soccer ball, you can come across it more. But in the end, it's really about the drop. A bit like the toss in tennis, I reckon. I'd carry a football around my flat and try to drop it perfectly. Glen and I even played a bit of a target game with cones after practice. When I started beating him, he lost interest in playing. Pity. I quite liked that little game.

"Hey, Ringo," Bunch called on the way out to the parking lot, jogging to catch up.

"Hey, Manny," Mickey replied, pleased that Bunch would use his nickname.

"I was just wondering how your friend was doing. I didn't mean to listen in, but I heard you talking to DC a couple weeks ago. Just wondering how she was doing," he queried, almost apologetically.

"Some days better than others, I guess. But getting through it on the whole, I reckon. Thanks for asking," Mickey said with a smile.

"I just . . . I know that's tough stuff. Cheryl's sister and her husband went through it about a year ago. They're expecting again now," he added, crossing his fingers. "Well it's not my business; I was just wondering." He paused for a long moment, seemingly dissatisfied with how he had closed.

"Hard to be all the way over here at times like that, I bet," he finally prompted.

Mickey nodded, moved by the mention of it, "We've seen each other at least once a week for as many years as I can remember. She's my best mate. I miss her a lot at the best of times . . . but that was extra hard. Husband's a great bloke too. Just lovely folk."

"I bet," Bunch nodded with a smile.

"Emanual, can I ask you something?"

"Sure, Mick."

"Do you remember that day in the weight room? When we were talking about fitting in and the like?"

Bunch was already fighting a knowing smile. "Yeah, I remember."

"Well, I've really just tried to be a good teammate to *all* the lads, regardless of colour. And most of them have kind of . . . accepted me, so to speak. Some of whom are black." Mickey tried to read Bunch's face as he spoke. Unable to get a good read, he started to rush.

"At any rate, whenever I'm getting on ok with teammates who are black, I sort of feel like you don't approve. Like I should feel guilty or something."

Bunch nodded, listening intently, without signs of discomfort.

"Well, I was just . . . I guess I just . . ." Mickey sputtered.

"You don't need to feel that way . . . I think that's the answer to the question that's probably coming eventually," Bunch teased. "Look, we'll have the whole conversation one day, Mick. But for now, if it helps," he paused, weighing how much he was willing to say, "this is how I feel; You're a great teammate. You make us all better, in very subtle ways. And I can tell that you've been mindful of that conversation, which I appreciate, . . . I may have come off a little harsh, though I don't remember exactly what was said. But no, . . . working to be someone you're not doesn't help any of us. My Daddy taught me that much."

"Sounds like a smart man," Mickey offered.

"Smartest man I know," Bunch beamed. "Taught history and philosophy at the local college until he retired a year ago."

Mickey listened, his curiosity piqued.

"Another time, Ringo. Gotta run, bro," Bunch patted Mickey on the shoulder and turned to walk towards his car.

Mickey stopped and smiled as he fished his key from his pocket. He wasn't sure what label to put on what he was feeling. But he knew he was feeling more of it than he had felt since he arrived.

Mickey had been feeling a bit sorry for himself for most of practice. Both his mother and Abbey had remembered to call him in the morning to wish him a happy birthday. He promised to stop by the post office after practice to pick up the care package that the two of them had collaborated on. He hadn't been forgotten; he just felt like he was awfully far away from the people that could help him celebrate.

The practice was unremarkable, except that he got to take a couple of reps during special teams practice as a punter and he pretended to line Sands up for a big hit on his return, adding a commentary.

"Ooooohhh, Sands is absolutely plastered into the television camera! He's very slow getting up, John!"

"Dream on, Ringo! Kicka won't never get close enough, baby!" Sands teased back.

"Let's watch it again in slo mo, John. A complete shagging train wreck!" Mickey carried on.

At the end of practice, Mickey was walking to the locker room when he was met by about a dozen teammates, led by Sellers with his frighteningly mischievous grin.

"Happy Birthday dear Ringo," Sellers sang softly stepping towards the diminutive kicker.

"Oh, thanks lads, who told you?" Mickey exclaimed unwittingly.

About five minutes and five rolls of athletic tape later, Ross Killackey walked out to the practice field to survey the damage, spotting Mickey at one end, thoroughly taped to the upright, really more tape than kicker.

"Oh hey, Ross. Lovely of you to stop by," Mickey began, trying to act less distressed than he was.

"Hey could you be a good lad and fetch a tape cutter from the training room? I'd really be in your debt, mate."

"Sure, Mickey," Ross laughed, "I've got a couple calls to make and I'll be right out," he teased.

"Oh, brilliant . . . great, no rush at all, mate," Mickey played along. He was unfamiliar with this custom, was more than a little confused by it, and probably still a bit in shock.

"Oh, bugger, Ross! Go easy, mate! I'm hairier than I look, you know!" Mickey pleaded as Ross liberated him from his athletic tape confines, waxing his legs in the process.

"Sorry, Mickey. Just like a band-aid, brother. Better if I just do it quickly," Ross laughed through the process. "Got any plans for your birthday?"

"Um, no, not really, mate. Just have to stop by the post office. Then maybe a movie and grab dinner out somewhere," Mickey imagined.

"By yourself? Well, that won't do. Where do you want to eat?" Ross asked, as Mickey was finally able to pull free of the upright. "Le Mont up on Mount Washington? You name it; I'll set it up," Ross promised.

Mickey smiled widely with one place in mind, "How about Dell's?" he requested.

Ross smiled back, appreciating the sentiment in Mickey's choice, "I'll give them a call."

A few hours later, Ross picked Mickey up from his waterfront condo. Mickey could have driven himself, but for a ten minute drive, it was pretty complicated. He'd have to cross both rivers and could easily wind up downtown without trying to. He was flattered that the Killackey family had chosen to spend his birthday with him. He walked into Dell's eager to partake of their hospitality again. What he saw, he had not expected.

A full third of his teammates packed the restaurant on a Wednesday night, along with many wives, girlfriends and a handful of children. He met Emanuel's wife, Cheryl, and couldn't help but stare at the soft, perfect curls of his three picture-perfect daughters. He'd seen them in photos but the life-sized versions were even more striking.

Ricky Wild's teenage daughter came along with one of her friends, and they helped to corral the young kids. Coach Baker's two year-old grandson went AWOL for a few minutes after supper but turned up in the lounge after a short search.

Not surprisingly, Vaughn and DC were the life of the party, carrying on a playful but respectful banter with the owners, posing for photos, and constantly calling 'Mama Dell' to dote on them. She obliged, matching them all evening with her humour and charm.

Except for a moment of sadness when he watched Cheryl Bunch tend to her youngest (it triggered an image of Abbey and her would-be child), the evening was perfect. The whole restaurant joined in for "Happy Birthday to Ringo" followed by pans and pans of Tiramisu.

In the end, it was good that Ross had picked him up, as he'd had enough wine that driving wouldn't have been a good idea. He stumbled happily into his apartment, set down his stack of birthday cards and the Beatles box set that the team had given him (meant as a joke, but met with "Ah, brilliant!" all the same) and climbed into bed for a long, untroubled birthday sleep.

The remuneration from the team was very good. My flat on the waterfront was great, but I'd actually chosen a pretty modest place relative to my teammates. And I was leasing a Jaguar (my one big splurge) that I didn't drive any more than I had to. But what I really wanted and needed was to be really good at something. That much I've always known. But my journey to the U.S. revealed a need of more salient priority; I wanted to belong, to be part of something special. The difference now was I offered something that my team needed, not just appreciated. Don't get me wrong. Harold Sheffield's compliment was not lost on me. It meant a great deal. But I felt like what I could offer my new mates was not subtle or sentimental. It was integral to their goals and dreams.

Being good and acknowledged as such was a good thing. Being in a position to contribute to something great, something bigger than myself or my own aspirations; that was a great thing. Perhaps the best of things. In return, they had started to invest in me, to let me be a part of their lives, not just an observer.

There was a curious oscillation of emotions that characterized my time in America. At times I felt like I was starting to belong. Between my teammates, the Killackeys, and the people who had become a comfortable part of my day-to-day, much had been done to make me feel welcome. The Polish family that owned the meat market close to my flat; Leonard, the 'smiley' security guard at the training facility who I couldn't seem to walk past without a ten-minute conversation (I'd simply factored it into my travel time to and from); Jeanine, the girl who cut my hair and kept thinking I was from Australia—I took to pretending I was until she caught on (a bit more clever than I took her for, as it turns out); and Diane, the sweet but unimaginably incompetent bank teller who eventually, through painful trial and error, managed to help me wire money home to me mum and dad. She was determined to figure it out because she thought I was such a nice 'young fella' to do that. Not all her fault, granted; apparently banks in America don't interact with foreign banks without considerable administrative effort. But at any rate, these people were all making Pittsburgh feel like home.

Other times, I'd see or hear things that made me feel painfully foreign. Generally speaking, any reference to pop culture had to be explained to me, which usually killed the joke. And the ones that occurred to me were the same way, so I was often left to giggle to myself, at my lonely little inside jokes. And the bloody time change often meant waiting several hours to call Abbey and share them with her.

The experience of race, as I've already mentioned, was not what I expected, but bothered me less as time passed. The sociologist in me became quite engaged in the pastime of observing the differences. Abbey got a kick out of it when I told her that whenever the black players put something on the stereo, it featured someone talking to a beat, while at every turn they seemed to be singing (perhaps to make up for the lack of singing in their music). And she of course had to ask if what they say about the 'endowment' of black men was true. And it is . . . the buggers.

But quite unexpectedly, there was a sadness that crept into my bones as I started to feel more at home in America, like my connection back home was eroding by default. It's an odd thing to be teased about your 'American accent' *by your mates in the UK and then find yourself teased about your British accent in the locker room on the same day.*

There's an uneasiness in transition, when one doesn't feel like he fully belongs anywhere. And the feeling lingered intolerably. It's the sort of deep-seeded thing that you work hard to distract yourself from, because figuring it out is bound to turn up answers you won't like.

But despite the peculiar blend of unsettling emotions, I was rescued more often than not by the exhilarating freedom that I felt. My path was uniquely my own, my environment fresh and new, and my body and mind were deeply engaged in my new craft, as peripheral to the game as it may have been. Without question, a penetrating happiness was part of my new adventure.

5

*Let me embrace thee, sour adversity,
For wise men say it is the wisest course.
~ William Shakespeare*

Indianapolis. Week 5.

Despite the relatively early point in the season, the build-up for the meeting between the Steelers and the high-powered Indianapolis Colts gave the pre-game a playoff feel. The experts waited anxiously to see if the tenacious Pittsburgh defense could curb an Indianapolis offence that was averaging nearly thirty points per game. Something would have to give, as the aggressive blitz package of the Steelers would be thrown at the NFL's most adept blitz-breaker, in veteran quarterback Kyle Latour.

With the game tied at ten, nearing the end of the first half. Mickey listened in with interest to the on-field chatter as Latour lined up on the hash nearest the Steeler bench.

"I'm comin' fo'ya, baby! I'm a comin'! Here come tha hurt, dog!" Percy Dawkins antagonized as he bounced from gap to gap at the line, feigning the blitz.

As the shotgun snap came up to Latour, Dawkins and the other linebackers dropped into coverage, but the stealthy Emanuel Bunch got a sprinter's jump and quickly turned the corner, blitzing from Latour's blind side and delivering a devastating blow in the middle of his back, whipping his head back. The Steelers' bench exploded at the hit, with every player up on his feet or up in the air. Impossibly, Latour had held onto the ball, but his team would have to punt after the nine-yard loss.

DeMarco Sands bounced on the spot downfield, awaiting the Indy punt. The kick was high but deep, and Sands would have an opportunity for a return. After fielding the punt, he juked side to side quickly, freezing one downfield tackler, and causing another to fly by him. Then he accelerated upfield, darting through the wedge that his blockers had driven through the Colts punt cover team. The home team breathed a sigh of relief as Sands fell on a shoestring tackle by a diving defender. The whole stadium glanced at the clock to assess the probability of the Steelers taking their first lead of the game.

Ricky Wild worked the 2-minute offense masterfully, chewing up nearly 50 yards before his only incompletion of the drive, a twenty-yard toss to Sands in the corner of the endzone, knocked away in the nick of time by the Indianapolis cornerback. He calmly called their last time-out of the half, with six seconds left on the clock. Then he jogged to the sideline to allow the nearly perfect Mickey Doyle to chip the 33-yarder through, to give his team a 13-10 lead heading into the locker room.

Mickey's routine was the same as always. The snap was on target, the pin perfect. But Mickey watched helplessly as the 'easy chipshot' hooked wide of the uprights. His stomach tightened as he heard the home crowd surge at his expense. He felt a tidal wave of loneliness as he jogged to the sideline. No one looked at him except for the special teams coach, Butch Jardine, whose hands were raised, staring Mickey down. His gruff voice pierced the still of the Steeler bench.

"We've gotta fuckin' have those, Doyle. Simple as that. That's just unacceptable. Right?"

Mickey nodded his head in acknowledgement, then hung it as he joined the silent procession into the visiting team locker room.

What had happened? Everything was the same. The snap was good, the hold, the steps, the stroke. It all felt the same. What had gone wrong?

Mickey replayed the kick interminably, trying to dissect it and find the flaw. Over and over it played in his aching head. Eventually he had twisted and distorted it in his head enough to blame an excessive follow-through for the miss, resolving to correct it on any subsequent attempts.

Dillon patted his head on the way by, winking at him.

"It's a'ight, Ringo; ain't none of us perfect, baby," he offered with a smile.

Mickey nodded in thanks but said nothing, resolving in his silence to truly lock in, the next time he was called upon. His team was relying on him.

The second half kick-off did little to ease his punctured psyche. His determination to drill the kick through the end-zone was sabotaged by the tension in his body, and the kick was long and low, nearly a squib, giving the returner lots of time and space and working the cover team extra hard to contain him.

Part of Mickey anxiously awaited the opportunity to make up for his miss and restore his team's faith and his own confidence. Another part recoiled from the idea of another attempt, for fear of another miss. And apart from a third quarter conversion after a rare 16-yard touchdown scamper by the usually pocket-bound Ricky Wild, Mickey was forced to wait well into the fourth quarter for a shot at redemption.

Meanwhile, the proud Steeler defence continued their statement of supremacy, frustrating the usually unflappable Indy pivot, Kyle Latour. Although they had no sacks in the second half, nearly every pass attempt was recorded as a hurry, and Latour finished more plays on the ground than not.

The Steelers offensive line was making its own proclamation, a blunt force pounding at the line of scrimmage that was wearing visibly on the Colts front four. Dillon turned each gap that promised four or five yards into six or seven, inspired by the Clydesdales in front of him. Though the lead was only seven well into the fourth quarter, the sense in vibe in the stadium was unanimous. The Colts were getting beat up, at home, slowly and unmercifully.

The Steelers offense had mounted a clock-munching seven-minute drive, mostly on the ground, and now stood to take a stranglehold on the home team if Mickey could hit from thirty-seven yards out. The good news was also the bad news; he had a chance to redeem himself with a relatively short kick . . . from nearly the same spot on the field as his early miss.

He went through his pre-kick routine, trying to shut out the heckles of the Indianapolis defenders and their fans. This time, he would not hook it. He would make sure of that.

The snap: on target. The pin: flawless. The kick; . . . wide right. He'd punched it. Again the roar. Again the deflation. This time a collective eye-rolling by the Steeler players and staff. Mickey jogged to the sideline, glancing up at a stone-faced Coach Jardine, too angry even to look at his disgraced kicker.

Head coach, Shawn Baker, quickly refocused his troops.

"Alright 'D', finish this thing for us," he barked with forced confidence.

But the energy drained from the Steeler bench was piped, like an oxygen tank, to the Indianapolis bench and, most dramatically to their offensive general, Kyle Latour.

Despite the tight coverage and still-relentless push of the Pittsburgh pass rush, Latour and his receivers put on a clinic, nipping patiently at the flesh of the Steeler defense. Seven yards; eight yards; five yards; 15-yard screen; 9-yard slant. Coach Baker began glancing nervously at the clock, going from 'willing it to run' to almost hoping for a quick score so that they'd have a chance to answer.

He didn't get it. And after a tying major with less than thirty seconds to play, a lost coin toss, and nearly as impressive an overtime drive, the Steeler bench watched hopelessly as the Indianapolis kicker split the uprights perfectly from forty-two yards out.

The kick pierced Mickey's heart like a harpoon. The Steelers' record sustained its first blemish, and Mickey tried unsuccessfully to wish himself across the ocean. His stomach dropped as he overheard Coach Baker's quiet query to Jardine ahead of him in the solemn procession into the locker room.

"Merritt's knee still on target for a December return?"

Jardine nodded slowly.

"Good," Baker concluded, finding some assurance that this new problem was temporary, unsure what had come over his replacement kicker, but not wanting to work very hard to figure it out.

The travel home was uneventful, though Mickey wished it hadn't been so. He was hoping for someone to hold him accountable, to voice anger. But no one said anything, and the silence opened the gates to his own demons, the ones that lurked just under the surface and fed on his confidence whenever he failed in some way.

The team would have a short workout, stretch, and video session the next day before the four-day break of their bye week would commence. Coach Baker entertained no thoughts of shortening the break as a punishment for the loss; the team had played arguably its best game of the young season. The film review before the break would allow them to learn what lessons they could from this game, then put it behind them. The reaction that Mickey had hoped for would come then.

A handful of players were changing into their workout gear in the locker room when the 'Do we really need kickers?' rant took shape. Percy Dawkins led the charge. Emanuel did not engage, checking the entrance uneasily from time to time, hoping that neither of the kicking specialists would overhear.

"Seriously, y'all. Just like the playground. Touchdowns only. Two-point converts. Kick-offs and punts would have to be by a player that plays another position. Some big lumberin' motherfucker like Hollweg," Dawkins added, entertaining everyone who would listen. A few agreed, but most just tolerated the blast as an acceptable venting of frustration. Most of the players in earshot would quickly forgive their diminutive import kicker. One who had not . . . was Mickey himself, who suddenly emerged from the corridor and joining quietly in the discussion, without making eye contact with anyone.

"We don't really fit in, do we? Probably on to something Dawk," he conceded quietly, inspiring the sudden silence of his teammates while he quickly changed and headed for the weight room.

Emanuel was the first to speak.

"Man, what's the matter with you?! Would it kill you to play shit once in your head before you say it? Or at least try to be a little discreet?" he challenged Dawkins.

"Hey, be cool, Bunch. He'll be a'ight. Dawk's just blowin' steam, dog. He did cost us the game. A little accountability ain't a bad thing," Sellers defended.

"And 'a little' would've been alright. Tease him a bit, get mad at him, whatever. But to say, even in jest, that the game of football shouldn't even have kickers . . . because of *his* failures. That's not a little," Bunch concluded.

"Manny, you makin' this bigger than it is, dog. Come on now," Vaughn challenged.

"Are you sure, V? No one works harder to fit in with this group than Mickey. Am I right? So what's he feeling right now?" No one in the room needed to respond. Bunch was making perfect sense. Percy acknowledged with a nod, already feeling sheepish after Mickey caught him in the act. Even Vaughn suppressed his kneejerk tendency. And the bottom line revealed itself poignantly with Bunch's concluding statement.

"He's got two weeks to think about those two kicks. Shouldn't we be helping him get back to the headspace he was in before? The shit we say to each other matters y'all. It's all part of the vibe. So let's bring him back."

Bunch closed his eyes and rubbed his face. It had just dawned on him that he had done much more to alienate Mickey a few months earlier than Dawkins just had, so he walked up to the shamed linebacker and quietly pardoned him.

"I ain't always good at this stuff myself, Dawk," he said as he shook his hand and patted him on his huge chiseled shoulder.

"You right though, Triple A, I know. Just bad timing is all," Dawkins said solemnly.

Mickey was sitting with Justin on the bikes when Percy came in to apologize in his own way.

"You know I's just kiddin', right Ringo? Just blowin' off a little frustration. Know what I'm sayin'?" Mickey nodded. He did know. But this gesture was still helping him immensely.

"So we good?" he checked, taking Mickey's much smaller hand in his and cupping the back of his neck with the other, jostling him gently.

"Yeah, we're fine, mate," Mickey reassured.

"Good. Now back to 'automatic', a'ight? Know what I'm sayin'?" Percy urged, his eyes wide and his smile even more so.

"You got it, Dawk," Mickey agreed.

Percy sauntered back to the bench he was working at and Justin and Mickey resumed their discussion.

"I wish I'd been there, bro. Cuz I could see it on TV," Justin began. Mickey listened carefully. "See you're not *learning* how to kick. You *know* how. Your body gets it. And I'm not saying we can't always be working to get a little better. But not at game time. Game time is about trust. It's about believing in whatever you've programmed in. It's about thinking *less*.

"See you take any kicker in the league. They all can kick. They all have the stroke. Most have a lot of leg. But get any one of them thinking about their last misfire . . . and they're fucked, bro. Including me, and . . . obviously you too," Justin added, snickering apologetically. Mickey smiled, excusing him. Justin went on.

"So when you miss, instead of trying to diagnose it, you go back in your head to what you want it to feel like. 'What's the *right* feeling?' Rather than 'what's wrong'. 'What's wrong' is reserved for practice time. Game time is when you protect the temple of 'I'm the fuckin' shit'," Justin said grandly, drawing a huge roof in the air with his hands.

"Fear and doubt got no place in your kitchen at game time, Mick," he added, pointing to his head. "No place at all," he repeated for emphasis. "You follow, bro?"

"Step for step," Mickey assured. "That's exactly what happened. And I should know better."

"You do. Just forgot, bud. That's where I can help," he said warmly as he climbed off his bike. "Time for a little physio," he said to close their conversation.

It astounds me how hard we can make it on ourselves to recover from our failures sometimes. It should be such a natural process. Every failure is more data on how to get back to center, right? But we can sabotage it so easily. I had absolutely crucified myself the night before. And in my emotional carnage, you'd have thought I hadn't made a kick all season. Instead of recognizing my drift away from confidence, away from the 'right feel' as Justin put it, I allowed that one kick to become the biggest thing in the world. I was so focused on it that I couldn't see anything else. Then when it should have been clear what a bad idea it was to dissect it, when I'd missed the second one, any amount of rationality says 'woah, Mick. However you were thinking about that first kick, it didn't work; where was your head before your good kicks?' But had I learned my lesson? No. Rationality was nowhere to be seen. Insecurity, guilt, fear, all my bloody demons from the past, suddenly they were main floor tenants in my mind, all working very hard to convince me that I was a loser, that I wasn't good enough. So I was in the process of beating myself senseless and analyzing the living shit out of both kicks when Justin caught me. The truth is, I likely wouldn't have caught myself for the full two weeks, instead punishing myself interminably for the previous game, with the expectation that I was to make up for it in the next game. And how would I do that with my confidence in the toilet, my mind on what I didn't want, with a running mantra of 'just don't bugger this up, Doyle?' Hardly an inspired battle cry. Maybe it's not as simple as knowing better. Maybe sometimes we need someone to remind us. In any case, as luck would have it, I had that someone. And my mind was already starting to repair itself, to remind me what I had done in the past, remind me that I was good at this, perhaps even great. But even in my renewed state, I could not have predicted what happened next.

"Whassup, Ringo?" Vaughn bellowed as he slapped Mickey on the back in his squat rack, nearly knocking him off his feet.

"Just finishing up my lift before video," Mickey replied. "Time to face the music," he added, although he was nearly at peace with the events of the day before and would gladly own his responsibility for the loss.

"Whatcha doin' for the break?" Vaughn asked.

"Hadn't really thought about it, actually. Not enough time to go home. Probably just mill about in town, I guess."

"Nah, dog. You comin' home with me. I ain't lettin' you sit alone for the break!"

Mickey was stunned, equal parts of 'moved', 'shocked' and wondering if Vaughn was 'having him on'.

"Uh, . . . where's, uh, where's home?" he stammered, barely entertaining the idea.

"Florida, baby! Ah yeah, come on home and chill at my parents' new crib. I bought them a dope old house close to where I grew up. All my cousins and shit are always there. You gotta meet my nephews, dog; they're a trip," he said excitedly.

"Well, w-w-when?" Mickey asked uncertainly.

"Flyin' out tonight. We'll get Debbie to put you on the same flight (Debbie was in charge of logistics for the team and often took care of travel needs). Ah yeah! Mama's home cookin for a few days, sit on the deck with my papa, hit the beach; this just what the doctor ordered, Ringo! I ain't takin' no for an answer. Pack your bag, baby."

Mickey smiled in resignation.

"Right then. Off to Florida. Brilliant," he digested, the idea quickly growing on him. "Your folks have lots of sunscreen . . . or should I get my own?" he quipped, watching Vaughn carefully to see if he knew it was a joke.

"Nah, that's all you, dog," he snickered, getting it. "Now come on; time for your whuppin' from Coach Baker," Vaughn laughed. "Come take it like a man, boy."

Their journey got off to a shaky start. Mickey had never met Vaughn's Rottweilers, Malcolm and Cassius. They snarled, barked, and nipped at Mickey over the back of his seat as he sat terrified in the passenger seat for the duration of the ten-minute drive to Demarco Sands' home where the dogs would stay. Vaughn's Escalade rocked as the dogs egged each other on. Vaughn was not very supportive.

"It's cuz they know you're scared, Ringo. Come on, just chill, dog," he insisted.

"I *am* scared, Vaughn! Bloody hell!" They think I'm a shagging steak!" Mickey snapped at Sellers, wincing with each sharp movement of the rotties.

"Well they can smell fear, dog! Whataya expect?"

"I can't . . . change my smell, Vaughn!" Mickey exclaimed in exasperation.

"A'ight, but you'll have to get over this eventually," Vaughn said as he leaned over the seat and shouted "OFF," nearly sending Mickey through the roof but silencing the dogs.

"Are you kidding me? You could have done that ten minutes ago!" Mickey protested, inspiring one last bark from Cassius. Vaughn raised the back of his hand slowly, displaying it to both dogs. They both shrunk down in the backseat, whimpering. Then Vaughn glanced over at his perturbed little passenger who was still waiting for a response. Vaughn's smile melted into apologetic stifled laughter that would last most of the way to the airport.

Mickey was not impressed, but Vaughn's failed attempt to stop eventually rubbed off, and Mickey finally shook his head, smiling.

"Daft bugger."

After nearly soiling myself on the way to drop off the dogs, I was seriously second-guessing my decision to take Vaughn up on his offer. But after that, it was one pleasant surprise after another. Vaughn truly did go all out in buying his parents a new home. It was a stone's throw from the water, a big old white house with a veranda that went all the way around. And once I'd met 'Mama' (I've been calling her that since my visit and expect I always will), I understood completely what had inspired his generosity.

When we arrived at their house, she met him half way up the walk and gave him the biggest, longest hug I've ever seen. When he said "Hi Mama" he sounded like a child, his defenses dropped and his emotions high. She was round, as I'd imagined, but also very sturdy and strong. She was also very pretty, which probably should not have surprised me given Vaughn's features. In truth, he's quite a nice looking man, but his many other um . . . qualities kind of grip you before you can notice. In any case, her eyes each squeezed out a tear as she hugged her lad, and I suspect if Vaughn had been facing me, his eyes would have looked the same.

Then she turned her attention to me and said, "Now you must be Ringo," to which I couldn't help but laugh. I felt kind of badly correcting her; it sounded really nice when she said it. But no sooner had I said 'actually, it's Mickey," and held out my hand, than she wrapped her big arms around me and gave me a hug too. "Well we're glad y'all could come, Mickey," she said in a tone that wrapped me like a blanket, "Any friend of Vaughn's is welcome here".

I was undone. She was the sweetest woman I'd ever met. Absolutely unabashed warmth. For the first time since I'd been there, I felt like someone looked straight past my skin colour and really saw me. Vaughn later explained that 'y'all' was referring to me only. Apparently, in the south, y'all is singular and 'all a y'all' is the plural.

Curiously, despite his physical similarity to Vaughn, Vaughn's father or 'Papa' bore little resemblance to him in personality. He was very quiet and never seemed to stop smiling. A retired carpenter, he greeted us inside, hugging Vaughn then shaking my hand with his enormous hand that nearly came to my elbow. Then he happily sat and listened to Vaughn go on telling stories into the wee hours, keeping one eye on the games that he'd 'Tivo'ed the day before. I became curious about where Vaughn's aggression and quick trigger had come from, as it didn't seem to come from either of his parents. I made a mental note to try to gain a better understanding of it if I ever felt comfortable enough around Vaughn to ask him that direct a question.

We slept in and woke to the smell of bacon and 'flapjacks' as they like to call them. The four of us sat and ate and laughed until almost midday. Mama told me stories about Vaughn as a young child. "Chald" she'd say. He made me promise on my life that I'd never tell any of them. The best was about him and his sister playing dress-up. Oh, bugger, I did promise. Never mind.

Anyway, we spent the afternoon at the beach, mostly standing around listening to him talk to people that recognized him, either from pro football or his time at "the U", their rather bold moniker for The University of Miami, where he had attended college (must check whether he actually 'attended' . . . actually). Somehow I went unrecognized. Not a big deal.

The evenings were amazing. The whole Sellers clan converged on the house and somehow managed to make the living room look small. Vaughn's the youngest of five children, and all of them, except for him, bred like rabbits. Vaughn was wonderful with the children, taking on all dozen nieces and nephews, except for the wee Fiona, who retreated to her grandmother's knee when the horseplay began. He'd tease and tickle and tackle each, making sure each of them was noticed at some point.

Eventually the rough play escalated and the fiery Terrence, almost nine, hauled off and popped Vaughn in the nose. Vaughn's sister, Carol jumped from her seat and yanked Terrence right off his feet.

"Terrence James, what's the matter with you," she scolded.

But Vaughn just laughed and assured her, "It's a'ight, Carol; shit, you used to hit me a lot harder than that," which drew laughter from the whole room and restored the levity, except for Mama's gentle reminder from her big chair.

"Vaughn, baby, don't curse around the 'chidren'," she said. Oh, she's wonderful to listen to.

But as I listened to the stories and watched Vaughn command the spotlight, it made more sense. Vaughn was the youngest of five children, and I think by the time he was born, his parents were more passive and permissive in their parenting. And Vaughn definitely has a fiery temperament (perhaps why he was so tolerant of young Terrence). So perhaps he was indulged by his parents, both of them so easy-going, so he had few checks on his behavior. And by the time he hit grade school, his size, ferociousness, and athleticism had already given him 'chosen one' athletic status. And so it went, or so I imagine it.

Regardless, by the time we were flying back to Pittsburgh, my nose was red and peeling, I'd probably gained five kilos from the food, and my face hurt from smiling and laughing for three days straight. Just what the doctor ordered. All this with the man who had bullied me tirelessly for the first month of my stay in America. What a curious . . . and wonderful turn of events. And somehow, the very idea that someone like 'Mama' was mum to one of my new mates made the place feel even more like home.

Minneapolis, Minnesota. Week 9.

The conversation with Justin had restored Mickey's focus. The trip with Vaughn had restored his mood and energy. And going five for six (his only miss from 46 yards with a crosswind) in his next two games had restored his confidence. The team won in a blowout against Cleveland, then dropped a sleeper to the New York Jets in which Mickey accounted for all the scoring (13-9).

Now the team was leading the Minnesota Vikings in their indoor stadium by a score of 21-7. Mickey was swimming in confidence after a warm-up that featured a 60-yard kick on only his second try before heading back into the locker room before game time. With no wind to deal with, Mickey sat chomping at the bit to kick under perfect conditions.

With less than a minute to play in the half, Wild orchestrated a quick drive, moving the ball to just inside the Vikings' 40-yard line. But the Minnesota defense stopped them in their tracks and on fourth down, a dozen seconds on the clock, Coach Baker gave in to the faintest of smiles then turned to Mickey and said, "Let's test that leg of yours."

Mickey could feel his energy surging as he lined up. Knowing he was a little nervous, he took a slow, deep breath to take the edge off, and imagined himself splitting the uprights from this distance. When the snap was down, he drove his foot powerfully through the ball. He watched uneasily as the ball began to drift to the left. It crossed the left upright but had the distance to break the plain above it so it was difficult to tell whether it had snuck through. After a delayed reaction from the officials (it was that close) the referee signaled that the kick was good. 24-7.

Mickey now had a 55-yard field goal to his credit, and coach Baker's smile (he didn't try to fight this one) was ample evidence that the back-to-back misses a few weeks before were far from his mind. As the team headed in for the half-time break, Mickey sustained a barrage of celebratory helmet slaps from his teammates. Amidst the raindrop rhythm of the pats, Mickey gave in to a smile as he heard coach Jardine remark to coach Baker, "that had the distance for sixty".

The visitor locker room was abuzz. Not only were they handily beating one of the top NFC contenders, but they had the added momentum of an unlikely bomb of a field goal from their rookie kicker. Between DC's 58-yard romp to open the scoring and Mickey's kick in the dying seconds of the half, the offense felt like they could score from anywhere, at any time. Meanwhile the defense had ruthlessly held the NFL's fifth ranked offense to only 120 first half yards. Mickey sat contently in his spot in the corner, savouring the vibe.

"DC, that fuckin' hole big enough for you?" Hollweg crowed.

"Hell yeah, baby! Ringo's grandma coulda' gone through there with her walker, y'all," Dillon teased, adding the actions.

"Bullocks! from the corner, "Nana would have beaten you to the hole," Mickey teased back. The room rang its approval.

"Can Nana kick, dog? Maybe she'd be a better safety on kick-off," back from DC, not to be outdone. He was making a reference to a failed attempt by Mickey to beat the Cleveland returner to the sideline two weeks earlier. Thankfully, one of the special teams speedsters had run him down. Mickey snickered at the dig, knowing any comeback would have fallen short.

"Touché," he conceded.

Then DC built him back up.

"Nice '3', Ringo! Shit, you money, kicka'!" he added, walking over for a 'smack & snap' celebration.

"That's a nice half, fellas," from the veteran quarterback, "but we ain't done yet," he cautioned to refocus the troops.

But the damage was done. The will of the Vikings had been surgically resected on both sides of the ball, and the game became a slow, chippy, penalty-filled affair. With just under five minutes to play, objecting to consecutive late hits on Carmichael, Coach Baker strode almost halfway across the field, shouting at the Minnesota head coach, Keith Manz, whom he had once mentored,.

"Hey, Keith, get your goons on a leash; this isn't goddam wrestling!"

"Deal with it, coach," back from Manz, "It's a physical game," he provoked.

"Physical game," Baker muttered before calling back, "We're beatin' your asses up and down the field in this physical game, you insolent little prick."

The Steelers players giggled quietly to themselves, not sure if it was okay to laugh when their coach was this irate.

"Let's run it up on these sons-a-bitches," he said to Demarco Sands as he sent him in with a play, "Let's go Deuces left, Hooks flood, and tell him to throw you the backside seam whether you're open or not," he said quietly, eyeing the opposing coach across the battlefield and smacking his turbo-charged wideout on the backside. Sands smiled confidently as he jogged to the huddle.

Wild's forty-yard rope to Sands trampled the already broken backs of the Vikings, sending Manz into a personal rage directed at Baker. But then he rambunctiously applauded the penalty call against the Steelers. Holding; the play was coming back.

Baker's emotion had rubbed off on the Steelers players. They were chattering excitedly at both the Vikings players and their coach, stoking the already bright embers. Mickey stood on the sideline, charged up like a school boy watching a playground fight. He wished he could deliver a blow on his coach's behalf. He got his chance.

Baker glanced at the yard markers and then over at Mickey. They were just inside of mid-field. 4th down; fifteen yards to go. Then he called to Jardine matter of factly.

"Hey, Butch. What's the field goal record?"

"It's like 62, 63 yards," he laughed, delighted by his boss' spunk.

Baker glanced at Jardine, then once more at Mickey.

"Field-goal!" he called smugly, giving in to a mischievous grin, "Let's see that bomb of a leg again, Ringo."

Coach had never called him Ringo. It gave him goosebumps. Meanwhile, Mickey's teammates bounced around the sideline, jabbering excitedly, none of them daring to believe he could hit from sixty-five yards, but thrilled their coach would give him a chance all the same. On the other sideline, Manz shook his head in disgust, finally gesturing to Baker with his middle finger, an indiscretion that would no doubt be fined heavily.

Mickey marked off his steps nervously, butterflies colliding violently inside him. The snap was a little low but deftly managed by back-up quarterback, Theo Branch. Mickey struck the ball with all of his might, not really having the luxury of aiming his kick from this distance. It left his foot like a mortar and the team held their collective breath as they watched it rise. Impossibly, it appeared to have the distance, but its line looked wide and you could feel a 'too bad' sigh come over the Steelers sideline. But Mickey saw it first, indeed he had sensed it from when it left his foot; the ball was hooking. It had a long way to go, but it was drifting inward towards the tiny uprights. He bounded sideways, willing it to get through while it registered on the sideline that it had a chance.

Vaughn was bouncing the other way towards Mickey in anticipation. The back judges looked at each other in disbelief, then signaled in unison that the kick was good. Mickey was mobbed by his teammates, Vaughn reaching him first and pouncing dangerously on top of him. At the bottom of the pile, Mickey lay breathless . . . and absolutely elated. What an enormous thrill. It wasn't the record, he reckoned in the moment, but the intense affinity he felt from 'the lads'.

Then the bubble burst. In the excitement, it took a few moments for it to register with anyone that a whistle had gone right after the play began. Coach Manz had signaled for a time-out to freeze the kicker, a split second before the ball was snapped. And the side judge had obliged. The play would not count.

But when the second attempt went well wide, and a little short, his teammates ignored it and carried their kicker off the field on their shoulders. Mickey was a little embarrassed, given the outcome, but didn't let it tarnish the moment. It was special all the same.

Thankfully, the game ended without further incident, both sides subdued by the surreality of what they had witnessed. History had been made . . . unofficially. It would not go into the books, but it would be etched into their memories for decades to come.

The team's charter flight home was a fun one. About halfway through, Coach Baker sat down beside Mickey, his eyelids droopy from fatigue and a couple of beers and started to recount his most memorable football moments. Evidently, Mickey's 'would-be-record' had cracked the list. Mickey listened patiently, just thrilled that their head coach, who might have spoken a total of twenty words to him all year, chose him to sit with for over an hour, talking to him like a son. It was a great day.

"Mickey, that's unbelievable! You'd better not be shitting me or I'll smack you!" Abbey threatened hollowly.

"I can scarcely believe it myself," Mickey admitted, buzzing from the all-but-finished Iron City six-pack he'd guzzled, unable to sleep.

"I wish you could have seen it, Abbey; it was . . ."

"Hold on," Abbey interrupted on a hunch. "I'm gonna 'YouTube' it. Oh shit, here it is, I bet," she continued, watching a video load after typing in his name. "Holy fuck, Mick! That's unbelievable! You're a shagging star over there . . . aren't you?" she prompted her friend to acknowledge.

"I'm having a lot of fun," he answered, not quite ready to assume that grand a status.

"Oh Christ! Is that Vaughn bloke on top of you?" she asked, glued to the conclusion of the video clip.

"Oh probably," Mickey supposed, unable to see her computer. "Still hurts a bit when I inhale actually," he added, not kidding, but not particularly bothered by it.

"There's another one here," Abbey noticed, "Kicker turtles?" she read aloud, "What's that?"

"Oh, piss it," Mickey muttered, realizing the clip was his most embarrassing moment immortalized in cyberspace, "Please don't watch that."

Too late.

"When was that?" Abbey queried, dissolving into laughter.

"Opening day . . . not my finest moment," Mickey subtitled unnecessarily, "Can we be done with that now?" he insisted.

"Hold on; just let me watch it once more," Abbey tormented.

"Oh lovely . . . by all means, enjoy," Mickey invited dryly. "Are you quite finished?" he asked impatiently. "Can we go back to my nearly record-breaking moment please?" he begged for a reprieve.

"Oh the moment's done, Mickey. Don't let it go to your head," she teased. "Oh, I'm only kidding, Mick. That's truly amazing. I'm so thrilled for you, love, honestly."

"Thanks," Mickey returned with a tired smile. "Had to share it with you."

"Glad you did," Abbey validated before giving in to her pesky side once more. "So . . . shagged any prostitutes lately?"

"Good night, Abbey."

6

A man wrapped up in himself makes a very small bundle.
~ Benjamin Franklin

So about now, you may be wondering if this is another cautionary tale about success going to another poor bugger's head. Well it's not. At least not from my perspective. There's no denying that I was enjoying a sudden and unfamiliar foray into elite success and status, but a number of things saved me. First and foremost, of course, was my mate, Abbey. Ever since we were children, whenever she saw me having some success and got the slightest inkling that I might be feeling self-important, she'd knock me down like a tower of blocks, the more grandly the better.

But the opposite was also true. She knew better than anyone else how much my self-worth could blow in the wind as a minor league footballer. And she was so steady. She's reassembled my pieces even more than my mother, whose support has also been unwavering. Ole Shanty, bless his heart, was absolutely manic depressive about my sporting career, not doing anything to help me keep it in scale, but at least always making me feel like I had a passionate supporter. But Abbey could care less; and for that, I owe her a great deal.

You see, the brightest minds in psychology have told us for years that the key to emotional health is having someone in your life whose approval and love was not contingent upon anything. So that life can be about being yourself, rather than proving yourself. And for the most part, the parents of young lads playing football would love them whether they were scoring goals or not. But here's the illusion that derails a lot of us. Parents are generally happy when their children are happy. And success and mastery are pretty reliable agents of happiness. So picture this; little Johnny scores a goal and jumps about like a loon. His parents see how excited he is and get equally excited. Their little Johnny's got a smile a foot wide after all. But between jumps, Johnny spots mum and dad also jumping about, flashing him a thumbs up, high-fiving the parents of the lad that set him up. On the way home, they relive the magical moment together and stop for ice cream. Play it back now and deduce what an 8 year-old lad will make of it. I score; mum and dad jump for joy. See it? Success equals love. Then a couple games go by when he doesn't score. He's disappointed about it, and his parents are respectfully quiet on the way home. Again, what message does the 8 year-old take away? Where's the love gone? Where's the bloody ice cream now? And so goes the addiction. And just like the drink, or the heroin, or the pornography, it takes more and more to bring about the same effect, the same emotions, both externally and internally.

Unless of course there's some sort of stopper. A source of love without a trigger. The last time I was cut from the major league side (predictable but still gut-wrenching), Abbey and her Jeffrey took me to the pub, got me bloody inebriated, endured a blubbering bout of self-pity that I'm glad I can't remember, then placed pillows on their bathroom floor so that I'd be comfortable between fire hose bouts of vomiting. Then they made me breakfast at noon the next day and walked me back to my flat, recounting every humorous detail of the night before (how humorous depended on your perspective, of course).

On the evening of my greatest professional football triumph, a second division win against the Manchester farm, I called Abbey to let her know that the lads were taking me out. Abbey let me recap the game in agonizing detail before finally clarifying, "so I assume the short version of all this is we're not meeting up at the Anchor, as planned". Doesn't sound like spectacular support, I know, but it is. You see, who scores more goals in a football match doesn't really matter a fig, does it? Doesn't save lives, doesn't take any (hooliganism notwithstanding). But it doesn't stop all of us from blowing the outcomes fantastically out of proportion. Page 1: Chelsea upsets Man. U. Page 2: God is dead; the Great War has begun.

I know people look suspiciously at Abbey and me, with all the time we spend together, especially Jeffrey's best mates. But it truly is a friendship uncontaminated with sex. Never have, never will. Not that I've never fancied a shag with her, but just because what we provide for each other has so little to do with that, which makes our relationship so much more unconditional than even a marriage. That's right, think about it. How many blokes would hit the door faster than a Beckham kick-at-goal if they knew their wives would never shag them again? Frightening, isn't it? But they stick around and generally behave themselves, not necessarily for the promise of sex, but merely for the modest probability. It's a bit sad really. An institutional equivalent of the slots. Besides, once she and Jeffrey finally have children, and I'm convinced they will, a few extra pounds on her will help to extinguish the idea completely. Hey, I'm just being honest. I never claimed to be above my gender.

But managing success also comes from what you aspire to. I've been around enough Rodney Banks' to lock onto some pretty strong values about success and humility. I believe that a man's worth is principle-based. Sure I admire talent. But talent guided by principle, now that inspires. The Harold Shefields, the Emanuel Bunches, my mother come to think of it. But I also count my father among my heroes, for his devotion, his passion, his humour, his honesty. I had a lot of time to myself for the first few months in America. I imagined what success on that stage would be like, who I might become. And I can honestly say that my yearning was not for shiny, new, beautiful friends, but rather for a chance to share it with the old ones. This 'little Johnny' wasn't hoping to draw a crowd; I wanted a clear view of me loved ones on the sideline, that we might be happy together.

But alas, as moving as all this rhetoric might be, the ultimate grounding influence for any success I might have in America was the simple fact that I was a kicker. While Vaughn Sellers was dismembering opposing quarterbacks and ball carriers, I was chipping in extra points. While Dillon Carmichael was hammering away at opposing defenses like a superhero, I was marking off my little approach. While Ricky Wild was picking himself off the turf after each strike he threw, I was kicking into my little net. My lot was to live amongst the gladiators without really being one, to reward them for their efforts through a consolation, a field-goal, when no touchdown could be scored. To punch through the celebratory point-after, more of a formality than a legitimate football play. But that was fine. There's something to be said for having humility built into one's existence. My father cut steel for almost fifty years, to no ovations, with a pittance of a wage. And he's probably the happiest bugger I know.

Week 12. Home to San Diego.

There was an electricity in the locker room for this match-up that Mickey hadn't felt since opening day. After a dominant 35-13 thrashing of the Atlanta Falcons (Mickey didn't see the field except for kick-offs and converts), the team had fallen to New England on the road. The score of the wet, snowy contest had been 14-13. Mickey was 2 for 3, impressive considering the New England coach didn't even let his kicker attempt fourth down kicks of 37 and 41 yards because of the conditions. Mickey's miss was from 44 yards in the first quarter. He'd slipped spectacularly and the kick barely made it over the line. His shoulder pads hit before his backside, yet another Youtube video with his name on it. But he cautiously pumped through kicks of 29 and 39 yards after that.

The game appeared to be in hand, when the offense was chewing up both time and yardage in the closing minutes before a botched exchange between Wild and Carmichael had resulted in a blooper fumble return that was fumbled once more, picked up, lateralled (forward incidentally, but not overturned) and finally rumbled in by a hometown defensive end. The game had haunted Carmichael for the week, despite a strong performance in the snow and mud. But Mickey was also very aware that his miss could have been the difference, though everyone else had been much more forgiving.

But tonight, a victory against the recently hot Chargers would give them a strangle hold on the division title. The chasing Bengals had lost a last second heartbreaker to the NFC leading Cowboys earlier in the day. They could all but seal the crown if they moved to 8 and 3, but the explosive Dexter Selwyn-Johnson, as fast as his name was long, would have something to say about it. He and Dillon Carmichael were neck and neck in the all-purpose yards race, swapping leads weekly. While Dillon was the whole package at running back: big, strong, fast, agile, and intuitive; Selwyn-Johnson was the ultimate speedster, deadly swift out of the backfield, even more lethal on kick-off returns. Extra practice time had been devoted to kick-off cover, indulging Coach Jardine's well-founded fears about the game-breaking potential of the Chargers' return. The thought of being the last man back against this human cruise missile terrified Mickey.

The opening kick-off validated the extra work. Selwyn-Johnson snaked his way to a seam and the home crowd held its breath before the back-up cornerback, J.D. Coleman snuck through the wedge unblocked and put the unsuspecting returner on his back. But impossibly, he sprang up as if nothing had happened and smiled through the trash talk, content that it had still been a 28-yard return.

While Selwyn-Johnson was effective, the Steeler defense managed to limit his yards after the catch, preventing any long, momentum-shifting open field runs. Meanwhile, on the other side of the ball, Dillon's timing was perfect, sensing where the holes would be and hitting them as soon as they opened. The Pittsburgh O-line, anchored by the colossal Hollweg, took great pride in the numbers that Carmichael had put up (he never forgot to acknowledge their efforts post-game) and he happily rode their stampeding heals to open field. And with the head of steam that they afforded him, he too was battering the Charger defense. They too managed to prevent any particularly long gains by the Steelers' back, but his cumulative carries were akin to a slow but steady hemorrhage that the Chargers would need to patch or die a slow, painful death at the hands of Hollweg and his paving crew.

The Steelers took a 10-0 lead on a 1-yard plunge by Carmichael at the end of a long drive. But on the ensuing kick-off, Selwyn-Johnson shifted the momentum for his team, as he had in numerous previous contests. Seemingly contained, he paused within the closing walls of his blockers. Two players had a hand on him and were dragging him down when he somehow spun free, froze an oncoming tackler, then darted for the sideline, taking off almost straight sideways, flaunting the laws of physics that Mickey had thought were fairly reliable. With a burst of acceleration, he turned the corner and outraced the angle of the Steelers cover team. Mickey had anticipated the move and made it to the sideline before being pushed out by a Charger's blocker from behind. Mickey scrambled to his feet in time to see Selwyn-Johnson dance into the end-zone, trailed by an entourage of celebrating San Diego blockers. 10-6. No flags.

Coaches Baker and Jardine scurried over to the nearest official, pleading their case for a clipping penalty on the shove that had sent their kicker onto his face out of bounds. Their argument would not be heard. The convert was good. 10-7. The Steelers took a 3-point lead into the locker room, unsettled by how quickly their 10-point advantage had vanished, still riled by the protest of their coaches.

"It's a'ight, y'all; we where we wanna be," Carmichael encouraged.

"Nice half, DC," back from Bunch, alluding to Dillon's 70 yards in rushing. Bunch had two knock-downs to his credit and had single-handedly brought Selwyn-Johnson down three times in the half. He too was in the zone.

"Lookin' good, hogs!" Vaughn bellowed at the offensive linemen, "Keep hammerin' baby." Hollweg winked his thanks.

The team quickly put the long return into perspective, restoring their confidence after a strong half of football. Their replenished energy showed in the opening minutes of the second half, confidently marching sixty yards to set up a 30-yard three from Mickey. But the Chargers offense took advantage of the extra attention the Steelers were paying to Selwyn-Johnson by turning to their unheralded receiving corps, and answering with a drive of their own. Good from 35; 13-10 Steelers.

Both offenses sputtered after that, trading punts well into the fourth quarter before Selwyn-Johnson squeaked through an opening and romped nearly 50 yards to pay-dirt. The Chargers had taken their first lead of the game, 17-13.

But not to be outdone, just inside the 2-minute warning, DeMarco Sands snagged a Ricky Wild bullet thrown up the seam and split two defenders with his own burst of blinding speed, loping into the end-zone to the deafening roar of the sell-out Pittsburgh crowd. Extra point is good. 20-17 Steelers.

But then 65 thousand nervous fans turned their eyes on Dexter Selwyn-Johnson, who anxiously awaited the kick-off, and a chance to land a knock-out counterpunch. Coach Jardine had instructed Mickey emphatically, holding his mask, before patting him on the rear end on his way onto the field.

"Nice little squib, Mick. Just keep it in bounds and outta that sumbitch's hands," he said, gesturing at Selwyn-Johnson.

Mickey's kick appeared to fit the bill, but it rolled mercilessly through the Charger's return team to the feet of the San Diego cheetah. Mickey bounced into his center-field position, trying in vain to swallow. Selwyn-Johnson read the hole tentatively before bolting straight up-field behind the Chargers' wedge. The audible gasp of the entire Steelers faithful matched Mickey's as he saw the same daylight that Selwyn-Johnson could see from the other side.

Mickey's stocky legs fired like pistons as he skittered towards the sideline that the returner was racing to, having broken the first wave. Selwyn-Johnson gave Mickey a little head-fake to freeze him as he accelerated around the corner. But just as it appeared that the blazing return-man would turn the corner, Mickey launched himself like a torpedo, desperate, his eyes closed. Doyle's shoulder pad hit Selwyn-Johnson square in the chest, jolting him right off his feet and out-of-bounds. The impact of the hit shook the Chargers' sideline before the roar of the crowd rumbled it like an earthquake.

An excited J.D. Coleman, the closest cover man in pursuit, yanked Mickey to his feet excitedly, hugging him, before the two of them were mobbed by the rest of the cover team. Mickey pranced across the field to the Steelers sideline, nearly concussed by the peppering of head slaps, but too delirious with adrenaline to notice. Butch Jardine lifted him right off his feet with a hug (remarkable considering how NOT-huggy the players perceived Jardine to be).

The fired up Steelers defense sacked the San Diego pivot twice before cornerback, Bo Townsend, intercepted a desperate bomb into coverage. Ricky Wild took a knee, and pointed to the sideline at Mickey, whose teammates had already started to hoist him up onto their shoulders. The euphoric Liverpool goalie was carried off the field and into the locker room.

"Put that on shagging Youtube," he shouted to anyone who was listening.

Mickey sat in the locker room of the training facility a couple days later, taking in the banter, in no hurry to get changed. Now feeling much more comfortable with his place, he was better able to enjoy the chatter for its entertainment value. His attention was eventually drawn to Ricky Wild and the conversation he was having on his phone.

"Well, none of the other wives can help? . . . Right, most of them are coming to the thing," he attempted to problem solve with his wife. "Well, I don't know, Kay; we can't *not* go," he insisted, realizing that his voice had risen and glancing up self-consciously.

Vaughn poked in response, "uh, oh, *Married wit Children* is in trouble, y'all; what up, Al Bundy?" Wild often took some teasing for his domestic orientation, as did Bunch. Bunch shushed him, but smiled, content that it wasn't him this time. Wild gestured at Sellers with his middle finger.

"I know, Kay. I'm not saying we should leave her. Just . . ." Wild looked up at Mickey and rolled his eyes as he let his wife vent.

"Kay, listen. We're going to this foundation dinner. I will find someone to watch Brittany. Alright? I will come up with something. Ok? So calm down, go to your hair thing, and I will see you at home. Ok. Love you. Bye." Wild shook his head and snickered, glancing again at Mickey.

"Trouble in paradise?" Mickey dared to inquire.

"Oh, not really. Our oldest, Brittany, actually I brought her to your birthday thing," Wild prefaced.

"Yeah, yeah, I remember," Mickey acknowledged.

"Well, one of her little friends was driving with her in the car and they got pulled over on their way somewhere. They had open beer in the car,"

"Uh oh,"

"Yeah, so she's on house arrest for a couple weeks. We're supposed to go to this Children's hospital thing tonight and now Kay's friend who was going to come over can't, so I have to come up with something else. She's called around with no luck. Funny thing is our 14 and 11 year-olds don't need a sitter, but our almost-17 year-old does," Wild managed to laugh at the irony.

"Well, if you're stuck, I can come by," Mickey offered.

Ricky's eyes lit up, attracted to the ease of the solution.

"You're not going to this dinner?" Wild asked.

"Didn't even know about it actually," Mickey assured.

"Are you sure, Mick? Cause you'd really be saving my ass," Wild checked, already gracious.

"All I had planned was dinner and my book and I can do that anywhere, I reckon," Mickey confirmed.

"Ah, that's great, Mickey; I owe you huge."

"Ah, naw mate. Not at all."

Ricky sat back down and looked at Mickey, as if deciding whether to confide. So Mickey sat too.

"Man, we've been here four years and she's still not really settled. We were in San Fran for eight and we both grew up out west, so that was easier. Anyway, any time we get stuck with something like this, she really feels how far away from home she is. So it's kinda tough," he confided, though that much was obvious.

"I guess it's a lot easier for me, having a built-in group of buddies. Anyway, she's pretty involved in this gala for the Children's Hospital so she's already a bit stressed," he understated.

"Yeah, I can relate to the homesick thing," Mickey smiled. It hadn't occurred to him that others in his midst might be dealing with something similar, for which he shamed himself.

"Oh yeah, I guess," Wild blinked sheepishly, somehow having forgotten how 'foreign' Mickey was. "Our place is pretty easy to find, you know where Mount Lebanon is?" Wild began, about to explain it verbally.

"Rubbish," Mickey interrupted. "No place in this shagging town is easy to find," Mickey stated, having gotten lost more times than he cared to remember. "Write it down, *in detail* and put your bloody cell number right there on the directions so that I can call when I get lost," he demanded.

He was quite proud of himself when he successfully navigated his way to the Wild residence. It was a big house, but not showy or extravagant like many of the players' homes. It struck Mickey as a good fit for Wild's personality. Quality without pretention. When the middle child, Amanda, opened the door, the tension was palpable.

"Britt, your . . . um, *sitter* is here," Amanda provoked.

"Fuck you, Amanda," Brittany retaliated from down the stairs. Kay Wild emerged from her room upstairs, calling down to her oldest, still brushing her hair.

"Brittany Leigh, we do not use that kind of language in this house," she spoke assertively, but more calmly than Mickey had anticipated.

"This two weeks can easily become a month if your attitude doesn't change." No response. At least none that could be heard.

"And Amanda, please wipe that smile off your face and stop antagonizing your sister. It's not helping."

Then Kay's expression softened and her shoulders dropped as she smiled.

"Hi, Mickey. Sorry. Having second thoughts?" she joked.

"No. I'll be just fine . . . long as you have a little cubby or something I can disappear to if things get really nasty," he teased back.

"Come on in. Amanda, please take Mr. Doyle's coat," she instructed.

"May I take your coat, sir?" Amanda asked in her best English accent, holding out her arm with a graceful wave of her hand. She realized too late that she had inadvertently mocked Mickey's accent then shot up straight, her eyes wide.

"Oh my God. That was so rude; I am so sorry," she offered, rattled by her own indiscretion.

"It's fine," Mickey assured with a gentle laugh, "Actually, it's funny, in England we quite prefer our butlers to be American," he poked.

"Really?" Amanda asked, believing him.

"No."

"Oookaay," Amanda replied nervously, not sure quite how to take their guest.

"Very smooth, beotch," Brittany commended sarcastically on her way upstairs, having heard the exchange. Amanda was still feeling too sheepish to retaliate.

"Hi, Mickey," she uttered quietly, barely acknowledging him, but making it clear that she would be addressing him more as a peer than an elder.

"Hi Brittany. Good to see you again," Mickey returned softly, complying with her tone and hoping to avoid her disdain.

"Do you like sushi?" Kay asked, returning to the landing. "Shoot, I should have called and asked."

"Sushi's great," Mickey answered agreeably.

"Are you sure? Because we ordered in and the salads are really good too, plus there's still quite a bit of chicken left over in the fridge," she carried on back down the hall.

"Chicken's gone, mom," a boy's voice called from the living area. Mickey glanced around the corner at their 11 year-old playing video games. Kay marched back down the hall then stood looking down at her son.

"Tell me you didn't eat *all* of that chicken, Robert. There was almost enough for another meal there," she asked incredulously. Robert paused his game, wise enough to face his mother when she was upset or stressed out.

"I . . . it was me and dad . . . yesterday after school," the youngster admitted tentatively. "You were here," he added, thinking for some reason that would help his defense.

"My God, where does it all go?" Kay shook her head on her way back to continue getting ready. Her response was programmed; Ricky's 5 million dollar salary could buy a lot of chicken.

The whole scenario struck Mickey as funny and he giggled to himself as he wandered in and introduced himself to Robert, who bore striking resemblance to his father.

"Wanna play?" Robert offered up his control pad. Mickey sensed how significant a gesture this was.

"Oh, thanks, Robert. Brilliant offer, but I'll just watch you if that's alright," he responded.

"Cool," back from Robert who quickly reengaged in his game.

After Ricky and Kay left for their gala, the gregarious Amanda returned to form while they ate dinner. Brittany had gone back downstairs to her room and had not yet reemerged, so it was just Mickey, Amanda, and Robert.

"So what's it like in England?" she asked.

"What's it like here?" he countered, "normal, I guess, it's what I was used to. You mean how was it different from here?" he clarified.

"I guess," Amanda shrugged.

"Folks are generally more reserved, I suppose, more guided by certain principles, I guess . . . like being sensible and responsible, you know, words like 'duty' and 'proper'," Mickey emphasized the last word with a smile, playing up his accent, knowing it would make Amanda laugh.

"But having said that, we curse a bit more in the UK, I reckon. Call someone a 'cunt' here and they'll cut your sodding tongue out," he elaborated, triggering a burst of laughter from Robert, along with the inadvertent snorting of his milk and a prolonged coughing fit. Neither he nor Amanda could believe that the 'c' word had been uttered in their home, but they were shamefully pleased that it had.

"But we get pretty excited about some things, like our football."

"I thought they didn't have football there," Robert questioned.

"Sorry, what you call soccer we call football in England," Mickey explained.

"Hm. Weird," Robert thought out loud.

"Weird? American football features players trying to throw or carry the ball across a line, only ever touching the ball with their feet when the efforts to cross the line have failed," Mickey teased, "now that's weird."

Robert and Amanda just looked at each other and smiled, neither with a comeback.

"You losers leave me any?" Brittany asked on her way into the kitchen.

"Ah, the enemy approaches," Mickey teased cautiously with a smile. "Still lots," he assured her, heading off the sarcastic retort he thought might be coming from Amanda. He moved his stool over to make room for the eldest child. But she chose to stand and pick at the sushi plate.

"What do you think of Americans?" Amanda asked, resuming their conversation. Mickey finished chewing his bite while he weighed his response.

"Well, that's changed a bit since I got here, actually," he began. "But one thing that's striking is how divided you are." Mickey could tell that they didn't follow yet.

"Black and white, Republican and Democrat, North and South, rich and poor. It's like that everywhere, I reckon, but the distinctions just seem a lot sharper," he paused, continuing to think. "Ambitious. Americans always seem to be striving to have more or have something better. And people generally believe they'll get there, one way or another, I think," he continued. He squinted, trying to refine his thoughts.

"There seems to be kind of a worship of success here, it seems to me. Pop stars, athletes, even politicians draw a crowd and whip them into a frenzy, like they're larger than life. Many years ago, a little band from my home town came across the ocean to play," Mickey led.

"Your hometown?" Brittany asked, giving in to curiosity.

"Ah, little city on the water called Liverpool," Mickey answered sentimentally.

"The Beatles," Robert blurted excitedly.

"That's right," Mickey commended.

"Too bad the only reason you know is that stupid video game," Brittany taunted.

"Still knew," Robby replied smugly. Brittany shot him the 'big sister contempt look'. He mimicked it back to her. Mickey pretended not to see.

"Right, well when the Beatles got to America, they were absolutely mobbed. I mean, people were going completely mental," Mickey exclaimed, setting off giggles at the expression. "Young women screaming and fainting, even throwing their underpants at them, just right loony. And they'd never seen anything quite like that. I'll say this for you; you do get excited about things. About the only thing that stirs the English like that is football . . . soccer to you."

"Why? It's so boring," Robert inquired honestly.

"Boring? Are you mad? Constant action, for 90 minutes, blokes from both sides moving the ball with only their feet masterfully about the field, push and counter, to and fro, with explosive feats of athleticism to create chances, then bullet shots, headers, give-and-go's, bending it, lobbing it, deflecting it into goal! Unless the diving keeper can keep it out with his catlike dexterity!" Mickey raved excitedly, "Yeah, that's bloody boring, isn't it?" he teased. "Not like American football, 'hey, fancy a pint? Oh yeah, we just watched a two yard run; shouldn't be another play for five or ten minutes," he teased, although, in truth, he had developed an affinity for his adopted sport. All three were laughing, even Robert, at whom the playful rant was directed.

"We get excited?" Brittany challenged.

"Like I said," Mickey qualified, "the one thing. Anyway, all that said, in the most important ways, we're pretty much the same. Just want to belong, to be part of something special, to find some manner of happiness, I guess, . . . just looking in different places sometimes" he said softly, pondering the faces of his new friends in his head, losing his young listeners in the depth of that reflection. He reverted to lighter thoughts to bring them back.

"Service here is magnificent though; waitresses, servers, salespeople: wonderful. Might be commissioned, I guess, but still. Back home, you feel like an imposition when you're trying to get a waitress' attention. And God forbid she's the least bit attractive or you could spend the whole evening getting dirty looks and not a single pint," he chuckled.

"But do you miss it?" Brittany cut through the humour.

"The pissy waitresses?" he tried for a moment to keep it light.

"No, just . . . home," she brought him back to the heart.

Mickey smiled and looked her in the eyes, surrendering to a sadness he hadn't let himself feel in a while. Then he nodded, a silent laugh leaving his nose, and spared her nothing with his answer.

"Desperately sometimes."

Ricky's kids all locked in, awaiting his explanation.

"It's fine here, in America. Lots of great things, great people. Lots of things I don't like too. But it's not home. It's not about better or worse. Just not home," he concluded simply.

Brittany nodded slowly, recalling her own displacement a few years earlier.

"Kind of like when we moved here. I was thirteen and had to leave all my friends," she began.

"We all had friends that we left, Britt," Amanda countered.

"Yeah, but it's harder when you're older, Amanda," Brittany tried to explain, "Once you hit junior high, it's not just a matter or letting go and being open to new friendships; kids don't like newcomers at that age. They make it hard."

Before Amanda could disagree, Mickey spoke up in her support.

"I think you're right. I think it does get harder the older you get," he said, reflecting on his own experience again. "Gives you a good stretch though, doesn't it?"

"I guess," Britt conceded.

"But are you gonna stay?" Amanda asked, catching Mickey off-guard. For some reason, he hadn't really entertained the idea that this was more than a temporary trial. Nor had he really dared to believe that it would go well enough for him to stay for any length of time. He had felt all along like he was getting away with something, and once people were on to him, he'd turn back into a pumpkin and retreat back across the Atlantic. No one had even asked him the question until now, probably all assuming he intended to stay indefinitely. So his answer was honest and unpolished.

"I don't know. I suspect not."

Funny that it was a 14 year-old daughter of a teammate that first drew it to my consciousness. As my reply left my mouth, I was immediately fearful that it would be repeated and might affect my relationships within the team. But the truth is, my response surprised me as much as it did them. I discovered in an instant that in my gut I expected the experience to be temporary. Not just the experience, but everything attached to it, including the relationships. And what followed was equally unexpected. I was buckled with guilt. The group of people that I feared would never embrace me had. But quietly, in the recesses of my mind, I had resisted a trade-in of my visitor status. Leveled again by an emotion that I didn't see coming. That had been a dominant theme of the whole trial.

At the risk of overanalysis, I suppose I felt as strongly as I did because I had invested emotionally in my new friendships, in my new team. Curiously, my mind then shifted to sadness, anticipating the difficulty I would have when I left, having discovered that, in my mind, leaving was a foregone conclusion. What an odd cocktail of feelings: still missing my friends and family back home, but already guilty about leaving my new friends, and dare I say . . . my new family. What is it about children that lets them cut so poignantly to the heart? Little buggers.

7

Life is what happens while you are busy making other plans.
~ John Lennon

Week 14. Home versus Cleveland.

"Goddamit, Carle! All we ask is two things: high and deep. Fuckin' one for two wouldn't even be that bad," Coach Jardine barked at punter Davey Carle.

In truth, his mood was not solely the product of Carle's shanked punt. An 80-yard punt return after Carle had outkicked his coverage earlier in the first half had kept the Browns within striking distance at 10-7. The fowl mood permeated the whole sideline, as the offensive unit had sputtered, followed by consecutive short punts by Carle. The defense was performing well but losing some patience with a Steeler offense that wasn't earning them much of a rest, and kept leaving their opponents with a short field, a shortfall to which their punter had certainly contributed.

Jardine reached his threshold when the Browns short series still allowed them to tie the game at ten.

"Doyle, you're in for the next punt, . . . if we need to," he added out of respect to the offensive players, most of whom were within earshot.

Mickey stood quietly, suddenly feeling a great distance between himself and Davey Carle, who was something of a kindred spirit considering their similar peripheral place on the team. He wouldn't be called upon until late in the fourth quarter. Mickey's 28 yard field goal had given them a 13-10 lead. Then a much needed boost had come from the offense: a 63-yard catch and run by Dillon that put them up 20-10. But the Cleveland defense held, and a three-and-out by Wild and his offense gave the Cleveland offense hope that a good return might set up a quick score and give them a chance.

Mickey stood a few feet inside of his 10-yardline uncomfortably close to their endzone. The thought of mishandling the snap flashed in his head and he quickly played the opposite image. Soft hands cradling the fast-moving ball. Quick self-assurance that his hand-eye coordination had served him well as a goaltender extinguished the remainder of the contaminating thought. He took a slow, deep breath and shook out the last of his tension from his finger tips. *Just like practice. Nice smooth stroke*, he reminded himself in his head.

"Hut," he called surely, to assert his confidence. The pause between his cue and the snap seemed like a long one, but it was right on target and he handled it cleanly. The oncoming rush gave him a jolt of panic which he channeled into the ball, a hurried but smooth stroke coming off his foot like a canon.

The Cleveland returner caught the nearly 55-yarder chasing it diagonally backwards to the sideline. He fought in vain to stay in bounds before stepping out and slapping the ball in frustration.

Mickey jogged off the field slowly, a somewhat reluctant recipient of several high-fives from his teammates. Coach Jardine never looked right at him, but simply nodded his head slowly in validation before finally adding, "Goddam right; that's how it's done."

Carle shot Mickey no looks of envy or resentment, instead directing his contempt inward, bruised with the sudden realization that his job was not safe. He hung his head and retreated to the end of the bench where he would remain until the gun. The Steeler defense completed the job, easily foiling a 4th and 15 pass attempt into coverage. Ricky Wild took a knee three times and bled the rest of the clock. The game, and possibly Davey Carle's starting job, had come to a close.

Mickey had gone two for two (albeit both inside of 35 yards) and added a momentum-busting 53-yard unreturnable punt. Objectively, it had been a very good day. But the empty feeling inside him did not match his performance.

I wonder if this is what other keepers felt when it was me and not them relegated to lower rosters. I'd never even thought about it. What a shagging ache in my conscience. It put my sodding Jiminy Cricket in the ICU. Davey and I had spent hours on end together. Granted we weren't the best of mates, but we'd kept each other company through the relative solitude of our lot, never threatened by each other's performance.

The shit part is I'd quietly hoped for weeks that I'd get to have a go at the punting. His hamstring injury had nagged enough that I thought it would come eventually. Just never thought it would happen like this. Never did this math. It occurred to me that this might have been more kneejerk than anything and I was probably just one bad punt away from restoring the status quo. But for some reason, now that I had one under my belt, I felt confident that I would not relinquish the punting duties. Odd that I'd feel so sure after one go, but I did. And I knew enough to understand that once technique is refined and grooved, believing you can more or less seals the deal.

Eventually I talked myself out of my guilt. I had, after all, done my time as the runner-up back home. Why shouldn't I get to enjoy the top spot? Bloody right I should. Still . . . poor old Davey. I knew his hurt all too well. But my conviction about what I deserved would be tested yet.

The inevitable return of All-Pro kicker Justin Merritt was about a week away. He had started taking some reps in practice, but had been advised to play it fairly conservatively. Mickey had imagined that he would retain both punting and kick-off duties. He had followed up his punting debut with a solid second game, averaging nearly 45 yards on his five boots. But in Coach Jardine's eyes, the more important stat was how many of those were shorter than 40 yards: zero. Jardine had secretly hoped that Davey Carle would falter, as he had been watching Mickey's strong leg for several weeks, and noticed that his punts in practice had become as consistent as a train schedule. But he knew that practice and game performance do not always equate, so he would need the starter to stumble before he could justify a change with Coach Baker.

Mickey's kick-off average of just under 73 yards led the league. Even pre-injury, Merritt's average was a full five yards shorter than Mickey's. So he felt confident that he would maintain a significant role when Justin returned. For a short time, he tried convincing himself that passing the torch on the field-goal duties would be a welcome alleviation of pressure. But his competitive nature silenced this line of thought. He had developed a confidence-driven comfort with it. Almost a craving, as success in the face of this pressure had endeared him to his team, its fans, and the city as a whole.

But Merritt's track record as a clutch performer was irrefutable. And everyone knew that it is success in the face of playoff-grade pressure that sets the truly elite kickers from the pack. Justin had a wealth of such success. Mickey had yet to taste it. Would the fairly old school Shawn Baker roll the dice with a rookie kicker when he had All-Pro pedigree in the stable? It was doubtful.

The Steelers management was in an enviable position. If Merritt's return was a success, they would have an all-star caliber back-up kicker that they could dangle as trade bait. Although he wouldn't be play-off tested, his ability to handle the kick-off, field goal, and punting duties would make him highly marketable. His long range threat would further entice. The *Post-Gazette* had published an article articulating as much, already indulging in the speculation of potential buyers and their players who might come the other way.

Mickey had tried in vain to ignore the report, but those closest to him noticed his demeanor change the day after, and they had no doubt that they knew why. This shift moved three Steeler stalwarts to take their concerns to Coach Baker. Mickey would not learn about the conversation until many years later.

"Hey, coach," Vaughn Sellers greeted softly as he poked his shiny head through the door. Emanuel Bunch and Dillon Carmichael followed him in.

"What can I do for you, gentlemen?" Baker asked.

"Um, we wanted to axe you something, coach," Vaughn prefaced.

"Ask away," Baker prompted, turning his full attention to his three stars.

"Well, we're wondering what happens once Merritt comes back. Does Mickey get bumped?" Bunch asked pointedly.

Baker crossed his arms and tilted his head as he looked at his All-pro safety. "This about that Goddam article in the *Post-Gazette*?" he asked.

"Partly," Bunch answered honestly, "but we all kinda feel . . . no, we feel strongly that the starting role should be his to lose," he modified the boldness of his statement.

"You're suggesting that we sit a healthy all-star kicker, same guy that won us the wild-card game in New York in the last minute, the conference semi with three seconds to play . . ."

"He hasn't kicked in a game for almost a year, coach," Bunch interrupted. "Mickey's been almost automatic for weeks," he pleaded.

The three of them watched their coach very carefully, wondering if he would become irate when challenged. Coach Baker looked back at them, and all three sat curiously as they watched a smile come over his face. He took off his glasses, set them down on his desk, and rubbed his face, his expression revealing for the first time the difficulty he was having with the scenario.

"Look fellas, we all like Mickey," he began, thinking he understood what had drawn them into his office.

"Ain't about that, coach," Vaughn insisted.

"No? Well then explain it to me fellas, because your logic escapes me. Justin looks like the same old Justin to me, and you guys seem to have a pretty short memory about what he brings," Baker asserted, finally showing signs of impatience.

"It's a big picture thing, coach," Bunch began. "See you've created a certain culture here. It's based on work ethic, professionalism, and preparation," he continued, confident that the reference to these cornerstones would keep his coach's mind open.

"Mickey brings that every day. *Every day*," he stated slowly again to emphasize. "You say all the time that performing well when it matters the most is a product of uncompromising practice, the habits we form every day that we're here. Day in, day out. That's Mickey. And what's more, I think the whole team has bought in better since he came."

"Fourth down; trailing by a field-goal; five seconds on the clock . . ." Baker started.

"Mickey," Dillon said surely, breaking his silence.

"Mickey," Baker repeated. All three nodded their affirmation.

Baker placed both hands on his desk and stood up.

"I appreciate your input, men. And I assure you your thoughts will be given consideration. But when I make my decision, and I will have to soon, I need your leadership in keeping things positive in either case."

"Hey, we professionals, coach," Vaughn assured.

"I know you are Vaughn," Baker smiled. "Now I've got to break down this Cinci film before tomorrow. Those sons a' bitches are a lot better than when we saw them last."

"Sure. Thanks, coach," Bunch offered to close, shaking Baker's hand firmly to close. Dillon and Vaughn followed suit, then retreated from the office to speculate about whether their input would impact the decision.

Mellon Arena, Pittsburgh.

A handful of Steeler players lounged in one of the luxury boxes at a Pittsburgh Penguins hockey game. It was an open invite, arranged by Ross

Killacky, but Mickey noted that none of the black players seemed to be the least bit interested. With some coaxing, Dillon finally agreed to come along. Once Dillon admitted that he'd never seen a game either, Mickey was relentless.

Dillon and Mickey sat in the seats at the front of the box, closest to the action. Beside them was offensive guard, Kyle Chambers, who grew up in Canada and was happy to educate his teammates on the basics of the game.

"I went ice skating once when we went to Sweden for an exhibition match, and these blokes are making it look very easy," chimed Mickey, clearly impressed.

"I can't keep track of the play, y'all; that thing is too small," Dillon complained.

"The puck," Chambers plugged in the blank.

"Ah rubbish, DC, when the players on one side are all trying to smash someone, that's the one who's got it," Mickey explained.

"A'ight, but why they keep blowin' the whistle for no reason?"

"Not *no* reason, DC," Chambers snapped impatiently, "Just because you don't know the rules doesn't mean there aren't . . ."

"Ho, dog! Them boys is thowin' down right there on they skates!" Dillon interrupted excitedly. "Damn! Ain't no one stoppin' them neither!" he added, delighted by the on-ice scrap. Mickey also looked on wide-eyed.

"Hey, my cousin played with that guy in junior; said he was a fucking psycho," Chambers added for colour as they watched the Penguins pugilist fall on top of the other combatant.

"The refs just stood there watchin', y'all! That shit was off the hook," Dillon carried on enthusiastically.

"Yeah, why didn't they stop it?" Mickey asked, not sure whether he was thrilled, terrified, or both.

"They usually let them tire themselves out before getting in between. It's safer that way, plus it gives the players a chance to hold each other accountable; fans like it too," Chambers explained.

"Hell yeah," Dillon approved.

"Accountable? They beat the piss out of each other, KC! Bare-fisted! Like a bloody street-fight," Mickey challenged in disbelief.

"You don't have the same leverage on the ice, plus it doesn't hurt that much when you're all fired up. More so after the game," Chambers clarified.

Mickey's and Dillon's heads snapped sideways in unison to look at Chambers, both thinking the same thing.

"You used to play that shit?" Dillon prompted.

"Yeah, played both until grade 11; then focused on football," he replied, matter-of-factly.

This sent Mickey and Dillon into a fit of laughter at the thought of it: the 300 lb. Chambers speeding around the ice, annihilating everything in his path.

"I wasn't this big, obviously," Chambers dispelled the image, "besides, some of those dudes are pretty big. See #3 in red? He's like 6'6, 250."

"Quite agile for a big lad, eh?" Mickey noticed aloud.

"Must be some fucked up injuries in this sport, dog," Dillon speculated. "Especially with their sticks and shit."

"No worse than football, Chambers answered, as he spit into his 'chew cup'.

"Who's this with it now?" Mickey asked.

"That's Crosby. Arguably the best player in the world," Chambers filled in, equally mesmerized by the player on the ice.

"He's bloody brilliant," Mickey said with a crooked smile.

"White boy's got skills, y'all," Dillon bounced in his seat, his hand on the top of Mickey's head as they both watched the young center man turn a defender inside out. "Oh bulyea, baby; another scrap! Too bad Vaughn didn't come," Dillon commented as another scuffle erupted near center ice. "He woulda loved this shit."

"Yeah, he sure got out of the locker room quickly," Mickey recalled.

"Um, somethin' with his folks, he said," Dillon explained, "here to spend Christmas maybe," he added as a guess.

The mention of Christmas made Mickey envious. He knew he'd be missing out on the Doyle family Christmas, as the team was playing the following day. He had considered offering to fly his parents out, but chose not to, knowing that it would disrupt his sisters and their families. But the loneliness of the holiday was quickly replaced by the idea of Mama Sellers being with her boy on Christmas day. Mickey smiled to himself, but swore as he did that he remembered the Sellers talking about the full house they would have over the holiday. His attention was drawn quickly back to the game as the home team scored to retake the lead.

"I know, I couldn't believe it! And five minutes later they were back in the game!" Mickey explained to Abbey excitedly.

"Bloody Americans," Abbey attempted to sum it up.

"Canadians actually, about two thirds of them KC said, but quite a lot of Europeans too, believe it or not," Mickey informed as he got up from his couch to respond to a knock at his door.

When Mickey opened his door, Vaughn stood in front of him, wearing an expression Mickey had never seen on the face of his colossal teammate. It was fear.

"Abbey, I'll have to call you back, mate. Alright? Thanks."

Mickey hung up his phone and looked in the eyes of his friend. Vaughn stood speechless, his hands by his sides, almost childlike. Then just when Mickey noticed his lip quivering, Vaughn finally put his distress to words.

"Mama's sick."

Vaughn's face conveyed, without words, the seriousness of the word 'sick'. This was serious. Mickey took a slow, deep breath while he digested the news, then snapped out of his trance.

"Oh . . . sorry, come in, mate," he directed into his apartment, his hand on Vaughn's huge shoulder.

Vaughn walked slowly inside, paused in the hallway, then began pacing back and forth between the kitchen and the living room, his hands cupped behind his head. Mickey waited patiently. Vaughn finally stopped, placed both hands on the counter and looked sideways at Mickey.

"Got any milk?" he finally asked.

Mickey blinked away his confusion about the question and eventually answered.

"Um, . . . yeah, . . . yeah, I've got milk, mate."

Mickey reached into his cupboard for a glass while Vaughn pulled the two-litre carton from the fridge and began drinking directly from it. Mickey discretely put the glass back and leaned back against the counter.

"Tell me what you know so far, Vaughn," he prompted gently.

Vaughn walked back into the living room and sat down on the couch, preparing himself to speak. Mickey sat on the arm of the couch and listened.

"Started out like nothin', you know? Once in a while she'd say "this heartburn hurtin' me somethin' terrible," but she just took her pepto and a Tylenol and dealt with it; know what I'm sayin'? Then, um, . . . bout a week ago, she told papa she was havin' trouble swallowin' her supper; said her throat was hurtin' somethin' awful so they made an appointment to see the doc. But they couldn't get in fo' a couple weeks. Then, couple days later she starts passin' black, shiny stuff in her . . . you know, in the bathroom, and I guess that's what blood look like once it come through. Papa took her in to hospital and doc said she had some kind of adeno . . . somethin' that they was gonna have to take out with surgery," Vaughn looked up, grimacing at the idea.

"Adenocarcinoma," Mickey said softly.

"That's what she said," Vaughn nodded. "Is that really bad?"

Mickey sat quietly, wrapping his head around what he would have to tell his friend. He suspected that Mama, knowing her as he did, would have protected her boy, hiding behind the technical term that she'd been given. He shut his eyes tightly for a moment then looked Vaughn right in his.

"It's cancer, Vaughn."

Vaughn looked back at him, too overwhelmed to respond. Then he sat back in the couch and stared at the wall, his eyes wide and glassy. Then, as if a switch had been flipped, he looked back at Mickey with a look of protest.

"Cancer? No one said nothing about no cancer," he said, his demeanor switching to annoyance.

"That's . . . what carcinoma means, Vaughn. I'm sorry," Mickey assured him, committed to helping his friend process the reality his mother was facing. "Did she say what happens now?"

"Well, Killackey always talkin' about UPMC docs bein' the best in the world, right? So I flew her here," Vaughn rationalized.

"She's here? In Pittsburgh?" Mickey asked, wondering how much more the travel might have stressed her system.

"Yeah, that way I can look after her," he added.

The response moved Mickey. Perhaps being with her boy, who she clearly adored, would give Mama Sellers a much needed boost in the process.

"So what's the plan?" Mickey moved forward, conceding the futility in scrutinizing his solution to this point.

"Doc Maitland made some calls; tomorrow she gonna see a specialist. This dude is like some kinda guru with this stuff. Doc M said he could go in through little holes and do the whole thing, stead a' crackin' her wide open."

Mickey's uncle had died of esophageal cancer in Ireland a few years earlier. He barely knew him, but took the role of guiding his father through the process in understanding what was going on. He was fairly sure that this procedure, irrespective of who was doing it, was not particularly straightforward, and the promise of such made him nervous. He also knew that the convention was to treat the cancer with chemotherapy and radiation therapy leading up to the surgery. This would test not only Mama Sellers, but both Vaughn and his father. Even if all went to plan, rates of recurrence were fairly high, and once the cancer had made its way through the lining of the esophagus, the possibility of cancer turning up elsewhere was also high.

But Mickey had also heard Ross Killackey talk about the 'world class doctors at UPMC'. In fact, he was fairly sure he remembered him saying something on that ride in from the airport many months before. And if Dr. Maitland had spoken favourably about a particular specialist, odds were there were legitimate reasons to be hopeful. But regardless, this was exceptionally bad news.

"I'm taking her into Oakland in the morning, . . . with Papa. Into Presby (Presbyterian University Hospital). I was . . . , I thought maybe you wouldn't mind coming with us," Vaughn requested.

"Of course, Vaughn. Of course I'll go with you."

Mickey wasn't sure what Vaughn had imagined he could do in this process. But it didn't matter. He would do whatever he could to help. For Vaughn. For Mama Sellers. They had embraced him as family. He would do the same.

I'll never forget the look on Mama's face when I arrived at Vaughn's house. She had taken care of her husband and children for decades. In this new context, I began to see more similarities between Vaughn and his father. Rodney Sellers had worked hard in his life; he was a good man, a strong man. But behind his strength was a woman who had cared for him, on whom he had leaned and learned to depend. Now, facing the threat of losing her, he seemed shaken and small. Both he and Vaughn could feel their foundation shaking with the faltering health of Mama Sellers. And she knew it. Like any great mother, her loved ones' suffering resonated in her bones, making her ache.

She was Mama first, Regina second (I didn't even learn her first name until the nurse read it off the chart at the hospital), and even in her current condition, her primary concern was protecting her family. She had kept her brave face on that others could draw strength from it. But on that morning, two days from Christmas, I believe I gave her the gift of simply being herself, being Regina, if only for a moment. Her eyes spoke the words her mouth would not, and they were clear as a bell; 'I'm scared, Mickey. I'm not ready to die. Who's gonna take care of my babies?'

She smiled a tired smile and enveloped me in a hug that was weary but complete. Then she kissed me on the cheek, gave me one more little squeeze for good measure and said simply, "Thanks for comin', Mickey; this means more than you know."

When I heard my own mum's voice in hers, I started to well up. So to cut the tension, she added, "Oh, come on now; I ain't dead yet," to which we both managed to smile and summon a tiny dose of laughter.

Then Vaughn's dogs suddenly realized that there was an 'intruder' in their midst and came running to the entrance way. Mama sensed my fear and acted instinctively.

"Cassius, Malcolm, NO!" she shouted in a voice that must have scared the wee Vaughn under his bed as a lad. "Now go on!" she added. I laughed out loud, in spite of myself, when the two mammoth Rotties scattered like mice out of the room. Mama looked back at me and smiled apologetically, "They good dogs, just get a little fired up is all," she explained. 'They're completely bloody mental,' I thought to myself, managing not to say so out loud.

"What do y'all do for Christmas back home?" Mama asked, seeking a distraction as they sat in the waiting area of the clinic.

"Pretty standard, I guess. We all pack into me parents' flat; I've got two older sisters and they're both married, three nieces and a nephew. The kids make it pretty fun, kind of restore the magic, I guess. Dad's usually half pissed by mid afternoon, but a happy pissed thankfully. My oldest sister married a bloke that none of us much like, but he stays pretty quiet when we're all there, so it's fine. Then once the kids are down, me and me dad usually find the bottom of a bottle of Jamison's before we stagger to bed," Mickey concluded, his mind far away in the happy place.

"Sounds lovely," Mama chimed with a light-hearted chuckle. Mickey laughed back, still distant.

"Last year was bloody hysterical; my nephew, Harold, got a Wii for Christmas and we played it most of the day. The more snookered me dad got, the more he cut the cue to play again. There's this dance game you can do and dad kept trying to do it, and got worse and worse until he finally stepped on a Barbie sports car and flew ass-over-tea-kettle onto the floor. Didn't know if he was hung over the next day or still suffering from concussion," Mickey relived the scene out loud.

"I'd love to meet your folks, Mickey; they sound fun," Mama said, still smiling.

"Well, we shall have to make sure you do," Mickey insisted, tapping Mama on the knee, "You and me mum would get on famously."

An Indian woman in a lab coat and dark dress pants walked by them and smiled. Her features were sharp and her hair was pulled straight back into a short ponytail. She was thin and relatively tall, and might have looked a bit intimidating had her smile not been so disarming. She held a chart that Mickey assumed was probably Regina's and stepped into a room with a tall, athletic looking man in a suit. Mickey and the Sellers' sat in relative silence for the last few minutes of the wait before a nurse escorted them to an examination room where they waited for a few more minutes.

Finally, the woman they'd seen earlier walked in and greeted all of them with a handshake and a smile.

"Good afternoon," she greeted, and Mickey was delighted to detect an unmistakable London accent with a hint of her original foreign tongue. "I'm going to guess that you're Regina," she said playfully.

"Uh, no, I'm Regina," Mickey joked, triggering the nervous laughter of the others.

"Right," the woman laughed, quickly returning to the business at hand. "Well, I'm Nivi Sahay. I'm one of the thoracic surgery fellows working with Dr. Mason. How do you do?" she began.

"Well . . . that depends on what y'all have to tell us," Mama replied honestly.

"Of course. Well, your doctor in Florida forwarded all of your test results to us, so that will help us to get down to business. Long day of tests, isn't it?"

"Oh mercy; I thought we'd never leave," Mama recalled.

"Well, here's what I can tell you so far; your esophagus is a tube, about ten inches long, that runs from your mouth to your stomach. And they found a tumor on your esophagus, close to where it attaches to your stomach. Little guy, about the size of your thumbnail. The good news is usually people don't develop symptoms until the cancer is more advanced, except in your case it appears that the tumor has invaded the inner lining of the tube but not the muscle tissue. So while we expected more bad news given your symptoms, it appears that we've caught this one relatively early, what we call a stage 1 tumor. And the earlier you catch it, the better the prognosis."

All four of them nodded along.

"That's what you were explaining to us, right Mickey?" Mama said, turning to Mickey, "So that's good," she added, trying to summon some hope.

Dr. Sahay looked at Mickey, wondering if he had some medical background. He did look a bit conspicuous in this group.

"The bad news, and I should say *possible* bad news, is that tumors are often diagnosed as stage 1 initially then upgraded . . . in a bad way, once we get in there for the resection. Your symptoms make us nervous that you might fit into that category," she explained honestly.

"Mm hm. That makes sense," Mama admitted bravely, taking the hands of Rodney and Vaughn. "And if it's into the muscle or the um, what did you call them?"

"Lymph nodes," Mickey filled in.

"Right, lymph nodes, . . . then the news gets very bad very quickly," Mama tested her understanding.

"That's exactly right," Dr. Sahay affirmed. She further explained what the surgery would entail, the convention of using chemotherapy and radiation therapy in combination with the surgery, and the fact that Regina was a good candidate to have the surgery done endoscopically (through small incisions, using a camera). This last bit was a ray of hope for all of them, though it didn't sound like this would affect the prognosis very much. The doctor then left the room and returned a few minutes later with the man in the suit.

"Hi, folks. How is everyone doing today?" he began, also shaking everyone's hand in greeting.

"Lookin' for some hope," Mama answered for all of them.

"Well, I think I can give you some of that," he smiled confidently.

"I assume Dr. Sahay explained your test results to you, what they can and can't tell us so far?" he checked.

Yes sir, she explained them very well," Mama replied, winking at Dr. Sahay.

"So you've got a pretty clear picture of what we're up against?" he added.

"I think so."

"Well let me level with you this much, Mrs. Sellers; the prognosis of esophageal cancer is not very good. But you have a few key things going for you. First, if this truly is a Stage I tumor, that is extremely good news. Second, and this is where I have to brag a bit, you are in the care of the UPMC Division of Thoracic Surgery. We do a lot of this and we do it well. We can also often do this procedure through small incisions using a camera, which is far less invasive."

"That sounds good to me," Mama approved.

"Now if you look at the published prognosis rates, open versus endoscopic resection appear to be comparable, but that is deceptive, because it factors in outcomes in hospitals that do not specialize in these kinds of procedures; it includes surgeons who are not as strong technically; it includes the learning curve while this procedure was evolving. So let me give you that dose of hope you were looking for. Take the overall success rate for this procedure and add ten percent. Take the rates of complication and divide them by about six. Take the mortality rate and divide it by four. You are in very good hands here. The fellows that this program attracts are the best in the country, even the world, though I'm sure Dr. Sahay was too modest to say so," he smiled, glancing at her while she looked down humbly.

"Like Doc Maitland said," Vaughn nudged Mickey, "these guys is the shit."

"I believe you're right, Mr. Sellers. We are the 'Pittsburgh Steelers' of thoracic surgery," he added to lighten things further. "I can also see that you have some very loving and supporting folks in your corner, Regina. You are in otherwise good health, and I'm going to guess that a good chunk of your son's strength came right from you."

Vaughn hugged his mama and left his arm around her. The flattery was blatant, but it was helping. Dr. Mason's confidence was rubbing off on the rest of them, though Mickey retained a level of caution in his optimism. He believed that the care would be good, and that a positive attitude would contribute to better outcomes, but he also knew, as both Drs. Sahay and Mason had both stated, that esophageal cancer is a death sentence at least as often as not, and his head involuntarily flashed forward to the devastation that this would cause his friend.

Thanks to Dr. Maitland's connections, the surgery was scheduled for the following week. The tumor was small enough that they didn't feel they needed to try to shrink it using chemotherapy in advance. What they found during surgery would determine their course of action post-operatively. Dr. Mason hurried out, leaving Dr. Sahay to answer any remaining questions. Everyone was feeling pretty overwhelmed, so the conversation was relatively short. She said that she expected that would be the case and gave them a card with a number to call if they thought of any questions. Then she walked them to the door and shook all their hands again.

As we walked away, I imagined that Vaughn and his parents were really 'sold' by Dr. Mason's confidence and optimism. He was a pretty charismatic bloke. But whatever comfort I left with, it was mostly inspired by Dr. Sahay. She carried herself with remarkable poise. She had the full endorsement of a surgeon who was a world leader in his field, but she seemed very realistic and humble in the face of the challenge they were facing. She also seemed very genuine in her concern, which probably afforded me the most comfort, as it suggested that she took the fate of her patients very much to heart.

She was probably a few years older than me, but she looked young and healthy, which I took to mean that she would likely be sharp and on her game in the OR, but her eyes revealed temperance and patience that would keep her calm and in control. I knew that I was constructing my own confidence around this physician, as the Sellers' had with Dr. Mason, but it was working, so I just went with it.

The ride home was excruciatingly quiet. I reckon Mama was pretty exhausted at the thought of it all, and the vacant look in the eyes of the other two probably meant they were starting to dissociate due to mental and emotional overload. I almost welcomed the sound of Vaughn's dogs (I said almost) when we drove through the gate. I gave hugs to all and headed to practice.

When Mickey arrived at practice, he was immediately summoned, along with Justin Merritt, to Coach Baker's office. Coach Jardine was leaning against the desk. Mickey had nearly forgotten that this Sunday would mark the return of his kicking mentor. Other thoughts were dominating his consciousness. His best guess about how this conversation would go had already played a number of times in his head: something to the effect of "You've done a great job in Justin's absence but your punting role is also very important and blah, blah, blah". But when it came, it bore no resemblance to his version.

"Have a seat please, men," Coach Baker began. When both players were seated in front of him, he leaned forward over his desk, and clasped his hands. "We've got a problem, fellas. But it's the kind of problem you hope for as a coach."

Mickey and Justin glanced at each other nervously.

"I guess I should start by thanking you, Justin. As ticked as I was when you got hurt, I'm even more pleased now, looking back on what a pro you've been, both in mentoring young Mickey here and working your way back to form."

Coach Jardine nodded in affirmation.

"Thanks, coach," Justin replied tentatively.

"And Mickey, what can I tell you, son? You've made a believer outta me, and I'll admit to you now that I thought Killackey was half off his rocker when he first told me the idea; that's the truth. I've watched you boys since training camp, probably more than you knew, and you've done real good work together. Mickey, I hope you know how much you owe this man for the success you've had."

"Oh, I do, coach. He's been bloody brilliant," Mickey said thankfully, looking over at Justin again. Coach Baker snickered, still not quite used to Mickey's vernacular.

"Right, well, . . . here it is; Mickey here is having a pro bowl season, Justin, under your tutelage. And my daddy used to preach, 'if it ain't broke, don't you go tinkerin.'"

Justin couldn't help but smile at Baker's variation of the common expression, even though he could see where this was going. Mickey was half in shock at what was happening, and half relieved that Justin did not appear to be too upset about it, again revealing his ultra-laid-back nature.

"So Justin, stay the course, keep workin', and be ready. Mickey, you're the hot foot right now. We'll go with you until you falter. But understand this; we have an all-star kicker waiting in the wings, so you'd best stay sharp," he concluded pointing his finger at Mickey.

"Yes sir," Mickey replied nervously.

"That's all, fellas. Let's hit the field."

The other players had already gone out to the field, so Justin and Mickey were alone in the locker room. Mickey felt profoundly uncomfortable with the silence.

"I don't know what to say, Justin. I'm feeling dreadfully guilty right now," he offered apologetically.

"Do you kick well when you're feeling guilty, Mick?" Justin asked, catching him off guard.

"Um, no . . . not especially," he responded honestly.

"Well then snap out of it, bro, 'cause you're the man right now. We need you confident, unburdened, and focused. Period. This is crunch time now, dude. I've got your back and I expect you'll have mine if there's a switch. Deal?" Merritt concluded with enough of a smile to alleviate the worst of Mickey's heaviness. The two teammates shook hands and jogged out to the practice field.

Mickey was again humbled. Who knew that the surfer-dude kicker from Minnesota would turn out to be such a shining example of unselfishness, teamwork, and leadership?

Justin might have bailed him out a little sooner, but he'd been deep in thought himself. He knew his stock would return to where it had been. He was actually fitter and stronger than he'd been before. And his stroke was back, perhaps better than ever, which he silently attributed to the quality training that he and Mickey had done together.

Mickey had rubbed off on him as well, with the meticulousness of his preparation and his dedication to training off the field. In a sense, they were their own miniature 'center of kicking excellence'. But Justin knew that it was temporary. One way or another, one of them would be gone at season's end. And with the market value he enjoyed from his years of success, the cap-strapped Steelers might be inclined to move him in the off-season, in favour of some less expensive depth elsewhere in the roster.

Mickey hadn't even considered the scenario, humble enough to still think of himself as being on a weekend pass, but also oblivious to the salary cap considerations that might make him the more attractive choice. His focus was much more immediate. *Perform or you get the hook*. And he knew his leash would be short. The pressure might have started to consume him, if Mama Sellers' condition hadn't put the game back into sharp perspective.

8

Courage is fear that has said its prayers.
~ Dorothy Bernard

"Hello, this is Dr. Sahay."

"Hi, Doctor. This is Mickey Doyle. I'm a friend of Regina Sellers; we were there this morning," Mickey reminded.

"Of course. Thought of some questions after all?" she invited.

"Had them then actually, just didn't want to ask then, if you catch my meaning," he explained.

"Understand completely. Fire away," she prompted.

"Sure, well actually, I'm in the building. Any chance you could spare a moment? I don't mind waiting," he added.

"Oh, up in the clinic?"

"If that's easiest,"

"Oh, um . . . could it be a quick moment? I haven't eaten since this morning and I was hoping to grab a bite before I go back into the O.R. I'm terribly sorry."

"Well, if it's not too much of an intrusion, perhaps you could eat while we chat?"

"Deal, long as it doesn't bother you; I'm absolutely famished," she admitted.

"Not in the least. I'll meet you in the cafeteria," Mickey suggested.

"It's up on 11 if you've never been," Sahay clarified.

"Perfect. See you there."

Dr. Sahay sat down across from Mickey with her tuna sandwich and a Diet Pepsi. This time she was in scrubs and a pair of green Crocs. Her hair was still back but a few stray hairs fell into her eyes, having escaped when she took off her surgical cap. But despite her less polished appearance, her surgical attire further enhanced the professional aura that Mickey had created in his head.

"I really do apologize. I simply wouldn't have made it through another case. We went straight from clinic to an emergency case in the afternoon," she explained with a mouthful of sandwich, her free hand covering her mouth.

"If it helps, I could eat the other half so you won't feel awkward," Mickey teased.

"Oh, would you like some? I won't finish it," she offered, laughing.

"No, only pulling your leg," Mickey assured, "I guess I'm looking for some pretty frank responses so I preferred face to face," he got right down to business. Dr. Sahay's attention sharpened and she nodded, her cue to go ahead.

"Dr. Mason talked a bit about the strength of the division here, very impressive incidentally, but he didn't talk much about the actual odds. And perhaps it's a gloomy outlook, but I took that to mean they probably aren't very good."

Dr. Sahay nodded slowly as she sipped her Diet Pepsi. Her expression was serious and she looked Mickey straight in the eyes.

"Well, a great deal does hinge on the staging," she began. If it's numbers you want, let me break it down for you," she began openly. "If we intervene surgically and her tumor actually *is* Stage I, then successful resection, which we achieve at a rate of about 94%, will give her a 1-year survival rate of about 90%. If the tumor turns out to be Stage II, then the survival rate a year out drops to about 65%. If it's Stage III and the lymph nodes are affected, that pushes her one-year survival probability to about 25%, not because we can't get all of the tumor, but rather because the cancer is bound to turn up somewhere, perhaps everywhere else." Mickey listened quietly, so she continued.

"National rates of mortality with this operation range from 5% in large centers to nearly 20% in smaller ones. The mortality rate for this procedure done on Dr. Mason's watch is about 1 ½ percent. And at the risk of sounding immodest, you're simply not going to find better numbers anywhere else. With esophageal cancer, that's about as good as it gets."

Mickey looked down at the table, his eyes wide and glassy.

"One-year survival," Mickey uttered quietly.

"If you knock about 10% off those 1-year numbers, that will give you your 5-year survival rates . . . roughly," she further clarified.

"Well, . . . I asked for it, didn't I?" Mickey acknowledged.

"I'm sorry, Mr. Doyle."

"You remembered my name," Mickey remarked, impressed with her memory.

"I knew your name. Two Pittsburgh Steelers came into our clinic today; it's all our nursing staff could bloody talk about," Sahay said with a smile.

"I suppose," Mickey smiled back, still not having digested his celebrity status.

"Well, Dr. Sahay, I'm trying to prepare myself to help my friend with this, and to help Regina and her husband with it. What do you think you're going to find when you get in there?"

"I really can't say," Sahay dodged.

"Well what does your gut tell you?"

"Mr. Doyle,"

"Mickey," he interrupted.

"Fine. Mickey do you really think it's appropriate for me to share my gut feelings about a case with a friend of a patient?"

"I don't know; can I have a bite of your sandwich while you think about it?" Mickey retorted with a smirk. Dr. Sahay laughed in spite of herself.

"Touché. Fine. I think you should do whatever you can to prepare the Sellers' for bad news," she said in brutal honesty. "I'm very sorry, Mickey. That's what my gut, for all it's worth, is telling me." A long pause went unfilled, save for the bustle of the early supper traffic in the cafeteria. "You're obviously very close to the family," Sahay surmised, her tone softening significantly.

"Yes. Impossibly, Vaughn and I have become pretty good mates," Mickey laughed, recalling their rather inauspicious start. "But Regina is an astounding woman; there's something so remarkable about her, something so maternal. She was 'Mama' to me from the moment I met her," Mickey shared openly, relieved as he did.

"I understand. I could feel it too, in a short time. And maybe that spirit will carry her through this, Mickey. If you dare to believe, maybe that will help her to. And frankly, holding onto hope is the one part of all this that is actually in her control," Sahay added poignantly. Mickey nodded.

Sahay suddenly pulled her pager off her hip.

"Oh, that's the O.R. I'm afraid I've got to go," she said apologetically.

"Oh, of course. Please, don't let me keep you," Mickey insisted, "Except . . . one last question."

"If you must," she teased.

"Is Nivi short for something?" he asked in genuine curiosity.

"Nivedita, but folks around here have a hard enough time with Nivi," she smiled, sweeping her hair from her eyes. "Take care of your friends until next week, Mickey," she said to close, as she backed away and began to turn.

"Oh, wait! One last thing," he remembered.

"I really have to go."

"Right. Just, . . . would you like tickets to the game on Sunday?" he offered, pulling two tickets from his coat pocket.

"Steelers tickets? God, you could get me killed if people know I have those," she exaggerated, only slightly. "That's very kind of you but I really shouldn't . . ."

Mickey cut in, "miss an opportunity to see a game," he filled in playfully.

Nivi gave him a scolding look, unable to keep a straight face.

"Fine. Thank you. Now bugger off. I really have to go back to work," she parted, with one last laugh, turning and walking quickly back down the hall.

Mickey caught himself watching her slim backside as she walked away. *Scrubs never looked so good*, he joked to himself.

Oh, bloody hell, he thought, his shoulders dropping at some realization. *Now look what you've gone and done to yourself, Mickey.*

Week 15. Home to Baltimore. December 26th.

The dressing room was eerily quiet without the booming voice of Vaughn Sellers pumping up his teammates. He sat in complete silence in his stall, his eyes fixed on the wall across from him. Mickey was probably most unnerved, concerned that, in his state, Vaughn might be a ticking time bomb. They would find out soon enough.

He watched anxiously from the sideline as Vaughn jogged slowly onto the field. On the first play from scrimmage, Ravens' running back Dante Jones tried to go off tackle but Percy Dawkins shot through the hole and turned him back inside. No sooner had he changed direction than he was crunched heavily from the back side by Vaughn, who had beaten his blocker cleanly.

On third down, Vaughn bull-rushed into the backfield, only slightly slowed by the guard and the blocking back, hurrying the throw by the Raven's quarterback, Carson Wahl. Incomplete.

Vaughn's defensive teammates tried to celebrate with him but he was non-responsive, shuffling to the sideline, still expressionless. There he sat in silence until the next set of downs, which followed a 21-yard field goal by Mickey. On first down, he plugged the intended hole in spite of another double team, allowing the outside pressure to get to the helpless runner. On second down, he chased down the sweep from the back side and assisted on the tackle. On third down, he spun around the tackle and jolted Wahl right off his feet right after he had hurried another pass into coverage. This time, Bunch was in position for an interception, playing centerfield on the throw that was well short.

That day, the Steelers' faithful witnessed arguably the most dominant individual performance by a defensive player of the decade. By game's end, Sellers had sacked Wahl three times, was credited with five hurried passes, had seven solo tackles, and assisted on five more. He was a one-man wrecking crew.

His defensive teammates were confused by the vacant look that occupied his face for the duration of the game, eventually deciding collectively that 'when someone is in the zone, you don't mess with it'. Dillon and Manny were privy to Mama Sellers' looming surgery, having been filled in by Mickey. They too were awestruck by Vaughn's performance. At the conclusion of the game, Vaughn hurried to the locker room, ignoring the throng of reporters waiting to debrief his spectacular performance. They were equally puzzled by his demeanour, as he was usually happy to oblige interview requests post-game.

When he got to the locker room, Vaughn pulled off his jersey and shoulder pads, sat down at his stall, and draped a towel over his head. The concerned whispers around him eventually brought most of the team up to speed about the condition of his mother. The room bore no resemblance to that of a winning team. Out of respect for their great warrior, they would celebrate in silence on this day, despite having stopped their surging division rivals in their tracks, a sound 16-0 victory, anchored by the freakish play of Sellers.

Mickey, Manny, and Dillon watched uncomfortably as they all noticed Vaughn's head shaking under the towel, and in the quiet of the room they could hear his stifled sobbing. They looked at each other, desperate for the words or deed to help him. Instinctively, Manny finally acted on their behalf, gesturing for the team to come closer.

"Little team prayer, y'all. Take a knee and join hands," he said quietly, his voice soothing his teammates as they gathered around. Flanking Vaughn were Dillon and Mickey, each with an arm around him.

Then Manny Bunch's low but gripping voice resonated among them.

"Lord Almighty, we humbly ask that you embrace the Sellers family with your love as they go through this difficult time. We ask for your grace in healing Mrs. Sellers, and we pray for your guidance in helping all of us to keep the most important things front and center in our own lives. We ask all of this in the name of our Lord and savior, Jesus Christ. Amen."

The players quietly dispersed to get changed. Vaughn finally wiped away his tears with the towel and pulled it off his head, glancing up sideways at Manny.

"Thank you, my brother."

As concerned as I was for Vaughn and Mama Sellers, I still have to admit that I was fascinated by his play that day. It went against everything I thought I knew about performance. You take care of the basics, the most essential things, so that you can be quiet minded and focused when you perform, so that you won't fall to distraction. But Vaughn was clearly distracted, his foundations clearly shaken and contaminated by uncertainty, and his performance was one of epic domination. Why?

When you break it down further, it starts to make sense. In no way am I advocating personal crisis and turbulence as a performance agent, but consider this. Once someone has automatized their skill set, once the elements of their performance are what we would call 'instinctive', the toughest job is to shut off that inner voice that instructs, guides, and at the level of mastery, interferes with our performance. For elite performers to have peak performances, they have to quiet that voice, to trust their 'program' enough to simply let it run. But that trust can be obstructed by the implications of our performance, the pressures we feel, wanting it too badly to empower our 'autopilot'.

But on that day, Vaughn didn't give his performance a second thought. So once he was on that field, he was running entirely on instinct, completely surrendered to the 'program'. And was that default program adequate in an important National Football League game? Well I think it was decidedly so. From age 5 to present, he'd been honing and refining that program. It was all he needed.

I assume his fear and anxiety were also given a physical outlet on the field, which was probably a healthy thing for everyone but the poor souls that he maimed with his play. But when the game was over, the energy of those powerful emotions was spent, but the core of them remained, leaving him with nothing to do but cry. Cry about Mama. Cry about the cruel reality. Cry about his powerlessness. It was a purge that he needed desperately.

Presbyterian University Hospital. Three days later.

Mickey sat with Rodney Sellers, Vaughn, and his sister, Carol in the surgical waiting area. They had been up to the cafeteria for a coffee shortly after Regina had been taken in to the OR, but did not stay long, as they wanted to ensure that they were there when Dr. Mason came out. Not surprisingly, Dr. Mason had assured them that he would do the procedure himself, with the assistance of a fellow. The big guns always did the cases of those patients deemed to be VIP's.

Carol had oscillated between tearful and outwardly optimistic, working to convince herself that the surgery would go fine. "Mama's the toughest woman I know," she kept saying. But the more time went by, the harder it became to stave off thoughts about the procedure being complicated in some way. Mickey's reassurance was of some help.

"He met the lot of you. He knows how precious Mama is to you. I'm sure he's just being extra careful to do a top notch job," he stated surely, convincing them enough to draw nods. But his confidence was more show than not. He was clock-watching with mounting anxiety.

Several minutes passed excruciatingly without a single word being spoken by any of them. The silence was finally broken when Rodney Sellers began to cry quietly, fighting hard to contain it in front of his children. Mickey looked at Vaughn who had not said a single word since their return from the cafeteria. Vaughn put his arm around his father and, nearly expressionless, finally spoke.

"Come on now. It'll be a'ight, Papa. She'll be a'ight." He rocked his father back to composure, still looking straight ahead. Then the agonizing silence was restored. Mickey wondered what was going through his friend's mind. Ever since Manny Bunch's prayer during the post-game, Vaughn had appeared curiously calm.

Mickey glanced discretely at his phone that had been vibrating with inquiries from Dillon, Manny, Ricky Wild, and Percy Williams. Each time he thumbed the simple response, 'nothing yet'.

Mercifully, Dr. Mason finally emerged through the doors and smiled compassionately at them.

"She's doing fine," he said quickly to release them from the worst of their fears. The room itself seemed to exhale.

"Dr. Sahay and I were able to get all of the tumor, although it was a bit of a tricky job," he said frankly. "She's in the recovery room. We'll let you know when she comes to and you can see her."

"Thank you so much, Dr. Mason. Thank you *so* much," Papa Sellers chimed graciously, shaking the surgeon's hand so hard he nearly brought him to his knees.

"You're very welcome, Mr. Sellers. But please, have a seat, so that we can chat," Mason insisted, his tone sounding less heroic than it had so far. Mickey suspected he knew why.

"The surgery was a success, and the news is significantly better than it might have been," he began. Mickey closed his eyes in sober anticipation. "But it appears that the tumor had started to invade the actual muscle tissue of the esophagus. Only slightly, so I'd call it that grey area between a stage I and II tumor."

"W . . . What does that mean, Doctor?" Rodney Sellers asked, not having had the full briefing that Mickey had.

"It means that the likelihood that the cancer may have spread elsewhere in her body goes up a little. But it's much better news than if we'd discovered that her lymph nodes had been affected, or that the invasion of the muscle tissue had been more extensive. So we can be very thankful for that," Mason offered in consolation.

"So now what, Doctor?" Mr. Sellers pressed.

"Now we let her recover from her surgery. Then we talk about the next steps. Today is a victory, Mr. Sellers. That is not a simple procedure. But it went very well," Mason added, patting Rodney Sellers on his shoulder and shaking his hand once more.

The rest of them shook Mason's hand and thanked him. As Rodney did, he spotted Nivi Sahay in the hall behind him and asked with his eyes for her to stop and talk. She stood by the reception desk for a moment and glanced at Mickey as if to call him over.

Mickey hugged Papa Sellers, Vaughn, and Carol then walked over to the Nivi.

"Well?" he prompted.

"Well, it's a pretty grey area, but better news than my gut had told me," she admitted.

"So what happens now?" he cut to the chase.

"Well what comes next would have been the same regardless, but now come the two hardest parts: the chemo and the wait," she answered honestly.

"Right," Mickey acknowledged heavily. Nivi put her hand on his shoulder.

"This was never going to be an easy go, Mickey," she leveled with him, knowing that he knew as much. "Right from diagnosis, this was the road. And we're in a much better spot already than we might have been," she added to bolster his hope.

Mickey rubbed his eyes, looking over at the tiny Sellers huddle.

"It's not fair," he stated simply.

"No. It's not," Nivi acknowledged. "But we've won an important battle, Mickey. Let's start with that." Mickey nodded, looking into the eyes of his new friend, trying to borrow from her optimism.

Nivi took a card from the desk, scribbled a number on the back, and handed it to Mickey.

"Give me a call later. Perhaps I could buy you a drink. You look like you need it," she offered, her head tilting in sympathy.

Mickey let out a quiet half laugh as he looked up to the ceiling, the florescent lights humming above him.

"A drink would be lovely."

Several hours later, Mickey anxiously scrolled to Nivi's number in his phone then hit call.

"Hi, Nivi, sorry, I'd have been on time but I'm bloody lost again," he admitted in exasperation.

"That's alright, where are you now?" she tried to help.

"Uh, . . . lost," he replied simply, not feeling entitled to be annoyed by the question.

"Are you on Shady?"

"Was. Looks like I'm not anymore," he revealed as he checked a street sign.

"Did you go through an intersection with a bunch of turnoffs?" she prompted, gathering data.

"Um, yeah, about five minutes ago," Mickey replied.

"Ok, and have you turned off since then?"

"No."

"Good. Ok, find a safe spot and turn around. Come back the way you came. When you get to that same intersection, get onto Shady. You're probably on Penn Ave. if you tried to keep going straight. Right after that intersection, you'll see it on the right; take the first right and park on the street."

"Ok, see you shortly, . . . hopefully," he appended sheepishly.

"You know, there's a Best Buy on the Waterfront; if you could find it, I bet they could find you a GPS," she teased.

"Shove off. See you in about five."

A few minutes later, they sat together at the quaint Shadyside pub, near the hospital. Nivi had a beer waiting for him when he arrived. Mickey was still a little frazzled from the drive but was drawn quickly out of his state when he saw the softer look of his new friend. Her hair was down rather than pulled back and she wore a fitted pink blouse that hugged her petite frame. Her scrubs-to street-clothes routine was only about three minutes long, but her thirty seconds of make-up made her look like she'd primped much more than she had.

"Sorry, it might be a bit warm. Might remind you of home at least," she joked.

"True enough. Cheers," he tapped her glass with his.

"Seriously, do you have some aversion to buying a GPS?" she dug playfully.

"No, just . . . doesn't seem that I should need it," he explained.

"Because a man shouldn't need directions?" she poked.

"No. I know I'm missing that part of my brain. But I only have to get to three places: my flat, the practice facility, and the stadium," he admitted, marveling as he did how many months had passed without his doing much exploring.

"Not planning to be around long enough to make it worthwhile?" she pried, hitting the mark.

Ouch, he thought, only managing a shrug for a response.

Nivi looked right through him. He could feel her reading him as a smile came over her face.

"Tell me what you're thinking," he urged impatiently.

"Well, at the risk of being presumptuous, I think I understand why that's hard for you to answer," she responded honestly.

"Do tell," he prompted, looking down and blushing a little.

"Well, when I moved to England to school," she began.

"From?" he interrupted.

"India. Went to Cambridge, then to King's College in London for med school," she completed the picture.

"Wow. Cha-ching," Mickey chimed, "part of the upper class are we?" he probed.

"No. America isn't the only place with a wealthy middle class, you know. My father's made quite a penny in electronics," she admitted.

"Ah, let me guess: GPS. Now I see the hidden agenda," he laughed.

"No, really just trying to save you from yourself on that one," she poked back.

"Anyway, when I got to England, at first I was pretty thrilled. I was young and had kind of romanticized the whole thing. And don't get me wrong; Cambridge was an amazing environment. But it wasn't long before I really felt like a stranger in a strange land. Mostly focused not on what it was, but rather what it wasn't, how it was different from home. I was able to bury myself in my studies and hide away, in a manner of speaking. Just the dorms and the lecture halls, then my wee little flat and the hospital. Eight years of 'visitor status'," she added poignantly.

"You know, that's interesting because one of the striking things is how English you sound. Seems like you were pretty committed to integrating," Mickey challenged gently.

"Deceptive. My English instructor in India was from London; my accent was pretty well-trained before I even got there. Anyway, at the end of each school year, I went home for a couple of weeks before heading back to spring and summer session. But each year I went, it felt less like home. And eventually I wasn't sure where I fit, even *if* I fit."

Mickey's smile faded as he ran his finger around a coaster, staring at it. He felt exposed, completely naked emotionally.

"Ringing a bell?" she asked quietly, touching him on the hand.

He looked up at her, unsure whether he wanted out from under her lens or whether being so transparent was something of a relief. Probably some of both.

"So what brought you here?" he asked, deflecting.

"Had more to do with my training really. Throughout medical school, I was always a little frustrated with what I thought was an ultraconservative approach to patient care. I definitely fit in better over here from that perspective."

"Then you did all your surgical training here in Pittsburgh?"

"No, I did my residency at Mass General in Boston. Then when the opportunity to train with Dr. Mason arose, I jumped," Nivi replied.

"He's that good, is he?"

"The numbers don't lie. But it's also helped me to find my own limits; he's pretty fearless in the OR, so we all need to realize pretty quickly that we're not him. Turns out I'm a little more conservative than I thought," she admitted.

"Is that good or bad?" Mickey asked.

"Neither. But knowing yourself is a good thing," she qualified.

"Fair enough. But I think you're being modest. Dr. Mason chose you over *his* peers to assist him with the mother of an NFL superstar. He's obviously got a lot of confidence in you," Mickey reasoned, hitting the mark.

Nivi shrugged, "just knows what to expect from me, I think," she evaded the compliment. But knowing he wouldn't let her get away with it, she added, "But if I'm good at my work, it's because I've had great mentors."

"I'll let you get away with that one, I guess," Mickey squinted playfully, feeling the same way about the success he had enjoyed this season. Then, sensing a breakthrough of his own, he returned to the heart of their conversation.

"So now you've been here, what, six years?"

"Seven."

"Oh, brilliant, so almost the same amount as in England. So do *you* feel like you belong here?" Mickey asked. Nivi smiled and took a long drink of her beer. She appeared to have a long answer cued.

"That's what's odd, I guess. For the first few years here, I was marveling at how British I felt, rather than Indian. Not a feeling I expected. But I guess it comes down to this, Mickey, as I sense this is what you're really wondering. I fit in India, England, and the US as much as I was willing to. I spent much of my childhood thinking I belonged somewhere else, somewhere more progressive; then I spent my university years in the UK, never really feeling like that was where I belonged; then I spent a good deal of my professional training here feeling British. But along the way, I made friends, had experiences, formed relationships, and grew attached to sights and sounds in all three. And I'll take all of those things with me forever."

Mickey looked at her thoughtfully, digesting what she had said, saying nothing. So she continued.

"And once I got over the fear and loneliness from feeling like no one could relate perfectly to me and where I'd been, I could really start to swim in the freedom of it. I think that's where I am now," she concluded with a shrug and a smile that piqued Mickey's hope.

"Thank you for that," he said earnestly.

"For what?"

"For your honesty," he said simply.

"Well it was that or punch you in the shoulder and tell you not to be a sissy. It was a coin toss," she teased, failing to keep a straight face.

"No, actually that might have been better," he teased back.

"So what about you? What brought you here? Searching or running?" she gambled, taking another sip. Mickey smiled, gaining comfort with the openness of their discussion.

"It was chance more than anything," he admitted. "I was a keeper on the 3rd squad in Liverpool. Modest living, but too bloody short to ever move up. One day, one of the lads brought an American football to the pitch. I kicked a few on a bet and someone caught it on video. Somehow it made its way over here; cheers to technology. And a week later I'm on a plane," he shrugged.

"Was it difficult to leave?" Nivi queried.

"Yes and no. *I* thought it was a no-brainer. Pretty amazing opportunity. But me mum and me best mate weren't keen on the idea," he recalled, "seemed to think I was giving up too much."

"Well, what's the verdict? Or is the jury still out?"

"Depends on the day? Some days I feel like a pound note in a pocketful of American change," he explained, steering his mind away from an unfortunate 'role of quarters' simile that popped into his head involuntarily. His snicker revealed nothing.

"And other days?" she prompted.

"Other days . . ." he reflected, peering up at the IC Light poster above the bar, "I'm just comfortable. I wouldn't say I fit *in*, per se, but I have a place, if you follow."

"I think so, like you've found your own little niche," Nivi paraphrased.

"Something like that. But people here have been pretty good to me, tried to make me feel at home . . . mostly. But I think I'm almost afraid of what I'll lose if I start to feel at home," Mickey confessed.

Nivi smiled, able to relate.

"I think I retain a similar caution," she shared, "almost like if I keep checking the 'other' box, at least I have my own little box to live in, . . . that I can furnish with little reminders of home," she added with a laugh gesturing with her hands.

"Do you miss football? Or should I say soccer?" she raised her brow, amused at the idea that he would refer to it that way.

Mickey looked right at her and smiled, an improbable realization making its way to the surface of his consciousness.

"My God," he began. "I've barely thought about it. It seems so far away now. The game. The lads," his wide eyes fixed on some spot on the floor. "Isn't that something?" he marveled.

"Then something meaningful must have taken its spot," Nivi deduced with a smile.

"Well that's the most unexpected part, I reckon. I wanted to come and be good at something. You know? To look out from the top for a change. But what I care most about now is my team. My mates. The games. The . . . ridiculous gladiator game they compete in. And I'm certainly not one of them, but strangely . . . I've become the thumb up or thumb down that saves or condemns them," he suggested, using his thumb to complete the roman imagery.

"Does that make it harder? That pressure?" Nivi asked curiously.

"No," Mickey shook his head confidently, comfortable enough to reveal it, to share it. "It locks me in, focuses me," he explained, then added, "once I learned to let it," remembering what his friend Justin had taught him.

"I must admit I'm curious about how you and Vaughn Sellers have gotten on so well," Nivi wondered aloud.

Mickey looked back at her and started to laugh, suddenly stricken by the improbability of it himself, shaking his head.

"Well that's the punch line, isn't it?" he started. "My first encounter with Vaughn was nearly fatal," he only barely overstated. "And now," again he looked off reflectively, "now I barely sleep at night, worrying about him and his mum," he admitted soberly, then added with a smirk, "his mama."

"You a'ight, Mama?" Vaughn called through the bathroom door.

"I'm fine, baby," Mama reassured, splashing water on her face, "makin' me feel just like the docs said is all, baby," she admitted, then straightened her blouse, brushed her hair back from her face and opened the door, smiling up at the face of her fretful son.

"I'm fine, baby. Now go on," she gestured with both hands, "go watch the game with yo' friends."

Vaughn was hosting Manny Bunch, Percy Dawkins, and cornerback, Bo Townsend for something of a 'business dinner'. The four defensive players ate take-out while they watched the Cincinnati/New England game with great interest. They would host the winner of the Wildcard match-up the following week. Despite having beaten Cincinnati in both meetings and having lost their only game against the Patriots, there was a clear preference to face New England. None of them liked the prospect of having to beat the surging Bengals a third time, and they all wanted a second shot at the Patriots, to whom they had lost by a point in the 'Snow Bowl' during the regular season.

Bunch did the majority of the talking, sharing his defensive analysis with the others, pointing out each team's key offensive threats and identifying play-calling patterns that corresponded to different formations. His mastery of the cerebral aspects of the game gave him the floor.

Vaughn's attention was divided between the game, intermittent chatting with Papa Sellers, and the occasional trip to the guest room to check on Mama. Mama and Papa Sellers would stay with Vaughn throughout the radiation and chemotherapy, through to what they prayed would be a 'good news' follow-up with Doctors Mason and Sahay in a couple of months. Vaughn's large but scantily furnished house in the affluent suburb of Sewickley was more than enough space for the three of them and the dogs. At Vaughn's request, Mama did some online furniture shopping for him, sitting up in bed with her son's Mac on her lap. She welcomed the diversion.

The combination of cisplatin and fluorouracil was assaulting her system. Nausea, vomiting, diarrhea, mouth sores, fatigue, and generally feeling not well were the prevailing effects of this combination of drugs. But Mama was determined not to worry Vaughn and her husband. She was fighting hard to appear well and not overly affected, a fight that she was finding as difficult as coping with the symptoms themselves. Much of her time was spent resting, and she drifted in and out, never fully dozing off completely; the pain prevented it. But every time they asked, the answer was the same; "Oh I'm fine. Don't y'all fret about me."

Mickey and Dillon had attended a Penguins hockey matinee against their cross-state rivals from Philadelphia. The two jumped right out of their seats at the last second heroics of the team's young Russian threat. Both had taken an interest in the team after their initial exposure. They both waved shyly when the audience cam spotted them and put them up on the big screen, to the raucous delight of the fans in attendance. Dillon sheepishly requested that Mickey not mention to any of the other 'fellas' that the activity was his idea.

"Ain't nothin' wrong with it, dog. Just ain't that popular with the brothers," he explained.

Mickey obliged.

They had promised to head over to Vaughn's after, not to be part of the defensive scouting session, but just to hang out with Vaughn, who seemed to request their visits with growing frequency. Vaughn greatly appreciated their warmth and support, though he was shy about saying so. They arrived close to half-time and Mickey buzzed in from the gate.

"Hey, Vaughn. It's Mickey and DC," Mickey announced through the intercom.

"A'ight, come on in," Vaughn invited.

"Uh, Vaughn?"

"What up, Ringo?"

A short pause. "Are the dogs outside?" Mickey queried, trying to sound nonchalant.

"Are the dogs outside?" Dillon squealed from his passenger seat, audible to everyone in the living room

"Those dogs hate me, DC; it's not bloody funny," Mickey defended.

"They in sleepin' with Mama, Ringo. Door's closed, dog. You a'ight," Vaughn assured with a chuckle.

The six of them and Papa Sellers watched the Patriots steal the game on a last minute touchdown drive, after being outplayed for most of the game. The late heroics and a fumble recovery and touchdown return in the second quarter were their only scores, but the resilient Patriots again found a way to win. 14-10 New England. The Steelers would get their match-up.

Mickey sat nervously as Malcolm and Cassius rumbled into the living room to see who had arrived. To his relief, the fact that he was already in the house and sitting with the group spared him the welcoming from the dogs that he had come to expect . . . and dread. Cassius ignored him completely, and after poking him in the groin with his muzzle, Malcolm moved on to the endeavour of charming Bo Townsend out of the last of his pasta. So Mickey watched curiously as Mama Sellers shuffled back into the guest room from the hallway bathroom. Another of many nausea false alarms.

A few minutes later, on his way back from the kitchen with a drink, Mickey slowed slightly as he glanced in the open door of the guest room.

He could hear the faint, stifled weeping of Mama Sellers and his heart sank at the thought of her discomfort.

"Mickey? she asked quietly.

He stopped and looked in.

"Mickey? Is that you, honey?" she asked again.

"Yes, Mama. Is there anything you need? Anything I can do for you? Mickey offered.

"Just come and sit for a minute, baby," she requested, reaching for a tissue to wipe her eyes and blow her nose.

Mickey walked slowly in and sat at the end of the bed. It was uncomfortably quiet for a moment.

"Game still on?" Mama finally asked.

"No, just post-game," Mickey answered.

"Who won? Wh-who you playin'?" she strained, her eyes closed, her head still pressed into the pillow.

"Patriots. 14-10," Mickey replied.

"Oh, . . . that's good. Nuth . . . nother shot at them boys," Mama smiled. Then her smile vanished as she shifted positions, trying to get comfortable.

"Quite uncomfortable, that? The chemo?" Mickey finally asked, forgoing more small talk. With that, Mama finally opened her eyes and looked right in Mickey's.

"Oh, I hurt Mickey, . . . somethin' awful. Can't keep nothin' down. Wouldn't want to eat if I could with these sores in my mouth, keepin' me awake. My body achin' and . . . tired, Mickey, tired like I ain't never been," Mama described to her friend.

Mickey took her hand gently. Intuition told him how desperately she had wanted to tell this to someone. And through a curious twist of fate, he had come into Vaughn's life and hers, and felt, in that instant, that he was destined to be that person.

"Is there anything I can do?" he offered.

"There is, Mickey," she began, "Look after my baby . . . if somethin' should happen to me . . . watch out for my boy, my Vaughn."

Mickey felt his breath leave his body, buckled by the magnitude of her request.

"He loves you like a brother. You know that? Darnedest thing," she snickered, "little white boy from cross the ocean somehow got into his heart."

Mickey breathed a silent laugh.

"Oh, he'll never say so, but he does. And me too, Mickey. You've done so much for us already. More than you know. But Vaughn won't do so good without his mama, I'm afraid. He's a good boy, but he gets lost sometimes. And I know you could help him find his way. Don't know how I know. Just do."

Mickey tried in vain to swallow. Regina shook his hand gently.

"Could you do that for me, Mickey? Look after Vaughn?" she asked again.

"I'll do what I can," Mickey said quietly.

"I know you will, Mickey. Thank you," she concluded.

"Anything else? Glass of water or something," Mickey laughed softly, and Mama along with him. They both knew that what she'd asked was well beyond the 'something from the kitchen' favour category.

"No, baby, I'm fine, thank you. But maybe . . . could you tell me more about whe . . . where you from," she forced out a final tired request.

For a few minutes, Mickey took her to the city of Liverpool, the coziest corners of it, until she finally drifted into a deep sleep.

"Mum?" Mickey checked, his voice small and childlike.

"Hi Love!" Mickey's mother chimed from across the Atlantic, "So glad you called, Dad and I were just talking about you. Everything alright?"

"Just really missing you guys. That's all," he admitted.

"Oh, I miss you everyday, Love. Every quiet moment I have, you're in my thoughts."

"Thanks, Mum."

"Right then, spill it, Mickey. What's happened?" she cut to the chase.

"Bloody hell, Mum, how do you do that?" Mickey laughed.

"Maternal appendix, sweetheart. Grows in us when we have our first baby, then presses on the bladder for the rest of our days," she joked.

Mickey told his mother about Vaughn and his mother. About how he'd somehow become a valued member of their family. About the heaviness of the favour that had been asked of him. Here in this strange land that he felt marginally connected to. Here in this place that he was visiting, away from *his* home. Feeling further than he ever had from his mum.

"Listen, Love. When you left, I admit I was afraid. Afraid that you'd lose yourself somehow. That you'd disconnect from what was most important to you. But now look at you; you're as 'Mickey' as ever," Elizabeth Doyle said with a smile that bridged the ocean between them. "You get into people's hearts, Mickey. Your dad's gift, and I like to think one of mine, if that's not too immodest. We're so proud of you, Love."

"Thanks, Mum," Mickey smiled back, dissolving to tears.

"Bloody hell, Shanty! Wait your turn!" Elizabeth scolded over her shoulder.

"Oh, Dad's there? Brilliant. Put him on. But . . . thanks, Mum. Helpful. I needed that."

"We all do sometimes, Love. Always remember where you can come to get it. Here's the old man."

"Mickey, you little scamp! How's the fruit a' my loins?"

*It's funny how sometimes we yearn for freedom, as if we're more likely to find our true selves out in the ocean, or at the top of a mountain, when we remove our shackles and spread our wings. But that's not necessarily the path, is it? We make connections and build for ourselves little castles of purpose and obligation and promises. To ourselves. To the ones we come to love. And then we live inside them, and sometimes feel bound by them. But we built them. Hopefully with love, with hope, with our values. When me mum held a mirror up for me to see, the fear of letting Mama down, the responsibility for my adopted brother, Vaughn, the ache I felt at the very thought of Mama dying, the responsibility to perform for my team, the yearning for closeness with me own mum and dad. Those are the walls that hold me. That's my castle. I built it. And perhaps, . . . vague as this metaphor is in my head, . . . perhaps I **am** that castle.*

9

Success is not the key to happiness. Happiness is the key to success.
If you love what you are doing, you will be successful.
~ Albert Schweitzer

Field. Conference Semi-Final.

There had been an air of tension in the few days leading up to the semi-final against the Patriots. On paper, New England was entirely unremarkable. No one at the top of the leader board for individual stats, middle of the road team stats, and yet, with their wild card win, they now sat at 10 and 7 for the season and had just knocked off the Bengals, who had won six of their last seven before the playoffs. They just kept finding ways to win, and had no glaring weaknesses.

The coaching staff had broken down a lot of film, trying to assemble a game plan, but no Patriots game seemed to resemble another. So the 'go-to' questions of "Who do we have to shut down?" and "Who do we try to exploit?" had no obvious answers. So a top-down anxiety started to grip the team.

None of them had forgotten that New England had 'hung on' for 3 ½ quarters against them before the botched exchange between Carmichael and Wild was scooped up and returned for the game-winning touchdown. Dillon was uncharacteristically quiet, no doubt replaying that play in his head and resurrecting the guilt that had long since passed. The slippery, sloppy, snowy contest from the regular season had returned to their consciousness with merciless repetition between their memories *and* the video sessions. And they had nervously watched the forecast which turned out to be right on target: a déjà vu dump of wet snow.

The usual checks were malfunctioning, as Vaughn had retreated inside his own head, much like the Baltimore game. Not a bad thing in and of itself, but inhibiting the running monologue that often helped to generate confidence on game day for the rest of them. Dillon was in the always dangerous 'make-up-for-it' mode, so his usual joy and levity were conspicuously absent. Bunch rarely did much to calm nerves; his role had always been the other side, keeping everyone *sufficiently* anxious and vigilant in their preparation. And Mickey sat quietly in the uncomfortable silence, doubting that it was his place to try to shake them out of their state, hoping that some early success would cure it.

But success would not come early, or for that matter, for most of the first half. After bobbling the opening kick-off, Bo Townsend darted up the middle of the field and was clothes-lined from behind, landing flat on his back. After a minute or so of breath-holding, he was helped to his feet and jogged off the field, just having been winded.

After two tentative Carmichael runs on first and second down, Ricky Wild took a shotgun snap and looked downfield on 3rd and 13. He rifled a pass up the seam to Sands who had split two defenders, but it slipped through his fingers, incomplete. The whole stadium groaned, wondering how valuable this would-be game-breaking play could have been. With Sands' speed and the step he had, he likely would have bolted the full 80 yards to paydirt. Instead, an energized Patriot defense had the Steelers hemmed in, 4th and 13.

Fortunately, the Steeler defense seemed to find a rhythm early, anchored by the dominant play of Vaughn Sellers and the intelligent guidance of their all-pro safety, Emanuel Bunch. For his part, Mickey benefited from the opportunity to get on the field frequently as the punter, averaging over 40 yards a boot in slippery conditions, but just as importantly, gaining confidence with his footing, before a single field goal attempt.

Still scoreless late in the half, Dillon broke two tackles and rumbled eighteen yards for their longest gain of the half. Then he took a pitch off-tackle for an additional twelve yards. You could feel the offensive unit gaining momentum, and the crowd and Steeler bench started to buzz. Wild noticed the Patriot defender taking an outside shoulder against Sands on the wide side and he audibled to a new play. He took a 3-step drop and fired a bullet to Sands on a slant route. But Sands had slipped when he cut and fell. Wild and the Steeler faithful watched helplessly as the Patriot cornerback stepped in front, snagging the gift interception, then scampering nearly 60 yards for a touchdown.

The stadium was eerily quiet while the team retreated to the locker room, down 7-0 at the end of the half. And that same silence permeated the Steelers as they sat quietly, awaiting the reaction of Coach Baker who was delayed by a field-level interview for the television broadcast. The head coach retreated to the coach's room where the group of them conferred for what seemed like a very long time. When he walked in, instead of standing in the center of the room from where he typically orated, he sat down next to Dillon on the bench, as a partner, a brother to his players. He took off his black Steelers ball-cap and rubbed his head before speaking.

"Shit, gentlemen," he began softly, "that team isn't doing anything special; nothin' special at all to be ahead in this game. All they're doing is waiting on us to shoot ourselves, counting on us to self-destruct. So far it's working. Right?" he prompted, almost laughing as he looked around the room. Most of the players smiled sheepishly, owning the subpar half of football.

"Defense, that was a real nice half of football. You do that again, or somethin' like it, and we'll win. I've got a hunch their offense is ripe for a couple slip-ups of their own, and you boys will make them pay . . . that I know," he added, his tone rising.

"Hell yeah," Vaughn agreed.

"Offense, . . . let's go out there and make some plays. Alright? Make some plays. We have a whole half of football that proved to us what happens when we're just trying not to fuck up. Don't we?" he added with another chuckle that seemed to drain the last tension and shame from the room. "Shit fellas, look around. Ricky Wild, Dillon Carmichael, Blake Hollweg, DeMarco Sands, . . . I can go on, but my point is simple; if you can't draw confidence from the faces of this offensive unit, then where can you? We have to outscore this team by seven points in thirty minutes of football. And make no mistake; we *will*. We *will* win this football game."

"Belie-dat," Sands affirmed.

"So chins up, gentlemen. Strap it on. We're the Pittsburgh Steelers, . . . and we have a job to do," Baker patted Dillon's thigh pad and leaned on it to stand up.

When Baker stood up, it wasn't to the boisterous cheers of a high school squad that had been fired up, but rather it was to the restored buzz of professional players conferring and problem solving within their smaller parts to solidify their tasks. Blocking assignments, pre-reads, blitz packages, defensive seams, opportunities to exploit gaps in the secondary, weak spots on the O-line, soft spots on both sides of the ball. Mistakes that would be corrected, plays and formations that would be effective with minor adjustments. The process. The score, the outcome, the implications of the outcome were all pushed from consciousness by the job, the execution of each player's role, distilled to its simplest form.

For his part, Mickey replayed his best punts from the first half in his head, locking in the feel of 'cautious sure-footedness' through his mental rehearsal. Then he applied that same footing feel to his place-kicking images, sacrificing a marginal amount of power for a confident, steady stroke.

The rehearsal paid off with a dead-center kick-off to start the second half, only a yard or two shorter than his dry conditions standard. The cover team swarmed like killer bees, penetrating the Patriots wall and quickly converging on the returner, limiting him to a short return.

"That a babe, Coach Jardine shouted as he high-fived J.D. Coleman who had torpedoed the Patriots' ballcarrier from the side. "Nice boot, Ringo," he added, giving Doyle a wink as he arrived at the sideline.

A hungry Steeler defense smothered the New England running back on both his first and second down attempts. The double team on Vaughn was freeing his teammates to attack the backfield at will. 3rd and 11. Patriots' QB, Jimmy Carr took a short drop, pumped, and rifled a pass into the middle of the field. A diving Percy Dawkins nearly held on before the ball squirted to the ground to a mix of cheers and groans for the defensive stop that was *nearly* an enormous break.

Sands strode confidently on to the field, his head bobbing, acknowledging the efforts of the defense.

"That's right, y'all! Yeah baby! Make 'em kick that shit to me, y'all!"

The Patriots' punter launched a long low kick that Sands fielded deftly over his shoulder. He cautiously began his return, careful to maintain his footing, then accelerated to full speed with the extra second that the low kick had allowed. Jarring blocks at the heart of the wedge by Coleman and two other special-teamers drove open a hole that Sands burst through in full stride. Mickey jumped about three feet off the ground on the sideline as he watched Sands gap the pursuant New England players with his speed. The stadium exploded with bone-shaking volume as Sands was mobbed by his teammates in the end-zone. Mickey high-fived every player within a ten-yard radius.

"Convert team," Jardine called triumphantly. Mickey stood there smiling in a stupor of joy, then snapped out of it.

"Convert! Right . . . that's me," he said as he sprinted onto the field.

Alright, Mickey. Calm down, lad. Task at hand, Mickey coached himself as he set up for the kick. He took a slow, deep breath and his shoulders dropped as he finally settled in. He played the stroke once in his head then nodded to the long-snapper. Theo Branch handled the snap cleanly and Mickey stroked it through. 7-7.

After the Steelers kick-off team again sealed the Patriots deep in their own end, the visiting team again demonstrated the resilience and poise that had served them so well all year. Carr and the Pats offense patiently chiseled their way down the field, slowly and unspectacularly gaining just enough yards to string together a series of first downs. The drive ended in a punt, but the Patriots had successfully sucked much of the life out of the crowd.

The two teams settled into something of a stalemate in which both offensive units assembled sustained drives, but neither could reach the end zone or even field goal range, especially on the slick, deteriorating field. Mickey kept himself busy on the sideline, stroking methodically into his kicking net between punts.

With just under five minutes to play, Steelers return man Bo Townsend juked his way through the Patriots punt team for seventeen yards. Not a gamebreaker, but a nice momentum boost for the offense, as they took the field to try to break the tie.

Dillon took the ball in the backfield and was met immediately by a Patriots defender, but he spun off the tackle, stutter-stepped to freeze the next defender, then raced to the sideline, his powerful acceleration kicking up mud as he turned the corner. He picked up six before being forced out of bounds.

Second down. Ricky Wild hit tight end, Michael Jefferson for twelve yards over the middle. After the play was blown in, the clock continued to run, and all of Heinz field had one eye on the clock and the other on the play. A hitch pass to Sands was complete for six more, and Mickey continued to kick into his net. Another twenty-five yards would put them in range for a 40-yarder, about as long as anyone would dare to try under the conditions. As if to reinforce the point, the slight sprinkling of wet snow turned to light rain, as if mother nature herself was daring Mickey to take the field.

Four hard-earned yards by Dillon, pounding ferociously up the right side behind Hollweg, gave them another first down and took them to the two-minute-warning. Wild jogged to the sideline to take instruction. They still had two timeouts but would plan to bleed the clock at this point.

First down; after a botched handoff, Wild tucked the ball and followed Dillon through the hole still managing three yards. On second down, Wild hit fullback Jack Baum on a screen pass for seven more. The clock stopped for the measurement. First down Steelers. New set of downs. Mickey talked himself down as he watched, knowing that they were nearing field-goal range, although nothing would be automatic on this field. *Nice smooth stroke; sure feet; head down; nice follow-through; money.* The last word was in a hybrid accent of Liverpool and Justin Merritt, punctuated by a mental image of splitting the uprights, intended to bolster his confidence and extinguish doubt.

Wild took the shotgun snap and dropped three steps, pump-faking to the flat then airing out a deep ball to Sands down the sideline. Sands had a step on the defender and laid out, trying desperately to make the catch. But the ball was too badly overthrown and skidded through the end zone. Ricky Wild bounced on the spot, patting his helmet with both hands in frustration.

"Fuck, sorry Sandy. Nice route," he apologized to his wide out.

"It's a'ight, babe, they on the ropes; we got 'em," Sands reassured.

Second down, Dillon instinctively cut outside one hole as a stunting linebacker plugged the original. Two defenders met him at the line, but his thick legs churned like a motor boat, pushing forward for nearly five more yards. On third down, Dillon's number was called yet again, a four-yard plunge behind the brute force of Hollweg's block. Fourth and a long one.

Coach Baker was crouched over with his hands on his thighs, a moment of intense thought, glanced sideways at Mickey, then stood up and barked his instructions surely.

"Time out, Ricky," he signaled to his pivot. "Field goal, let's go."

The attempt would come from 42 yards with just under a minute on the clock. The players lined up while Mickey surveyed the spot he would be kicking from, nudging Theo Branch over a half yard to find the best patch of grass. They lined up before the inevitable: timeout New England. The Patriots' coach would try to 'ice the kicker', make him think too much about the kick.

The field goal unit huddled up. Ironically, Mickey welcomed the regroup, as the initial set-up had felt a bit rushed. He stood calmly, soaking up the encouragement from his teammates during the stoppage.

Then they lined up again. Once again he pictured the stroke in his head, feeling it in his body as he did, the *feel*, the rhythm, the balance, the swing. Then he nodded to the long snapper surely. The snap was slightly off target but handled well by Branch and Mickey struck the ball hard, his footing sure. As he watched the ball heading towards the uprights, he felt the jolt of a rolling Patriots defender bowl into him from the side. He was knocked off his feet and fell to the ground, but pushed quickly up on his hands to see the outcome. A Heinz Field breeze pushed the ball gently to the right. Long enough . . . but just wide. Mickey closed his eyes in disappointment, relieved that he felt more shaken than damaged from the contact.

Branch helped Mickey up then nodded his head, clapping at the yellow flag that landed at his feet. The Steelers would get a fresh set of downs with 48 seconds to play, and the referee marched the ball to the 20 yard line.

"*Contacting* the kicker?" Baker protested, stepping onto the field. No reply from the officials except to usher him off the field of play. Baker griped on his way off.

"Jesus Christ! How hard does he have to hit him for that to be roughing?"

An attempt from here would be from 37-yards. The Steelers would likely be content to keep the ball on the ground, confident that Doyle would not miss two in a row, especially from five yards closer.

Dillon took the hand-off and darted off the hip of Kyle Chambers. Hollweg ploughed over the defensive end and the fullback knocked the inside linebacker back, almost off his feet. The hole split open like a melon and Dillon shot out of it like he was coming out of a canon. For an instant, he paused, shocked by the amount of open field in front of him. Then he raced for the opening, outrunning the angle that two Patriot defenders had on him. The last player that had a play on him was the free safety that met him at the five yard line. The safety played him well but Dillon lowered his shoulder and overpowered him, stumbling into the end-zone, still on his feet.

It was absolute bedlam at Heinz Field. The players mobbed Dillon. In fact, one of the security guards in the end zone was almost first onto the pile, overwhelmed with joy. Mickey joined in the celebration, simultaneously elated and relieved. Coach Jardine patted him hard on the shoulder pads.

"Hey, you alright?"

"Yeah, fine. Bit of a knock but nothing I'm not used to from the soccer pitch," Mickey assured.

"That was a nice kick on this shit, in the wind; almost got 'er," Jardine credited his kicker, nipping any doubts in the bud before they could form.

"Thanks," Mickey acknowledged.

Then Jardine pointed up at the out of town scoreboard.

"Conditions will be perfect in the dome," he noted.

Mickey looked up at the board. The Indianapolis Colts had dispensed of the talented San Diego Chargers, sending a powerful message: 41-14.

The temptation was to feel like it was a win that I hadn't really contributed to. But for some reason, I was past that. Seeing the joy in me mates' eyes washed those feelings away like sand in the waves back home. And in fairness, I had outkicked the Patriots punter by nearly 5 yards per go, and they hadn't even attempted a field goal, despite being inside the twenty-five on two drives. Regardless, having 'taken one for the team' seemed to have scored me some points with the lads. They always seemed to like me a little more after I'd taken a hit, even moreso after I'd delivered one. Fair enough. Little tastes of the coliseum, if you will. Momentary 'honourary' status in the ring.

But piss it; all that mattered was we had a date in the conference final, one game away from the big show, the Superbowl, . . . with which I was only vaguely familiar a year ago. Funny thing, life. Isn't it?

Vaughn had many of the players over to his house after the game. Ordinarily, they would have gone out and clubbed, at least for a little while. But Mama's condition kept him close to home as often as he could be there. And Mama was in great form, still thrilled from the game, and coping with the drug side effects better than usual. It seemed to be a much needed 'good day'.

"Let me bring you some more ribs, DeMarco," she offered.

"Nah, Mama Sellers, I'm good, thanks. Bout ta burst open if I have any mo," he said, leaning back and patting his belly.

"Ah, come on; look at you. There's nothin' to ya. Surprised you didn't get stuck in the mud out there," she teased.

"He did on that last drive," Wild teased from his spot on the couch.

"Ah, hey now," back from Sands, "that was an overthrow, Wild Thang."

"Yeah, it was," Wild admitted readily.

"Hey, where DC and Ringo at?" Vaughn asked as he set another round of ribs on the table. "Still a lot a cow here, y'all," he announced, draped in Mama's apron.

"Vaughn, take that off, boy; you look like a big fool," Mama laughed.

"You like that, Mama?" Vaughn mocked, pushing his belly out. Papa Sellers said nothing, just kept laughing in the corner, as he had all night.

"DC's bringin' some girly with him," DeMarco explained. "But he said we supposed to be real nice to this one."

"Hey, if my brother gets her name right twice in a row, I'll be nice to her," Manny joked.

"You'll be nice to the poor girl anyway," Cheryl Bunch slapped her husband playfully up the back of his head, "because he either likes her or she's being led to think so," she said, hitting the mark.

"Come on now, Mrs. Bunch," Vaughn protested, "you calling my boy a *playa*?"

"Vaughn, . . . do not start with me. I'm no fool," Cheryl cautioned. Vaughn's response was a big belly laugh, knowing he couldn't make any kind of an argument with a straight face.

"Mickey said he might bring a 'lady friend' too," Ricky Wild informed on his way back from the kitchen, holding as many cold *Yeunglings* as he could carry. It stopped Vaughn in his tracks.

"Ringo doin' the nasty and didn't tell nobody?" he asked incredulously.

"Vaughn Sellers, you show some respect, now," Mama chastised, "People gonna think I didn't teach you nothin'."

"I'm just jokin' Mama," Vaughn insisted, hugging Mama from behind. "You did good. I'm curious about Ringo's lady though," he admitted.

"Yeah, me too a little," Mama confessed with a guilty laugh.

Mickey had to shake his head when Vaughn opened the door and all the necks in the living room craned to see whom he had brought. Dillon, who had arrived with his new love interest to much less fanfare, had hopped off the couch and peered over Vaughn's shoulder inquisitively.

"Hello," Nivi said shyly, revealing her accent to the absolute delight of the living room patrons.

"Dr. Sahay!" Vaughn exclaimed reverently, pushing Dillon out of the way to clear the way for his honoured guest. "Mama! You belie-dat? Look who came wit Ringo!"

Mama scurried from the kitchen. Her eyes wide, centering the hat on her head and straightening her blouse self-consciously.

"Dr. Sahay? Well, my goodness, what a . . . I had no idea, what a wonderful surprise! Come on in!" she finally said excitedly.

"Hello, Regina," Nivi greeted warmly, "I love your blouse."

"Oh, thank you, Doctor."

"Oh, please just call me Nivi," she insisted.

"Of course, sorry, Nivi. That's such a lovely name; I meant to say so at the hospital, just was a little distracted was all," Mama rambled.

"Understandably," Nivi smiled, touching Mama on the shoulder.

There was a short pause before Vaughn turned to the smiling face of Dillon over his shoulders.

"Quit standin' there gawkin' like a fool, DC; you embarassin' my guest! Sit the f . . . , go sit down, man," Vaughn commanded, censoring himself.

Dillon giggled and tiptoed back to his date.

"I'm a' go sit down," he whispered playfully, "But I'm Dillon; nice to meet y'all."

Mickey smiled, remembering Dillon tutoring him that "y'all" could be used in the singular.

"Hello, Dillon. Mickey's told me all about you," Nivi informed.

"Mmm Hm," Cheryl Bunch smirked knowingly from her seat.

"All good," Nivi assured.

"Still more to tell then, huh Mick?" Manny teased.

"Hey now," Dillon defended weakly, his arms raised. Predictably, Mama came to his aid.

"Dillon's a good boy, Nivi, just with a big ol' dollup a' child in him still; but that's why we love him," Mama explained, giving Dillon a hug.

"Thanks, Mama," Dillon cried, feigning hurt feelings.

Ricky and his wife, Kay, glanced at each other sentimentally, both thinking Mickey and Nivi looked like an awfully cute couple; small, English, and both sporting Euro-style jeans.

Before long, Mickey and Nivi sat uncomfortably on the couch, having eaten far too many of Vaughn's famous ribs, his recipe passed secretly from Mama.

"Ugh, I feel like Mr. Creosote in the *Meaning of Life*," Mickey joked. Nivi got the joke but the others looked blankly at their kicker.

"Come on, *Meaning of Life*? Python?" More blank looks. "*Monty Python*? You've got to be sodding kidding me! 'Come on Mr. Creosote, it's only wafer thin'," Mickey recited a line from the English comedy classic. Nivi chimed in at 'wafer thin', recalling it nostalgically. Manny looked past Mickey and spoke.

"It's so nice that Mickey finally found someone he can talk to," he poked.

"You've never heard of Monty Python?" Nivi blurted incredulously.

"Is that like the British Crocodile Hunter?" Vaughn guessed earnestly.

"Culturally deprived, the lot of you," Mickey mumbled.

"Wait, isn't that with the 'Nobody expects the Spanish inquisition' thing?" Cheryl asked.

"Yes, thank you!" Mickey jumped out of his seat relieved.
"Yeah, I saw that. I didn't get what was so funny," she added.
"Oh, bugger me."

Nivi was certainly a hit. Apart from the cultural chasm of Monty Python, the evening was lovely, everyone still pleasantly abuzz from the win. Nivi and Cheryl really got on well which probably thrilled me more than it should have. Manny had really warmed to me but I admit that was still my greatest point of insecurity, that it wouldn't be okay for me to get on with all the lads equally. But I had certainly settled in more than I would have dared to hope after that agonizing first exchange months earlier. It was comfortable. I belonged, but I had also retained my heritage. At times, I reveled in my 'Britishness', and most of the lads had fun with it and, I'd like to think, even thought it was rather 'cool', as they say.

But there was a new factor that I was working hard not to get too excited about. I thought Nivi was absolutely extraordinary. Razor sharp wit, intelligent, independent, confident, world-class by her own right, and more attractive every time I saw her. One might have said her features were quite sharp, but I thought they matched her personality. And she had a strength about her that drew me to her; but she was also humble, compassionate, and playful. Alright, I was smitten, as they say.

But in another sense, she was like a slice of home. Ironic that it was an Indian-born, English-trained physician that would end up making me feel most at home in America, but she had. I hoped that her befriending me was not solely related to her sympathies for me and the Sellers family. But I didn't think so. It felt very real, very authentic. I also hoped that she had found in me half the comforts I had found in her. It was too early to tell.

"Sounds lovely, Mickey. Oh hooray for you," Abbey expressed sincerely. "Look at you. See you can find happiness without the kind of tart you're usually chasing," she added, unable to resist the dig.

"Easy now, mate. She might not be the least bit interested, . . . romantically, I mean," Mickey cautioned.

"Well, regardless, Mickey, nice to have a mate that's not on the team or . . . across a bloody ocean," Abbey added perceptively.

"It is. Quite right. Thanks for the clarity," he said appreciatively.

"You're welcome. More to life than shagging, you know."

"Easily said when you're getting shagged occasionally, isn't it?" Mickey kidded. A short silence. "Abbey? Things alright with Jeffrey?"

"Uhk, he's fine . . . he's ridiculously patient actually; I'm the mental one," Abbey finally let down.

"What's wrong, Abbey?"

"Well, we haven't been . . . intimate very often lately. Seems this whole . . . thing with the miscarriage has turned me a bit . . . frigid . . . for lack of a better term. Just . . . it's me, I don't know what's wrong with me, and Jeffrey hasn't pushed, hasn't complained, hasn't . . . ah, Mickey, what's wrong with me?" Abbey finally let down.

"Nothing wrong with you, mate. You were *really* sad and it probably just takes time . . . and maybe a bit of forgiveness, . . . of yourself, I mean," Mickey tried to explain.

"Not sure I follow, Mick," Abbey admitted.

"Well, I imagine the idea of it was pretty aversive after, . . . you know . . . all the . . . stuff that goes with that. But I imagine what got you back to it was guilt about not wanting to and the idea that you 'should want to' and 'should try again' and 'should be over the whole thing'. An awful lot of 'shoulding' on yourself . . . if you follow. Just . . . not a very good starting point for lovemaking, I wouldn't think, if I can pretend to be an expert for a moment," he tacked on a disclaimer.

"Just this once," Abbey managed a laugh.

"In any case, maybe you start out just being together, being close, you know? And just feel what you feel, instead of shaming yourself into it, trying to will yourself into the mood. Probably the more you rush it, the longer it will take. Kind of the opposite version of teenage shagging, you know, the more worried you are about finishing too quickly . . . ," he explained with a shrug.

"Great analogy, Mick. Thanks," Abbey snickered

"Well anyway, you get my meaning," Mickey finished.

"Well, I'd have to concede that you know something about relationships, . . . and I'm just not sure I'm ready for that, Mickey," Abbey joked, turning to levity.

"Right, of course. Well, bugger off then. I'm off to bed," Mickey concluded playfully, confident that his point had been acknowledged, happy to have been a small help.

"Mickey?"

"Yes?"

"Thank you."

Stop it. I know what you were just wondering. Do Mickey and Abbey eventually shag? Well, just get that thought out of your head, because this story doesn't go that way. Nor should it. Because we're best mates. I mean, I see how you got there; "he shagged a prostitute for Christ sake, this bloke has no boundaries whatsoever!" Fair enough. Still digesting that one myself.

Your best mate always takes you as you are, as I've already discussed. All your little imperfections and such. Oh, they'll call you on it when you're being a wanker, but they won't turn their back on you. But they also help to protect you from losing the best of yourself.

You see, sometimes, when we start to drift from the best in ourselves, our qualities, our values, it's our best mate that sees it first. They serve as an early warning system, if you will. If you're having success and it's going to your head, "Hey, cock-up, smarten up or you won't be able to get your shirts over that noggin"; when plastered and hitting on the waitress, "Go home to your wife, you stupid git, that tart'd be a 4 out of ten if you were sober"; when you have an opportunity that you've been waiting a long time for but you're starting to chicken out for fear of failure, "get over yourself, you yellow bugger, and just have a go". It's why I took Abbey's analysis so much to heart before I came.

It can be hard to see the ground sometimes from inside the tornado. Sometimes we need our best mate to give us a whistle and hold out a hand, "hey mate, down here". To nudge us, even shove us when we're off our axis. And of course they're apt to see it first; they've seen the best in you for years; naturally they'll see when it's gone missing, and they'll hold up a mirror so you can see it too. Of course they'll hear it first when your values take a backseat; they've listened to you go on about them for years, it's conspicuous when those things quiet or are drowned out by others.

In a sense, your best mate protects you from your blind spots, your weak spots, and they understand your triggers, so they can stand guard at the chinks in your armour. For Abbey and me, we often take our commitment to this role as seriously as our own pursuits. I know that one of the best parts of Abbey is her devotion to Jeffrey. He's wonderful to her, wonderful for her, and vice versa. I wouldn't compromise that if you put a gun to my head. Abbey knows that the drink sometimes clouds my judgment, so she's my guardian, my keeper, my 'wing person' if you will, and the flirtiest moments in our relationship were her deliberate attempts to fend off a lass she thinks is trouble. We quite simply have each other's back, in every way. Abbey even throws a decent punch, believe it or not.

It's not that she wouldn't be a brilliant shag. Given her likes and dislikes, I mean, . . . we talk about bloody everything, it would be a carnival ride, I reckon, complete with a hefty dose of laughter (an under-rated shagging ingredient, we *both agree). But we're the keepers of each other's soul, for goodness sake. Lots of best mates have been lost over a shag. I reckon not a single one was worth it.*

Mickey walked alone through the corridors of the Carnegie Art Museum, near the University of Pittsburgh. Mama Sellers had planned to go with him, but in the end apologized profusely, understating that she was having one of her "not so good" days. He pardoned her unconditionally, promising to scout the place out and take her to all the best parts. Nivi had hoped to join them, but was called away for an emergency case on her way out of the hospital.

So Mickey roamed alone, taking in some culture, but most of all reflecting. The museum featured pieces from many of history's great artists, including his favourite, Monet. He liked the impressionists most of all for the emotions that their paintings conveyed, textured with personality and mood. Naturally, much of the work came from Europe, and the landscapes took him home, back across the Atlantic. The cobblestones, narrow streets, and ancient, weathered buildings took him back to Liverpool and his childhood. The renaissance styles drew him back to the history that he had learned in school, and the conservative traditions of England. The images evoked both nostalgia and a yearning for home. He wasn't bothered by it, as he was accustomed to it swelling from time to time and had come to expect it in his quiet moments of solitude.

Then he wandered into a display of paintings by an African-American artist whose name he didn't recognize. Her style captivated him immediately, bringing to life the faces and figures of rural black folks at the turn of the 20th century. As he examined each painting, he was reminded of the history to which Emanuel Bunch had alluded during their exchange many months before. Their eyes conveyed the hardship and injustice that they had endured.

But the more he looked, the more saliently other qualities of the subjects rose to the fore. Whether it was the farmer wiping his brow, the old woman peeling potatoes, or two barefoot siblings pulling a dilapidated cart, there was a quiet dignity that transcended their condition, a resilience that took him back to Mama Sellers in his mind, first to the picture of her face, then to an emotional warmth inside of him.

As he slowly passed by the last of the exhibit, a set of charcoal drawings on canvas that had not been finished, he smiled to himself about how unexpectedly his new friends had gone from being part of his adventure to part of his life. Their history was not a part of his, but it would be, and his part of theirs. And they were the most prominent figures in his present. To the cynic, he was the red herring, the oddball, 'one of these things that's not like the others'; to the romantic, he was the interesting character that enters the story with fresh wisdom and perspective, the unlikely hero brought by destiny. He went back and forth between the two, sometimes within the same day.

10

Our deepest fear is not that we are inadequate.
Our deepest fear is that we are powerful beyond measure.
It is our light, not our darkness, that most frightens us.
  ~ Marianne Williamson

The first of the dreams came two nights before the New England game. At the time, I chalked it up as having eaten too close to bed and being anxious about the game. I had quickly calmed and fallen back to sleep, and in the light of day I barely remembered having it. But I'd had three more since that were almost identical, except with growing intensity, and I'd now had them on consecutive nights, despite close vigilance over what I ate and when.

They were quite unnerving. In each case there was some dark, vague, formless being that was about to kill me. With each, I dreamt that the threat, whatever it was, was actually in my room, centimeters away when I woke. How or why I would be killed was unclear, but the terror was real, and the most recent one left me wondering momentarily whether my pulse would actually return to normal. Of course, once I was fully awake, there was nothing there. But it didn't stop me from combing my flat to be sure. I hadn't had nightmares since I was a child, and none of them had shaken me like these.

Compounding my concerns was another symptom. I had been having, from time to time, a constriction in my breathing, an occasional shortness of breath, almost as if my body had forgotten to inhale properly. It was too mild to warrant alarm, but taken with the dreams, a troubling profile was arising. Naturally I had begun my search in the daytime for an explanation, turning up very little. I felt I had settled in pretty well, finding real purpose in my pursuit and truly integrating with my team community, so there was no obvious trigger on that front. Although pressure was mounting as the play-offs rolled on, I can honestly say that I was more excited than nervous, so I really didn't feel like there was some intense fear of failure at the heart of it.

A visit with the team physician, Dr. Maitland, revealed only that I appeared to be in perfect physical health. On one hand, there was some relief in ruling out physical issues. On the other was the implication that the painfully gray psychological dimension was to blame.

The Liverpool club had a bloke that we could talk to about the mental side of the game. I remembered him saying that "nothing comes from nowhere"; all emotions have their origins in some idea or thought, albeit often lodged in the recesses of our mind. But whatever was contributing to these symptoms was buried deeply enough that I was having trouble making the puzzle pieces fit. And I'm a 'thinker'; it did not sit well.

The mood at practice was light. A confidence flowed through the ranks as they ran through their game plan for the conference final against the Indianapolis Colts. Although they knew they would have to be at their absolute best against the powerful Indy squad, the prevailing feeling was that they would be. They had somehow made it to this point of the season with no major injuries and few minor ones. Then it happened.

Back-up defensive end, Lorenzo Park turned the corner on a mock rush against the starting offense. The shot that Blake Hollweg gave him to knock him off course instead turned him and he fell off balance into the side of an unsuspecting, and therefore unprepared, Ricky Wild. Ricky buckled and grabbed immediately for his knee. The training staff hustled to his side to assess the damage. They helped him to the sideline and up onto a treatment table where they investigated more thoroughly. He winced through preliminary tests that suggested an MCL tear, but he was then rushed to the UPMC sports clinic for diagnostic imaging.

A wave of disbelief swept over the whole team and its staff as he was carted off the practice turf. Then all eyes turned on the wide eyes of Theo Branch, the second-string quarterback. He had been there all year, and blended into the scenery, as it was generally understood that he would carry the torch eventually, but not for at least a couple of years. He was a talent by all accounts, a standout during his college days at Oklahoma, but he was as green as the turf, and was very slowly digesting the many layers of a professional playbook. The prognosis for Wild was as yet undetermined, but everyone, including Branch, had to start considering how the team might function with a second year pivot at the helm, one that had taken about a fifth of the snaps in practice that the starter had, and hadn't taken a single snap in the regular season.

No one had paid much attention to Theo during the year. I think folks were content to let him absorb things slowly under the patient mentoring of Ricky and Coach Baker. But a palpable sense of doom gripped the team at the thought of rushing him into service under such extreme pressure. I don't think it was so much a vote of non-confidence for Theo as a reverence for Ricky's unwavering performance, poise, and experience.

But after Ricky, I had probably spent the most time with Theo, as he was my highly reliable pinner on field goals and converts, whom I trusted enough to forget that it was even a possibility that he could mishandle a snap. My perception of him was 'steady and calm'. And while I'm not naïve enough to equate being a reliable pinner with competently steering the offensive ship in a conference final, I was open to the idea that he could surprise us all. That his demeanour, athleticism, and training might have adequately prepared him for this very opportunity. I mean, don't get me wrong; I was praying for good news about Ricky's knee like everyone else, but I didn't believe that our hopes relied completely on it. At any rate, the confidence that was in the air at the start of practice had been replaced by a cloud of another sort.

In the locker room, the mood was subdued, no one daring to voice their fears about what this might mean while Theo Branch was in earshot. But Theo could feel it. He quickly showered and dressed. As it happened, he too lived on the Waterfront, close to Mickey's condo, so Mickey decided to reach out to help his young teammate prepare.

"Theo, why the rush, mate? Late for a date?" Mickey kidded.

"Yeah, date with my playbook," Branch replied, his tone sullen and heavy.

"Better eat something first, lad; come on, I'll buy," Mickey invited.

"No, seriously Mickey, I'm just gonna order something in and go through the whole playlist for tomorrow. Gotta be ready in case," Branch explained.

"Easy, TB," Coach Baker cautioned from the doorway of the locker room. He walked over to Branch and put his thick hand on his young quarterback's lean shoulder.

"We don't know what's up with Ricky yet. Don't go off half-cocked," Baker instructed, with an expression that Mickey tried to decode in his head.

"But listen, son," Baker began quietly, "if it is the case that Ricky can't play, and it looks like that's a possibility, we will shorten the playlist, simplify, and play to your strengths. Understand?" Theo nodded, already a little relieved.

"You will not be thrown in over your head. Ricky's a pretty special player in terms of his head and his experience, so we're kind of unbound in terms of what we can do when he's out there, what kind of play selection, what kinds of reads and adjustments we can ask of him. But you bring some things that he doesn't, with your mobility, your basic athleticism, and those are the things that we'll feature if you're behind the center. Capiche? So go through your playbook if it makes you feel better, more prepared, but rest assured; we will defeat the Colts on Sunday, whether it's you or Ricky. Now go let Ringo buy you dinner. Take him somewhere good, Mick," he closed with a wink.

Baker slapped Theo on the back and walked quickly out of the locker room, already on a mission to retool their playlist for both scenarios.

Mickey, Theo, and Ross Killackey sat together at PF Chang's restaurant on the waterfront. Killackey had tagged along, insisting that the team would pick up the tab. He had pushed to draft Branch with their first pick two years earlier, and there was a part of him that was excited to see what the young pivot could do in a game of this magnitude. While they waited for their drinks, Killackey received a text message from the team physician: partial tear of Wild's MCL. He would not play on Sunday. A return in time for the Superbowl was not out of the question, but Branch would definitely start in the conference final.

"Well, it's gonna be your show, TB," he announced.

Branch took a deep breath and nodded.

"You'll be brilliant, mate," Mickey added.

Branch acknowledged them with a smile. He had lost some of his swagger in his two years since college. While he was developing steadily, and was a diligent understudy, he felt dwarfed at times by Wild's mastery of the cerebral side of his position. Physically, he was superior to Wild: quicker feet, stronger arm, not quite as big as Wild, but every bit as hard to bring down. But what Branch had discovered in his two years was that it was a precision game, a profoundly mental game. And the quarterbacks, more than any other position, had to possess an intelligence, an efficiency in decision-making that Wild had in spades, perhaps more than all but a couple others in the league. He didn't always make a perfect throw, but he almost *never* made a bad read. And that put him in an elite category.

Branch had, among his strengths, the quality of humility. His caution not to get too full of himself had made him studious and hard-working, sponging up every lesson he could from his mentors and coaches. But humility is a sword with two edges, because it can cause us to be dismissive of our strengths, our potential, when we most need to believe in them. Both Mickey and Killackey had sensed this danger, and their intervention was intended to address it. Killackey came well-armed. He pulled from his coat a Sports Illustrated issue that featured Branch on the cover and threw it in front of him. Branch smiled widely, in spite of himself.

"Where'd you find that?" Branch asked, turning it for a better look.

"I've got a bunch of old ones in my office. I keep everything that has you guys in it," Killackey explained. "That was a helluva year for you boys. Nine straight after a shaky start, including the Cotton Bowl, right?"

"Yeah, I don't know how you remember all that stuff," Branch answered shyly.

"How could I forget?" Killackey continued, turning to Mickey. "So Oklahoma goes into the Cotton Bowl against Florida, the 2nd ranked defense in the country, flanked by Terrence Cage."

"From the Bengals?" Mickey followed.

"The very same, but you should have seen him in college; he was a one man wrecking crew, absolutely unstoppable. The question wasn't whether he would get to the quarterback, it was whether he'd put him in the hospital."

"Bloody hell," Mickey cringed.

"Yeah, but poor Terrence went home disappointed that day; Theo here was made of vapour. Cage couldn't get a hold of him for four quarters. So Oklahoma has just under 200 yards passing, Theo adds over 100 more on the ground, and they down the Gators 23-10."

"Bravo!" Mickey exclaimed, as if he had just watched the game himself. Branch shrugged shyly.

"But here's the punchline," Killackey added, "When Theo pulled the ball down and ran as often as he did that day, and scurried out of the pocket to survive, everyone stopped thinking of him as a pocket passer and somehow forgot that he'd torn up the Big 12 as one, so he slips to the second round, and we trade up to steal him 35th overall."

"*Stealers* indeed," Mickey joked.

"So am I worried about Theo's ability to step in? Hell no. Can't wait to see him play again," Killackey concluded with a wink.

"Tryin' to fill awfully big shoes though," Branch stated respectfully but accurately.

"Sure. But has he taught you anything in the last two years, Theo?" Killackey pressed.

"A ton. Best teacher I ever had," Theo commended.

"Then put some faith in his teaching. Give him some credit for preparing you for this moment," Ross insisted.

Mickey had to smile. He loved this tact. If the humble, intensely respectful Theo Branch was going to believe in himself, what better foundation than the teachings of the mentor in whom Branch had such unwavering faith? *Brilliant*, he thought to himself. Branch looked Killackey in the eyes and nodded, buying his pitch completely.

"Well for my part," Mickey began, "I owe my success to the teachings of Justin Merritt, and the cool hands of my trusty holder," he said, patting Branch on the back.

"Now you're reachin'," Branch snickered, "any fool can catch a snap".

"Maybe," Mickey conceded, "but can any fool calm a bloke under pressure with his eyes? You've got a quality, mate, poise that permeates the people around you. It's just what the offense will need to settle and play."

"I hope you're right," Branch deferred.

"Look, lad," Mickey took a firm, fatherly tone, "your modesty is a real virtue, it truly is, and I'd even say it's endearing," Mickey started, embarrassing Theo into another smile. "But what does your team need from you?"

Theo looked up. "Performance," he answered simply.

"Bloody right," Mickey affirmed, "So let me ask you this; when you've played well in the past, when you were at your best, how did you feel?"

"Confident, strong, . . . prepared," Branch reflected.

"Good show. Well then listen. The next few days are not about studying. They're about getting yourself to *that* place. Whatever you have to do, whatever you have to say to yourself to get yourself to a place of confidence, of fortitude, of feeling prepared, well that's what we need you to do," Mickey asserted, recalling the 'temple of *I'm the fuckin' shit*' pep talk that Justin had given him. "Can you do that for your team?"

"Yeah. I can do that," Theo replied surely. His commitment to his team, to his mentor, to excellence was rock solid. Now he could see that faith in himself was not self-indulgent; it was *prerequisite* to fulfilling those commitments.

He's such a nice lad. And he's a magnificent athlete. That's what makes his demeanour all the more admirable. We barely talked about football for the rest of the meal. He kept asking me about home, about soccer, lots of stories that Ross had heard before but he smiled through them patiently anyway. Perhaps Theo needed a distraction from the gravity of his task. But perhaps not. He seemed at ease from then on, like he'd put his doubts to rest. I couldn't help but feel a little proud of the help that Ross and I had provided, and of him for being so easy to help. But when we finished our meal and parted ways, I knew I had one more important stop, one more friend to help.

"Oh hi, Mickey," Kay Wild greeted him at her door.

"Hi, Kay. How's our lad?" he jumped to the point.

"Pretty quiet," she began, "Not Goddam fair, is it?" she said softly, painfully digesting the heartache of her husband.

"Not at all," he agreed.

"He's up in the living room, icing it."

"Mind if I go up and bother him a little?" Mickey asked.

"Of course not. Brought some pain meds with you?" Kay half-laughed, pointing to the paper-bagged bottle in his hand.

Mickey withdrew a bottle of Jamison's whiskey with a guilty smile.

"For all occasions," he added, in mock advertisement.

Mickey climbed the stairs and peeked around the corner.

"Hey, Mick. What's up?" Ricky barely acknowledged him, his eyes returning quickly to the television.

"Thought you could use a drink," Mickey proposed, holding up the bottle.

"Perfect," Ricky broke a faint smile, turning the bottle in his hand to examine the label. "Not supposed to have alcohol with T3's right?"

"So they say," Mickey smirked.

"Good. It'll put me to sleep," Ricky deduced with a laugh that eased them both.

Kay came into the living room carrying two glasses with ice.

"Here you go, honey," she doted, kissing Ricky before leaving them.

Mickey poured them each a couple of ounces and handed one to Ricky. He didn't think it was a time for toasts but for some reason was compelled.

"To sedatives," he offered feebly.

"Cheers," back from Ricky. They each took a drink then sat in silence for what felt like an eternity to Mickey. But his instincts told him not to speak first.

"Fuckin' fluky little accident and I'm done," Ricky finally muttered.

"Fluky is right," Mickey agreed.

"Well not all fluke, probably. Probably wouldn't have hurt it ten years ago," Ricky continued. That his age was partly to blame was obviously one of the demons circling the injured quarterback's head.

"Don't do that, Ricky. There's no point," Mickey challenged gently. "Could have been anyone. Besides, there's a chance it could be playable in time for the Superbowl, isn't there?"

Ricky shrugged, "slight chance. I'm not holding my breath."

"Well, . . ." Mickey began cautiously, "maybe tonight should be about lamenting what's lost. It's not bloody fair. Just shit luck," Mickey intuitively licensed his friend to carry on being upset. He was entitled. But then, as if that weight had been lifted, Ricky reopened the door to optimism.

"Theo will be alright. More than alright. He's ready, and twice the fuckin' athlete I am," Ricky assured, simultaneously cursing his own body. Mickey took another swig and spoke.

"He needs you now, mate. Needs your head, your eyes, . . . your reassurance." Ricky said nothing, so Mickey carried on. "He thinks the world of you. All of us do, but him most of all."

"He's a great kid," Ricky said affectionately, then drifted back in his memory. "You should have seen him in college, an absolute natural. I wondered how long I'd have before I got the hook to get him in there. Then he shows up at camp and he's just like my little shadow. Followed me around, hung on my every word." Ricky laughed as he continued. "One day he drops back and launches this canon about seventy yards to DeMarco. Everyone's yippin' and high-fivin' and he slinks back to me and says, 'should've thrown the flare, shouldn't I?' and I'm like, 'kid, if I could do that, I'd go deep every play.'"

"Well mate, he just wants to live up to you," Mickey disclosed.

"Well, . . ." you could see Ricky's mental computer switch on, "we'll watch lots of film. Indy plays a lot of cover-2; he'll have to recognize it or we're in trouble. And they'll probably throw the kitchen sink at him. Stunts, backers, safety blitzes, overloads. But he'll be ready. Short playlist and have him ready for everything. He's a smart kid. He'll be ready," Ricky concluded, downing the rest of his drink.

"Want another?" Mickey asked, already reaching over to pour.

"Nah, man. One's good, thanks. I think I'll go in nice and early tomorrow. Get some physio then start dissecting film," Ricky planned out loud, once again impressing Mickey, and revealing saliently the mental qualities that had made him one of the best in the game for a decade and a half.

Lucas Oil Stadium, Indianapolis. AFC Championship Game.

If Theo Branch was nervous, he showed no signs of it during the pregame. His persona had shifted dramatically. His walk, his tone of voice, his posture, all conveyed a quiet confidence. Mickey suspected that some of it was a show, what Theo felt his teammates needed to see to dispel their own doubts and play without that burden. But by game time, it rang as authentic, as if stepping into that 'character' with his body language had awoken it in his soul. It would be tested. But he did seem to possess it at the start.

The team benefited from the renewed music of Vaughn's confident voice. The stabilized condition of Mama appeared to have unlocked his game day spontaneity.

"Curtain's up, y'all! Steel curtain's up in Indy, baby!"

"Ah, yeah," back from Dawkins.

"Whassup, TB? Ready to rock this mofo?" Vaughn asked, turning his attention to the young quarterback. "He gots the golden gun, y'all! He gots the golden gun!" he shouted, patting Branch's right arm and making him laugh, easing some of his tension.

Pittsburgh won the toss and elected to receive. Mickey had hoped to kick-off, inviting the release that had calmed his nerves quickly in previous contests. And one might have thought that Baker would choose to put his defense on first, rather than pressing his back-up quarterback into duty for the opening drive, with a hostile home crowd rattling the covered stadium. But Baker wanted to convey his own confidence to the young pivot.

Sands took the opening kick-off at the 5 yard-line, broke one tackle and sped towards the sideline. When he tried to turn the corner, he was pushed out, short of the 20. Not that remarkable a start, but enough to rev the home crowd up even more.

Branch jogged coolly out to the huddle and called the play. The Colts would be expecting a run, a straightforward play to allow Branch to settle. So Baker would bait them with one.

"Alright, let's go Bama split right, 46 boot-hold, on go," Branch called assertively.

He took the snap, faked the hand-off to Dillon who helped to sell it, rolled the opposite way and threw a perfect strike to the tight end, Jefferson for a 14-yard gain. The Steeler bench breathed a collective sigh of relief.

He threw two more quicks, a 7-yard slant to Sands and an 8-yard curl to undersized wide-out Zack Jones. The manufactured calm that Theo had achieved in the pregame was starting to sink all the way in, and he strolled confidently to the line before each play.

The crowd regained its energy when Dillon was stopped in the backfield for a loss of two yards. Second and 12. Theo took the shotgun snap, read the defense, and rifled a pass to Jefferson. The ball was tipped slightly by a linebacker dropping into coverage, went off the outstretched fingers of Jefferson reaching back, and was plucked from the air, before it could hit the turf by the Colts safety. Sands dragged him to the turf, but the damage was done.

Branch jogged to the sideline, patting his chest to take the blame. Wild tucked his clipboard under his arm and grabbed Branch's mask to get and hold his attention.

"Hey, you know what? That's just a great, athletic play by their backer. Alright? Right read, pretty good throw, just a great play to get a piece of it. That's all. Ok? Just hit 'reset' and let's go back to work." Branch nodded to acknowledge.

First down Colts, at mid-field. Colts pivot, Kyle Latour, dropped to pass on first down and lobbed the ball to the outside shoulder of his wide-out. The receiver hauled it in, cut around the cornerback, Townsend, but was tattooed by Bunch, who nearly flipped him. A great hit, but the receiver held on. Gain of almost 25.

On first down, he dropped back again, paused then retreated from the pocket. Vaughn ran him down dragging him to the turf before he could throw the ball away. Loss of eight. Or so they thought. A flag had been thrown in the defensive backfield. The officials conferred.

"Illegal contact, number 27 on the defense. Five-yard penalty and repeat first down."

A furious Bo Townsend was restrained by Bunch as he protested the call. Two more quick strikes by Latour, and the Colts were in for their first major. Convert is good. 7-0.

Wild's reassurance seemed to help Branch to settle back down, but the offense was unable to put together a sustained drive for several possessions. Fortunately, the Steeler defense had recovered impeccably, under the stubborn encouragement of Sellers and the level guidance of Emanuel

Bunch. So Branch's counterpart, the usually unflappable Kyle Latour, became demonstratively frustrated as his punter and Mickey booted back and forth for most of the half.

But after a 30-yard punt return was called back on a hold, Branch and the Steelers started their drive from inside their own 10-yardline. They ran the same play-action pass they'd started the game with, but the defense didn't bite, so Branch was forced to run. He found a bit of daylight and scampered towards the sideline, managing to reach the line of scrimmage.

But when it looked like he was going to step out of bounds, he cut back. A Colts linebacker had him in his sites and just when a collision (that Branch would lose badly) appeared inevitable, DeMarco Sands earholed the unsuspecting defender and Branch squirted into the secondary. The impact of the block seemed to stun both sides as, for a split second, everyone but Branch seemed to pause. Downfield blocks by Jefferson, Jones, and the fullback, Jack Baum, sprang Branch into open field.

That was all he needed. The mortified Indy faithful looked on in shock at the athleticism that had tamed the Florida Gators erupted like a dormant volcano. Branch blazed over ninety yards to the endzone, but probably traveled about 150 in the process. The Steeler bench was absolute pandemonium, except for a cool Ricky Wild who leaned into Coach Baker with a smirk and said, "That's exactly what I would have done." Convert is good, held by an out-of-breath Branch. 7-7 at the half.

Despite being tied, the locker room radiated with hope. The Colts hadn't been held to single digits in a first half of play since mid-season. They were deadlocked without the services of their veteran All-Pro quarterback. And the spectacular scramble and run by Branch would no doubt put the Indy defense on their heels to start the second half. Vaughn and the defense had not only limited the Colts to one score; they had punished Latour, his receivers, and the two Colt running backs that shared the load on the ground. History suggested that it was only a matter of time before *the defense* would put up some points of their own.

But the Colts had a history of their own. One in which they had won every game that they were not trailing at the half for almost two seasons. Nothing was settled yet. But the second half promised to be an entertaining one.

But it was not the fleet feet of Branch or Sands that stole the show in the third quarter, but rather the brute force of the Steelers offensive line. Without a single run longer than ten yards, the Steelers work horses started to exert their will over the highly athletic, but undersized front four of the Colts. Dillon Carmichael's legs churned for nearly six yards per carry, taking pressure off of Branch, who threw only five passes in the quarter, completing four of them. The Pittsburgh bench again generated the only noise in Lucas Oil Stadium when Jack Baum punched into the endzone, capping an unspectacular 73-yard drive by the visitors that ate nearly eight minutes of play. 14-7 Steelers.

But there were good reasons why Kyle Latour had played in enough Pro Bowl games to merit buying a condo in Hawaii, where the games were played. And he orchestrated a drive of his own, chewing up the rest of the quarter and the beginning of the fourth. Using all of his receivers and every tiny crack in the secondary that he could find, Latour nickel-and-dimed his way down the field, slowly and methodically marching 80 yards to tie the game at 14.

The Steeler bench started to deflate when their cold offense went three-and-out after watching Latour's surgery against their highly touted defensive unit. After a would-be momentum stealing 58-yard punt by Mickey, Latour again went to work with his scalpel, and the Colts chipped their way down the field again.

On second and goal, Latour threw a fade into the corner of the endzone where only his 6'3 wide receiver, Jerome Perkins, could get it. Or at least that's what he thought. The 5'10 Bo Townsend, who had been victimized repeatedly on this and the previous drive, took flight, out-jumping the slender receiver to snag the ball, dragging his heels as he landed. Everyone waited in silence while the play was being reviewed to determine if he had stayed in bounds.

"After review, the player had control of the ball and both feet touched the ground in bounds when he landed. First down Pittsburgh at the 20," the official announced to the boos of the home crowd. Meanwhile, Townsend was mobbed by his defensive teammates on the sideline.

Branch and the Steeler offense trotted excitedly onto the field. Just under six minutes remained on the clock. A short plunge of less than three yards on first down. On second down, Branch dropped back to pass and was under pressure immediately. He hurried a pass to Sands on the sideline that skipped short. Third and eight.

The Steelers lined up in a shotgun. Branch took the snap and took a step back, then darted forward through the hole that the pass rush had left up the middle. A gutsy call that paid off. Twelve yards and a first down.

The whole stadium clock-watched as the Steelers bulldozed their way down the field, Carmichael hitting the holes aggressively, but having to settle for five or less per carry. After 50-yards, all on the ground except for short receptions of 8 and 6 yards by Sands, the clock reached the 2-minute warning. Mickey had been kicking into his net repeatedly, locking in the stroke that he would attempt to reproduce, given the opportunity, but also using the rhythm to calm his nerves. The ball sat on the 30-yardline of the Colts. From here it would be a 47 yard attempt: well within his range with such ideal field conditions.

On second down, Jack Baum battered his way forward for four more. Third and two. Dillon took the ball on a pitch, waited patiently as he accelerated easily towards the corner, then blasted upfield, on the heels of the charging Blake Hollweg. The hole opened wide and Dillon broke through and bolted to the sideline, bashing the Colts safety as he was forced out of bounds, inside the 20.

Thirty-six from here, Mickey thought excitedly. *Oh, bugger*, he amended. The play was coming back. Holding. Repeat the down. Third and 12. The kick would be 53 yards from here. Branch had one more chance for another set of downs or a shorter kick. He took a short drop and whistled a pass to Jones on a slant. Jones was dragged down after a gain of 8. Time out. On Baker's command, Mickey and the field goal team took to the field. Fifty-two seconds on the clock. Game tied. It would be a 45-yard attempt.

Mickey marched off his approach, every step of his routine programmed, down to the patting of the thigh of his kicking leg. He played the kick in his head once he was set. A whistle. The predictable icing of the kicker. Mickey stood up and shook the tension out of his shoulders, then returned to the huddle, to the positive energy of *the lads*.

Again the routine. Again the rehearsal in his head. Good snap. Clean hold. Perfect stroke. Mickey didn't get to see it go through as he was mauled by Branch who knew as well as he that it was going through. The kick was plenty long, . . . and dead center.

After the celebration, the Steelers looked up at the 47 seconds on the clock. An eternity in the hands of Kyle Latour, especially considering he only needed to get into field goal range. The kick-off return to their thirty-six burned seven more seconds. He had 40 seconds to work with.

First down: twelve yard sideline strike. Almost to midfield already. Thirty-two seconds to play. First down again: nine yards over the middle. Second down: 8 yards on a curl, and the receiver managed to fight his way to the sideline before being dragged down by the Steeler nickelback, Coleman. Clock stopped at 25 seconds. The Colts' kicker had hit from outside of 50 yards only once this season. It would be a 52-yarder from here.

Latour took a shotgun snap and surveyed the field. He pump faked to his wide receiver who then turned up the sideline. But before he could step and throw, Vaughn Sellers tomahawked the ball from his hand as he jolted him from behind. A massive scrum ensued, all scrapping ferociously for the ball somewhere under the pile. The referees buzzed around, trying to determine who had the ball at the bottom. But it was Bunch who saw it first. He leaped into the air, then bounced all the way to the sideline, pumping his fist as the referee signaled: Pittsburgh ball. Lying at the bottom was Vaughn, clutching the ball like a lab with a tennis ball. The Steelers were going to the Superbowl.

11

But what is happiness except the simple harmony between a man and the life he leads?
~ Albert Camus

It was nearly 10pm by the time Vaughn and a handful of his teammates and their significant others converged on the Sellers house. But Mama and Papa Sellers were still up and had mounds of food cooking in the kitchen, including Mama's famous ribs. She had napped after the game and was in good form.

"Smells gooood, Mama," Dillon commended on his way in.

"Hey, Dillon! Come on in and dig in, child. You must be starvin'. You were amazing today," back from Mama, along with a hug.

"Thanks, Mama. Hey, that Pendergrass you all playin'?" he asked.

"Oh yeah, me and Papa love ole Teddy," Mama laughed.

Dillon looked back at the steel eyes, shaking head, and pursed lips of Vaughn and wisely decided to leave the joke alone. His lady friend, Tanisha, didn't need to see him in a headlock on such a happy occasion.

It was a full house, with Manny and Cheryl Bunch, Ricky and Kay Wild, Bo Townsend and his fiancée. Theo Branch, Percy Dawkins, DeMarco Sands, J.D. Coleman, and Michael Jefferson came in with a group of young women with no obvious pairings. And of course, Mickey and Nivi sat cozily on the couch together, soaking up the energy.

"So how are you feeling, Regina?" Nivi inquired.

"Real good, Nivi. Least ways more good days than bad lately. Thanks for askin'," Mama replied with warmth and gratitude. "Y'all been busy at the hospital?"

"Oh, always. But it's going very well. Lovely people that I'm working with; the O.R. staff are amazing."

"Oh, yes, they were wonderful!" Mama exclaimed, still visibly thrilled that Mickey had brought Nivi into their social world. "I'm 'a go get the rest of the ribs. Mickey, will you come give me a hand, baby?"

"Of course, Mama," he was on his feet before he even answered.

Together they stood in the kitchen, consolidating platters of food to bring it all in one load.

"Loads of meat, looks like. Still corn, bread, potato salad, . . . what?" Mickey prompted, looking at the smiling face of Mama.

"She sho is lovely, Mickey," Mama smiled, already feeling a little guilty for prying.

"Yes. She is. Think this is one trip or two?" he attempted to change the subject.

"Don't you let that girl get away, Ringo. You won't find another one like that for a lifetime," Mama continued, the urgency of her sentiments swollen by her condition.

Mickey smiled back sincerely. In truth, his reluctance to talk about it was more about protecting himself in case it didn't work out than wanting her not to know. But there was a general uneasiness about talking about his future that he hadn't really pinned down yet.

"I believe you're right. But she could probably find lots of 'Ringo's," he said dismissively. She wasn't going to let him get away with it.

"Oh now, that's nonsense, child! You one of a kind, love. Now you know that! Don't go fishin'. We don't tell you we love you enough, baby?" she teased then gave him a big 'Mama hug' to reinforce her point.

"Well, a bloke can hope, right?" he finally conceded.

"He sho can," she assured. "Always room for hope."

They carried the food into the living room and set it in front of the group. Already well fed, they still sprang up for more. Mama's food inspired this kind of stuffing.

"Drinks for anyone?" Mickey asked.

"Hey just drag that whole cooler in, Ringo," Vaughn suggested from the couch.

"Good call, mate," Mickey replied and headed toward the kitchen. On his way, he was caught off guard by a shortness of breath. He steadied himself on the wall and ducked into the bathroom. Manny Bunch noticed and discreetly jumped to his aid.

"I'm 'a help Mickey with the cooler," he said quietly as he jumped off the couch.

"Mickey? You alright, dog?" Manny asked as he slipped into the bathroom. Mickey held his chest and was working to get a breath in, his eyes starting to register panic.

Manny seemed to know just what to do. He held Mickey's shoulders with both hands and spoke.

"Hey, Mickey, look at me, ok? You're gonna be ok. We gonna take a little breath together. Little breath. Good. Ok, another one, little bigger. There you go. Another, together, ok? Great. Together now, again. Good. Feel it? It's passing. Right?"

Within thirty seconds or so, Mickey was breathing again, on his own. He nodded to assure Manny he was okay.

"You sure? You're ok? Alright. Take a moment, my brother," Manny coached patiently. Mickey leaned against the sink and closed his eyes, relieved that the episode had passed.

"Thanks, mate," Mickey whispered.

"Hey, I'm here for ya, baby," Manny reassured. "But, um, . . . what's up, Mickey? What triggered this?"

"Not sure, mate. Honestly. I've been trying to figure it out. It's new, last week or two," he admitted, seeing no point in concealing it.

"Other attacks like this?" Manny asked, trying to complete the picture.

"Not like this."

"Well, . . . we gonna talk about this. Alright?"

"Sure, mate. Couldn't hurt," Mickey agreed.

"Alright. Let's go get that cooler," Manny said to close.

"Did y'all go *buy* more drinks?" Vaughn teased when they came back in.

"Nah, just got chattin'," Manny answered to cover.

Nivi sensed something when Mickey sat back down, looking shaken. She wondered if he and Manny had had another cool exchange, having heard about their early tensions.

"Everything alright?" she whispered, touching him on the arm.

"Yeah, fine," he replied, glancing up, feeling like she was reading him. "I'll tell you later."

The vibe of the party faded soon after. They were all pretty spent from the game and all of the excitement. The single players lingered with the group of girls, tired but determined to close. Dillon teased Mickey and Nivi for ducking out.

"Where y'all goin'? We just getting started," he kidded them, the others, and himself.

"The good doctor's got to operate in the morning," Mickey explained.

"Yeah, right. Y'all are gonna . . . *operate* tonight. Know what I'm sayin'?" Dillon continued to tease.

"Dillon Carmichael!" Mama chastised, the same time Tanisha punch him in the arm.

"Ow! Sorry, Mama," Dillon smiled.

"Motherfucker, what'd I tell you about respecting my guests?" Vaughn charged.

"Vaughn! Watch your cursin', child!"

"Sorry, Mama."

"Right then. As entertaining as this is, we'd better get going," Mickey excused them, his hands on Nivi's shoulders.

"G'night, y'all," Mama sent them off with a smile. "Sure you don't wanna take some ribs home?"

A short while later, Mickey and Nivi sat in front of her rental condo in Oakland, still in his car. Mickey had admitted to her what had happened at Vaughn's and how Manny had helped him through it. While he felt embarrassed about it, that feeling was outweighed by the fear of it happening again, and his desire to make some sense of it.

"You're under a lot of pressure, Mickey. It's probably affecting you more than you think," Nivi suggested.

"But why then? Why at Vaughn's? Once the pressure was off?" Mickey searched.

"Is it? Not trying to set you off again, but doesn't today ramp the pressure up even more?" Nivi asked.

"Sure, but I wasn't thinking about it! Not at all! Furthest thing from my mind!" Mickey countered in exasperation.

"Well, what *were* you thinking about?" Nivi helped him along.

He'd been thinking about her, and about Mama. But he couldn't say so.

"Everything but," he offered as a cover.

"Well, don't worry. You'll make sense of it soon enough," she said, feeling the need to back off a little. "Now are you going to see me in or do I need to have my own little bout of anxiety?" she joked, hoping the phrase 'little bout' didn't offend him.

"Of course. Sorry."

They walked to her door and stood there for a moment. She looked him in the eyes and smiled shyly, then looked away, feeling self-conscious about something. She unlocked the door and opened it, then took him by the hand and led him in, still not looking at him.

Mickey's fatigue vanished in an instant as he dared to believe what was in motion. He took her coat off and hung it, feeling her hands tugging his off as he did. Then he turned to her and put his hands on her waist and leaned over to kiss her. She suddenly seemed smaller to him, more delicate, as in his mind he preserved her image as larger than life, giant-like in her attributes.

Their kiss was slow and soft, followed by a pause as they looked in each others eyes. Then they were both taken by a rush of excitement and anticipation, their kisses accelerating and as they pressed close to each other, his hands came up around her back and hers up into his curly hair. He lifted her up and she wrapped her legs around his waste. He started upstairs, but stumbled, putting his hand down to catch them both.

"You alright?" she giggled.

"Fine," he answered, carrying on up the stairs.

"There's a headline; Steelers kicker breaks arm in romantic encounter," she kidded, further cutting the tension.

She directed him to the bedroom, still laughing, having some trouble in reverse.

"Left. No. My left!"

They collapsed onto the bed in hysterics, and undressed each other quickly, all smiles and giggles as they continued to kiss.

She wrapped herself around him again, the touch of each other's bare skin making them both tingle. He paused, then pressed gently inside of her. She gasped, then surrendered to the sensation, her smile replaced by a look of concentration, her eyes closed. They continued to kiss as they moved together until her breathing quickened and she broke off their kiss, pushing her face into his neck, gnawing at it and his earlobe. Their hands were entwined above her head. He felt her grip his fingers tightly as she gasped again. His stomach contracted in climax and he squeezed her hands in return. He exhaled heavily, pressing his elbows down to keep from compressing her tiny frame. They smiled at each other again and kissed once more, delicately. Then a mischievous grin came over her face and she spoke, unable to resist.

"Maybe that will help you to bloody relax."

It was official; I was completely bloody mental. I come to America to fame and fortune, kick the winning field goal to send my team to the championship game, am embraced by my teammates in spite of, even at times because of, my differences. I meet the most complete woman on the planet, and an hour after our first shag, am I basking in the glory of my good fortune? Watching highlights of our glorious win? Sleeping soundly without a worry in the world? No. I'm curled up in a ball on my floor, my chest as tight as a snare drum, buckled with abdominal pain. What a shagging mental case. What was wrong with me?

"Well, I'm sorry, Mickey, but I'm as much at a loss as you are. I mean . . . you couldn't paint a best case scenario much rosier than all that, could you? Perhaps you should see the doctor again," Abbey suggested.

"Abbey, I just saw one. Did a complete work-up of every possible explanation, outside of anxiety. He tested me for everything. Believe me, these guys don't take chances with their investments," Mickey explained.

"So can't he give you some pills or something to help manage it?"

"Abbey, . . . you know how I feel about that stuff. I've just got to figure it out. Please, just help me to figure it out!"

"I'm trying, Mickey! And I'm sorry; I wish I had answers for you but, ... Well, I'm afraid I'm just not much help, I guess," Abbey conceded.

"No, it's not . . . I mean, it always helps just to talk it out with you, Abbey. You're helping. I'm just frustrated. I don't understand these chains that are holding me. This should be the greatest time of my life, and I've contaminated it with some pissing neurotic episode," Mickey admitted in exasperation.

"Well, you've always been shagging neurotic, Mickey. We shouldn't be caught off guard by that," Abbey finally reverted to humour.

"Right, of course. By the way, any chance you and Jeffrey could get away for a few days to come see the game?"

"Mickey, are you shamming? You could actually get us tickets?" Abbey asked excitedly.

"Yeah, the lads were talking about it at Vaughn's. They set aside a certain number of tickets for family and friends of the players. I'll pay for flights and stuff if you think you could get away," Mickey offered.

"Absolutely, Mickey! Jeffrey can get us flights through work. That's no problem. Oh, this is so exciting! Where's the game being played?"

"It's in Miami this year. Supposed to be lovely there this time of year actually," Mickey said nonchalantly.

"Miami! I could wear a swimsuit in February? Jeffrey! Are you still down there? Mickey can get us tickets to his championship game, the Superbowl, in Miami!" Abbey shouted, still into the phone. "Oh, sorry Mickey, that must have been loud."

"No worries. Great then. It will be brilliant having you guys there," Mickey started to perk up.

"So we'll get to meet the lovely Nivi!" Abbey chimed, almost as excited about that.

"Yeah, for sure! Oh, you'll love her, Abbey. And she you," Mickey said excitedly, the tightness in his chest nearly vanishing for a moment. "Alright, the game is two weeks from last night, er, wait, . . . still Monday for you guys, right? The Sunday anyway."

"Fantastic! Listen, Mickey, I'm ridiculously late for an appointment, gotta run, but we'll talk soon to work out details. Thanks, love," Abbey said to close.

"Right, bugger off. Talk to you soon."

After the Tuesday practice, Mickey was in the training room for a contrast bath. Manny sat on one of the treatment tables, icing both shoulders and an elbow, receiving ultrasound from their trainer.

"Got dinner plans, Mickey?" Manny checked quietly.

"No, well probably not. Nivi and I talked about grabbing a bite but they had an emergency case that pushed everything else, so it looks like I'm flying solo."

"Any chance Cheryl and I could coax you out to Fox Chapel for a meal?"

"Sure. Nivi finally shamed me into picking up a GPS, so I should be able to find it," Mickey admitted.

"Good. That'll help. It's actually easy to miss our turnoff after dusk," Manny informed.

"Right. Thank God for technology," Mickey exhalted, already quite enamored with his little device.

"Cool. After supper we can have a drink and chat about . . . stuff, if you're game," Manny suggested. "You drink Cognac?" Manny asked.

"I drink anything," Mickey answered honestly.

"Perfect. My father got us a nice bottle for our anniversary, but Cheryl thinks it's disgusting. Can't bring myself to drink it on my own though."

"Right, I'm a useful bloke to have about when alcohol surplus is your problem," Mickey overstated.

"Cheryl, that was magnificent," Mickey commended, leaning back from the supper table, patting his belly.

"Thanks, Mickey," Cheryl said appreciatively.

"Yeah, outdid yourself again, baby" Manny added.

"Mama, can Mickey read us our story?" the eldest daughter pleaded musically. The second daughter lit up, but was still too shy to second the request.

"It's Mr. Doyle, baby, and you'll have to ask him," Cheryl directed.

"Mickey, plea . . . uh, Mr.Doyle, pleeease," young Vanessa begged, her hands pressed below her perfect olive face.

"Of course, love. Long as it's not *War and Peace* or the like," Mickey agreed.

"Alright then, y'all go with your mama for bath and pajamas and then Vanessa, you can pick a book and bring it in," Manny instructed. The two girls scurried off excitedly, followed by Cheryl with the baby on her hip.

"You boys okay unsupervised for a few minutes?" Cheryl poked with a smile.

"Yep. Gonna sip at that cognac a little," Manny answered.

"Oh good, better you than me, Mickey," she teased.

"No, I'm quite happy to take this for the team," Mickey insisted. He and Manny watched Cheryl and baby leave the room.

You lot are picture perfect, Manny. The most beautiful family I've ever seen, I reckon," Mickey shared sincerely.

"Thanks, Mick. I'm sure you're on the same track," Manny replied. He poured two glasses of cognac, handed one to Mickey and cut to the chase.

"So that was new for you, the anxiety attack?"

"Yeah. Never had anything like that. Nivi insisted that we're *all* under a lot of pressure. But for some reason, I feel certain that wasn't the trigger, or why would it happen after the game?" Mickey queried, anxious to hear Manny's take, and why he seemed to know so much about them.

"Well, it doesn't always work that way. Sometimes adrenaline gets you through, then when it wears off, the wave can sneak up on you, when you're tired, and your guard is down," Manny explained.

"Have you . . . , I mean, has this ever . . . ?" Mickey asked nervously.

"Mm hm. Don't tell nobody, but I fought that battle about five years ago," Manny began. Mickey listened intently.

"Most innocuous thing, on the surface. My folks were here visiting, we're sitting at dinner, real pleasant evening. My father was starting to think about retiring from the college and made reference to a movement there'd been for him to be promoted to Dean when the current Dean retired. He was flattered, you know, modest to the end, but no one would have been more deserving or more capable. And I think he really liked the idea of guiding the college in the broader strokes. Then he tells me about this behind the scenes political push by some of the old boys at the college, all of them white, some of them threatening to leave. And, . . . I mean, . . . you'd have to understand my father; he gave everyone the benefit of the doubt his whole life. So if he believed this was going on, there would have to have been pretty blatant signs. Anyway, he said he went to the acting Dean and said he was fine to carry on as a professor for a few more years and didn't feel the need to push through that kind of resistance at that point in his career, . . . so the whole thing went away. So . . . there we are, sitting at dinner, . . . and I'm thinking, my father is the smartest, wisest, most positive and diplomatic man I've ever known, you know, . . . in my mind, the kind of person you look to for leadership and direction. And these old boys can sabotage the whole thing, quietly, behind the scenes, no process, you know, . . . in an institution of higher learning! And I'm thinking, really, . . . how far have we even come? Know what I'm sayin'? My father played by their rules, embraced his role, lived by principle his whole life, respectful and trusting, and gets stabbed in the back. I didn't make much of it at the time, but Cheryl was pregnant with our first, I was injured at the time, MCL, so, you know, . . . painfully aware of how quickly the game could be taken away, . . . and I'm about to become a father, to bring a child into a world that suddenly looked as backward as it was fifty years ago, you know, . . . just a little more subtle."

 Mickey nodded in acknowledgement, then Manny, reflecting on his own story, added, "It's no 'burnin' cross nigger story', . . . but it affected me a lot."

 Mickey sat, perfectly quiet for a moment, understanding at last the visceral nature of Manny's mistrust, then finally responded, "Sure, mate. Would have affected me the same way, I reckon. It's not really the event, is it? It's the meaning your mind assigns to it. How did it affect your dad?"

 Manny snickered, "barely affected him, really, . . . far as I could tell. Just poured his energy back into his teaching, back into the students, where he knew he'd get some energy back, knew he'd get a return on his investment. Shit, I'm the one with the business major, you'd think I'd figure that one out," he poked at himself. "You know, if they'd had a half decent football team, I'd have gone to Trinity just to see him in action. The man's got enough teaching awards to wallpaper his office," he added proudly.

"Where'd you go to college?" Mickey asked.

"Colgate. Great school, and a pretty good football team, Div I anyway. Not a powerhouse by any stretch, but we won more than we lost all four years I was there. Besides, I needed to get out of the south."

"Mickey raised his brow in inquiry.

"Lots of good things about the south, but folks are awfully slow to change there is all, social change most of all, as you can tell from the story," Manny tied back to where he'd started.

"So that's when it started? The attacks I mean," Mickey followed.

"That's when they started. Began as just a feeling of dread sometimes, about being a father, raising a family, about the uncertainty of the game, and just, . . . these debilitating doubts about my ability to care for a family . . . in this world, . . . where *I* had followed all the rules. Before I knew it, it was full-on attacks, like the one you had."

"When did they stop?" Mickey asked, desperate for a solution.

"Well, stopped would be the wrong word. The feeling still comes and goes. But I learned how to breathe through it, learned how to talk myself through it, learned to pay closer attention to the things I could control, . . . and let Jesus take care of those things that I can't. Cheryl's really good at talking me down now too, . . . since we've talked a lot about it."

"Hm," Mickey mumbled thoughtfully, staring down at the hardwood, so Manny refined the search.

"So I guess what I want to ask you is what is it that is making your walls close in, what's the feeling of dread at the epicenter, if you catch my meaning. When you first came over, what were you most afraid of? Failure?"

Manny's question seemed to awaken something in the recesses of Mickey's mind, and he sat up a little taller, feeling closer to an answer, his eyes squinting to try to make it out.

"No, I mean, coming home a failure was in the back of my mind. But there was something bigger, planted there by me mum and best mate, Abbey, . . . this is all their fault, really," Mickey accused, not really condemning them.

"What was that?" Manny demanded, engaged in the puzzle himself.

"They went on about what I was giving up, what I was leaving behind, . . . not geographically per se, but inside myself," Mickey explained.

Manny started to laugh out loud, catching Mickey off guard, but then explained himself before his little teammate could take offense.

"Sorry, dog. I'm not laughin' at you, baby," he assured patting him on the head. "It's just so clear now, . . . isn't it?" he checked.

"Indulge me," Mickey prompted, not yet making out the picture.

"You were afraid to *succeed* here, dog! Were right from the start. Shit, now I feel the fool for not seeing it sooner," Manny continued. Meanwhile, Mickey rolled his eyes at the idea, not buying it.

"No, come on, Mick, play it back now and you'll see it," Manny insisted, his hand on Mickey's shoulder. "Mama Doyle and your best friend in the whole world, Abbey, they plant this seed; you're selling your soul, leaving behind the most important part of yourself. Right?"

Mickey acknowledged that much with a nod.

"Oh shit, Ringo; you like a Paulo Coehlo book," Manny teased, still pleased with himself. "So what happens if you are successful here?" Mickey didn't respond, so Manny continued. "Then the ink on your contract with the Devil dries, dog. The deal is sealed. You've lost yourself. You've given up your soul."

Mickey's chest tightened at the idea, still unable to respond, but starting to make out the edges.

"The first time I referred to Pittsburgh as your home, you went white as a sheet. You're pretty white to start with, but still. Then you start to fit, start to grow roots here. Vaughn, his Mama, Dillon, the Wilds, . . . now your girl," Manny added, looking Mickey right in his eyes, cornering him with the logic in it. He saw Mickey's eye start to well, but was confident in where he was leading. "Damn, . . . every kick you made, every friend you made, . . . and then falling in love, my brother, that was the last straw; the deal was done, wasn't it?" Manny presumed, but wasn't the type to gamble if he wasn't fairly certain.

Mickey took a gulp of his cognac and looked back at his friend, completely exposed, his soul in plain view.

"So let me help you, dog, cuz it's all good news if you're willing to see it," Manny began his denouement. "If you had come over here and got wrapped up in your success: the money, the fame, the spotlight, and truly lost yourself, become someone else, then your mama and your friend, . . . their fears would have been realized. But what really happened, Mickey? You brought 'Ringo' to America, to the team, to each of us, to our families, to our community. And you've blessed us all, Mickey. You really have. Vaughn, . . . bless his heart, he'd have come unglued completely with this thing with his mama if it wasn't for you. Dillon, . . . I've been on that fool about how he lives and takes care of himself since he was drafted, and then you come along, set the right example without preachin', and he's finally comin' around a little. And for my part, Mickey, . . . you helped me to be a little more colour blind, though I still have a ways to go," Manny concluded appreciatively.

"But what if I leave? What if home calls me back?" Mickey asked fearfully.

"Then we let you, dog. We give you a big hug and wish you well. When a cardinal lands on your lawn for a minute, then flies away, . . . you don't curse it for leaving, hate it for robbing you of its colour. You lock it away in your head, where you can see it any time you want, and take it with you," Manny stated poetically.

Mickey wiped his eyes, more grateful than he could put into words. "You're your father's child, mate. That's for sure," he commended.

"Maybe, but when the pupil is ready," Manny started.

"The teacher will appear," Mickey closed.

"Thanks, Manny."

"No, Professor Doyle, thank *you*," Manny returned. "But um, . . . if you need a little fear of failure to balance things out, . . . then if you miss any kicks in Miami, . . . I'll tell Vaughn it was on purpose," Manny joked.

"Right. Brilliant. That works," Mickey laughed, quickly gathering himself. Just then, Vanessa popped over the armrest, onto the vacant spot on the couch next to Mickey. Young Cleo hopped up next to her and bounced into her spot.

Manny, Vanessa, Cleo, Cheryl, and Isabelle on her lap, sat and listened to a theatrical, highly animated reading of *Cat in the Hat* from a renewed, and less burdened Mickey, or Mr. Doyle. His accent made it all the more special.

The lads who had played in a championship game had a critical role during the lead up. The city was absolutely abuzz. While I had gotten used to being recognized when I was about the town, it was generally smiles and the occasional autograph seeker, particularly when I was with Dillon or Vaughn. But in the days prior to our departure for Miami, if I was in public, I was being cheered loudly or serenaded with the 'Here We Go' Steelers Superbowl song. It was like gameday times ten. Everywhere. The temptation is to get as excited as they are, to get swept up in it. But you can't. You can't afford to. It's dangerous because it's so much fun that you don't recognize it as a problem. But no one can expect to ride that kind of emotional wave for that long. We're just not physically capable. Once a wave crests, it's heading for a crash.

The blokes who had been through it knew that and worked to keep the rest of us level. Coach Baker was so even, it was comical. He barely cracked a smile for the whole week. He guides us through video sessions and practices with all the animation of an accountant. Fantastic poise. His words when we arrived at the airport in Miami; "the carnival's for the fans, we're here to work".

Manny was his usual analytical, cerebral self in practice, though even he couldn't help but break into the occasional 'unprovoked' smile. And for their part, Vaughn and Dillon, though not doing much to curb the excitement, were in great form with their banter, taking the edge off of the nerves with their humour.

Ricky Wild went to work as the personal coach of Theo Branch, taking no reps in the practices but being omnipresent during the offensive sessions. He had been rehabbing his knee aggressively, but nothing had been said about the possibility of his return. I heard Coach Baker making some vague reference to being 'ready for Tuesday', which I assumed was a target date to start taking some snaps again. Theo stayed close to the veteran pivot like a child with a blanket. He had done much to prove his readiness against the Colts, but his humble nature demanded his respect for the magnitude of this next challenge.

And the challenge would be substantial. We would lock horns with the NFC Champion New York Giants, who had dropped just two contests during the regular season, one to San Diego on a dramatic last-minute 90-yard gallop by Selwyn-Johnson, the other to the Philadelphia Eagles. They avenged that week 5 loss by thrashing them once in week 10, then again, 28-7, in the conference semi-final.

Their Head Coach, Brick Holden, something of a legend, was making his seventh trip to the Superbowl. He already had four rings. It's hard to imagine a seventy year old man intimidating the kind of blokes I played with, but this man's mystique caused the lot of us to clench, and I'd only recently been acquainted with his body of work. Must stop watching Sport Center. He had tooled a defense that many of the pundits argued was better than ours, just less hyped.

But if any aspect of either team had been underhyped up until that point, 'Superbowl Week' would more than remedy that. I'd been around our Premiership team during a championship run, but nothing could have prepared me for this: two weeks of waiting for the big game, no real stories save those that could be manufactured to occupy the masses while they waited.

There was some quiet speculation in the locker room about what kinds of stories might be dug up. That the media might latch onto Mama's health and its effect on Vaughn had crossed everyone's mind, including Vaughn's. But he said he'd simply talk about what strength he had drawn from his mother's courage, and use it as an opportunity to plug the caliber of physicians at UPMC, as kind of a thank you. But we all hoped that he wouldn't have to talk about it at all, that his hometown status might inspire gentle handling from the media.

Others reckoned that the crossing paths of Baker and Holden would be the big story, as Baker had been an understudy to Holden earlier in his career, then they'd had something of a falling out and hadn't spoken much since. But that story lost its legs quickly, as neither coach had anything to say about the other that wasn't complimentary (in spite of considerable goading by reporters).

The only game-relevant Steelers story, as far as anyone could tell was the status of Ricky Wild, and Baker wasn't giving anything away, saying only that his rehab had gone well but that it would be a gametime decision.

On the Giants' side, the preseason assault acquittal of wide receiver Corey McElroy was rehashed, inspiring little interest, as it appeared that his accuser had no intention of pressing charges until he found out who the bloke was that broke his nose in the scrap at a Manhattan disco. Er . . . beg your pardon, night club; I'm told 'disco' became terribly 'uncool' in America by the early 80's. You are a funny lot. Shamefully, I was surprised to discover that McElroy was white, already falling for the stereotypes most prevalent in the media. But the tattoo-clad Syracuse 'bad boy' may have even gained popularity in New York as a result of the story.

No, the story that sparked the most excitement caught everyone, especially me, off guard. Took my shagging wind right out, in fact. It was Monday night. We'd had our first light practice in the Florida sun and a team meal in the hotel, catered by the Kenney family. We were all milling about like kids, going back and forth from room to room, admiring our Superbowl 'freebies' from all the sponsors (funny how excited millionaire athletes can get about free stuff). I had just finished sending an excited text message to Nivi, when Dillon leaned gravely into Justin's and my room.

"Y'all have ESPN on? You'd better see this, Mickey," Dillon insisted, quickly locating the remote and turning on the T.V. Mickey, Dillon, and Justin sat and watched the tail end of the report before Dillon found a local channel that was starting the story from the beginning. Mickey sat in stunned silence as the blonde-haired anchor addressed the camera.

"Well, it appears Superbowl week has its first controversy. Unnamed sources report that popular Steelers kicker, Mickey Doyle, had a relationship with alleged call girl, Stephanie Page, better known as 'Chantale'. The source claims that Page caters to the wants of Steel Town's business elite. The couple looks friendly here in this file footage from a Pittsburgh Pirates home game earlier in the year. Neither Doyle nor Page has commented on the allegation or whether their relationship was professional in nature.

"Because no one bloody asked me, you ditsy tart!" Mickey retaliated from the edge of the bed. "Bugger, shit, fuck, cunt, balls, bugger, bugger, and once more bugger," Mickey exclaimed, his face buried in his hands. "How many people will see this, DC?"

"Um, . . . this is headline news, dog. The media pack is hungry, . . . and um, . . . this shit is pretty juicy. Sorry, my brother, . . . it's Superbowl week," Dillon assessed accurately.

Minutes later, after several failed attempts to call and text Nivi before she could hear the story second hand, Mickey waited nervously on the elevator, heading up to Mr. Kenney's penthouse suite. When he walked out tentatively, he saw Kenney peering over the shoulder of the team's media attaché, Jason Price, who was playing another network's nearly identical airing of the story. Ross Killackey had greeted Mickey at the door and walked him in. Kenney watched the last few seconds of the streamed video then turned to Mickey.

"Mr Doyle," Kenney addressed him grandly, "can you shed some light on this for us?"

"Yes, sir. There's really not much to it, honestly," Mickey assured.

"Good. Well, let's hear it."

"Well, I met Chantale, er, . . . I suppose Stephanie at a strip club that I went to with a few of the lads," he began.

"Strip Club? Killackey is there anything about, . . . establishments like that in our player conduct agreement?"

"Not specifically, Mr. Kenney," Killackey answered quietly.

"Well, long as they're not dancing on the tables, I guess it's their own business. Anyway, Doyle, . . . met her at a strip club," Kenney prompted.

"Right, she was our hostess at the club, and she and I chatted a bit and got on quite well . . ."

"Got it on?" Kenney interrupted.

"Uh, no, *got on* well, sir. English expression, like *got along with*," he explained, choosing to leave out the lap dance.

"Oh, . . . alright. Then what?"

"Well sir, I didn't know many people in town and Ross gave me tickets to the Pirates game, so I asked if she'd like to go."

"Ball game? Alright. Hence the footage. Well did you know that she was a hooker?"

"No sir."

"So you didn't pay her for sex?"

"No sir."

"Well, not much of a story there, is there?" Kenney concluded, glancing back at Price's computer screen. "Pretty little thing though, isn't she?" he offered with a smirk.

"Well, I thought so sir. Taught me quite a lot about baseball too, as it happens," Mickey added.

"Probably best if you don't say so tomorrow, Mickey. Two many double entendres their, if you follow," Jason Price suggested from his seat.

"If you say so," Mickey agreed.

"Alrighty then," Kenney transitioned with a clap, "who wants scotch?" he asked, seemingly content that the team would not be smudged in any meaningful way. He poured two fingers for everyone but Price who declined, then put his hand on Mickey's shoulder.

"So, . . . learned all about baseball from a girl, Doyle?" Kenney snickered. "Well that's almost as embarrassing as the hooker."

Mickey barely slept that night, checking his phone interminably for some response from Nivi. Nothing. As the night passed, he imagined what assumptions she must have drawn, and how he must have fallen in esteem in her eyes. He felt as helpless as he had when he had waited for Nivi and Dr. Mason to resect Mama's tumour weeks earlier. And he was surprised at just how sad he was at the prospect of losing her, how intensely attached he was already, yet desperately distant from his new friend and lover. And the emotions swelled and twisted in his stomach as he tossed and turned.

In the morning, he tried twice more to reach her before heading down to breakfast. He sat down next to Vaughn with a small plate of eggs and a bowl of oatmeal. Vaughn shifted his plates over to make room. The table was silent except for the eating sounds until Vaughn could no longer bear it.

"Ain't no thing, dog," he assured. "Ain't nobody's business," he asserted, shaking a piece of bacon in the air. "But um, . . . how come you never told us you was tappin' that?" he finally asked with a chuckle.

"I only 'tapped that' once, mate, . . . and it's actually rather an embarrassing story, . . . if you must know," Mickey admitted.

"Well, uh, . . . we know a gentleman never tells, Ringo, . . . but um, . . . was it for money?" Dillon prodded with irritatingly bubbly curiosity.

"No, it wasn't for money," Mickey answered quietly.

"Yes! That's my man, y'all! Woo!" Dillon exalted as he jumped up on his chair. "Too much mojo in the Ringo, y'all!" he chimed, slapping Mickey on the shoulder and knocking the bite of egg off his fork. Then he turned his attention to Percy Dawkins who moped over his waffle. "I told you, Dawk! Pay up, fool!" he demanded and Dawkins slapped a bill into his hand.

"You're incorrigible, the lot of you," Mickey muttered, finally unable to fight off a smile.

"Thanks, dog," Dillon replied earnestly.

"Can I turn this up, Mick? Or do you want it off?" Jack Baum asked, gesturing with the remote when an update came on the T.V.

"It's alright, Jack. Might as well hear what she has to say," Mickey replied.

He felt annoyed as he watched the aggressive push of the media, a barrage of microphones thrust in her face. She looked even more delicate than he remembered.

"Are the allegations true about your occupation?"

"I'm a hostess in an adult club."

"Was the relationship with Mickey Doyle professional?"

"No."

"How would you characterize it?"

"He was an acquaintance."

"Are you still in contact with him?"

"No."

"Did you have sex with him?" Mickey held his breath as he watched.

"Mickey Doyle invited me to a baseball game. I went. We had a great time. End of story. He was a perfect gentleman," Page stated confidently then pushed her way through the crowd of reporters and into a car that was waiting.

Mickey felt both relieved that the story was not a publicity stunt on the part of Stephanie, and curiously protective of the woman who was really the first to take any interest in him since he had arrived, in spite of the awkward pretense that brought them together. But most of all, he hoped that he might somehow convince Nivi that the whole thing had been innocent in its origin, with momentum that could at least be understood. And he hoped that Nivi might see Stephanie's charm and humanity, as he had, though it was a lot to hope from a sound bite.

Media Day. Sun Life Stadium.

Jason Price had prepared the team for the Tuesday circus, or 'media day' as it was called. It was an all-access pass for the press to both teams, before, during, and after practice. After that, access would be limited until the day of the game. The players were simply asked to be themselves, be polite, and be as cooperative as they could. Privately, Mickey was told that he wouldn't be expected to take a beating, and could draw a line in the sand if necessary. Price didn't realize what he'd given license to.

As Mickey made his way up onto the platform, where numerous microphones were assembled for multiple players to be up at once, he recalled momentarily the bullying that Stephanie had endured on camera and he felt a pulse of anger as he sat down.

"Mickey, any comment on your relationship with Stephanie Page?" one began predictably.

"Sure. We went to a baseball game together, as friends. That's all," he answered simply.

"And . . . ," the reporter prompted.

"And regrettably, the Pirates lost, . . . as I recall, but the food was excellent," Mickey replied, deadpan, to the amusement of his teammates and most in attendance.

"Nothing more to add?" the reporter tried once more in disgust.

"Um, . . . yes, . . . 5-3 Cincinnati, I believe, . . . but you could probably check that online," he carried on the joke.

"Did you have sex with her?" another barked impatiently.

"I beg your pardon?" Mickey's eyes searched ferociously for the face from which the voice had come.

"I said, did the two of you have sex?"

"I heard you! I just can't believe the nerve of your question. What unimaginable guile. How about you? Did you shag your wife last night? No? Someone else? I mean *her*. Did *she* shag someone else? There. How's that? Seems a bit inappropriate when it's aimed at you, doesn't it?" Mickey charged, then added for good measure, "wanker."

No more questions not pertaining to football came Mickey's way on media day. However, his brief tirade made virtually every network, was on youtube within ten minutes of its happening, and would no doubt be tucked away in the archives to be used on a Sport Center 'Top 10 list' at some later date.

Before his return to the hotel, Mickey was commended by countless media folks for his handling of the questions, one veteran sports reporter calling it the most fun he'd had at a press conference in twenty years. But his spectacle had served as an effective smoke screen for the *real* show.

Ricky Wild had taken about a third of the reps at quarterback during practice, smiling and winking at the cameras. Then he sat patiently and answered numerous questions about his knee and his ability to play, particularly against a defense as potent as New York's. He told them that he felt great, was right on schedule, and believed he would be under the center by Sunday. Then he quietly changed and retreated to the bus, where he buckled over and finally revealed to all in his inner circle that he was in unimaginable pain, and the whole thing had been a show. The New York Giants would assemble and practice two different defensive game plans, one for each Steeler quarterback. Baker had doubled Holden's defensive preparation, thanks to a courageous show by his veteran pivot.

"Hi, Mickey," Nivi's quiet voice finally responded, nearly catching Mickey off guard, having called dozens of times.

"Oh God, Nivi, thank you for answering! Please, I just need to talk this out with you," Mickey sputtered.

"Just tell me the whole story, Mickey. Not the media version. I can't promise it will change how I'm feeling, but I will listen," Nivi conceded that much, really looking more for closure than reconciliation.

"Ok, . . . when spring training finished, I went with some of the lads to a strip club," Mickey began honestly.

He told her the whole story, including the lap dance that Stephanie had given under pressure from the others, the ball game, their return to her place, the awkward revelation of her occupation, and their continuation of what was in motion, on her initiative, that they both agreed to keep to themselves. After, knowing what he then knew, he made no attempts to contact her and knew that their relationship ended there.

"But you knew, Mickey. When you had sex with her, you knew that she was a prostitute! And you went ahead with it anyway!" Nivi charged.

"I'm . . . it's not something I'm proud of, Nivi! I've shamed myself over this for months, . . . not my finest moment, I know, . . ."

"Oh, you think?" Nivi interjected.

"But I'm not going to pretend that I could just shut it off at that point, Nivi, . . . when she carried on. I am human, and . . . I know you don't want to hear this, but she's very attractive, and she seduced me, Nivi. And I was far from home, was feeling lonely, and . . . it felt really good to be wanted that way, . . . in any way. Was I weak and . . . morally retarded once the wheels were in motion? Yes. I'm not denying that, . . ."

"Do you know how girls fall into that profession, Mickey? Did that occur to you for a second when all this happened?"

Mickey thought to himself that 'no, while she had him pinned against the wall with her tongue in his mouth, that had, in fact, *not* occurred to him', but managed not to say so out loud. Nivi continued, her tone rising.

"They're raped, Mickey, or exploited, extorted, made to feel that's all they have to offer the world! And have you stopped to think what you might have been exposed to? God, it just makes me cringe. And to think that we were together after that, Mickey! I feel dirty! Why should I have to feel that way?" Nivi broke into tears. Mickey apologized to her, over and over, tormented by the physical distance that separated them, though she would not have let him touch her if he was there with her.

"Well, however we leave this, Nivi . . . I am who you've gotten to know. I've never pretended to be someone I'm not. In fact, I feel more myself with you than with anyone else I've met here. Was I completely open about this? No. But I could barely admit it to myself, . . . or believe it for that matter," Mickey pleaded for understanding. She said nothing.

"Will you still come to Miami? To the game?" Mickey urged gently.

"I don't know, Mickey. And sit with your parents, and your best mate?"

"And Regina, and Cheryl, and Kay, and lots of others you've gotten to know pretty well," Mickey added.

"I don't know, Mickey," Nivi repeated assertively. Mickey relented.

"If I come, I come. But please don't try to see me, Mickey."

"Understood. I just . . . in spite of everything, it would mean a lot to me if you were there." Nivi was quiet again, so Mickey closed, "Good night, Nivi. Thanks for talking."

"Goodbye, Mickey."

She said 'goodbye'. Bugger. I'd had my chance to clear the air, but it sure sounded like goodbye. The most complete and remarkable woman I'd ever been with. Well, possibly a tad more judgmental and unforgiving than a bloke might have hoped for but . . . oh, who am I kidding? When the harshest criticism you can come up with for a bird is 'a bit judgmental of the lads who sleep with prostitutes' you know she's a keeper. I'd really bloody blown it.

The League hosted receptions for each of the teams and their families on Friday night. It would be the last chance to see them before the game, as the players would be shielded from all distractions from Friday night on.

Mickey could barely contain himself on the elevator ride down, knowing that his parents, Abbey and Jeffrey would be in attendance. The team congregated outside the ballroom so that the commissioner could announce their entrance.

When the team walked in, to the applause of their loved ones, Mickey saw the beaming face of his father, Ole Shanty, already with a bit of a glow on, partly from the sun, partly from the free drinks. Beside him was the slender Elizabeth, her smile less 'cheeky', but just as warm, more thrilled to see her son than she was wrapped up in the grandness of the event. Mickey took them both in his arms and squeezed, burying his face between their heads to conceal his tears. Miraculously, southern Florida suddenly felt like home. Elizabeth dabbed his eyes with a tissue from her purse, then her own.

"Hey, I was told there'd be no sissies in this crowd," Abbey's voice came from behind. Mickey turned to greet her, and saw that she was equally moved by the reunion. She gave him a big hug and kissed his cheek. Then Mickey held his hand out to Jeffrey who ignored it and gave him a hug of equal scale.

"Ah, look at me," Mickey sputtered self-consciously, "I'm undone." Elizabeth passed him another tissue.

"I can't believe you play with these lads, Mickey," Shanty began, looking around, "they're bloody gigantic!"

"Well, I'm something of a specialty player, not really right in the trenches," Mickey admitted.

"Still, . . . must take a good pair to step on the field with 'em," Shanty commended.

"Thanks, Dad," Mickey replied, suddenly a little nervous about his father's casual vernacular.

"Now come along, lad. Let your old man buy you a drink."

"The drinks are free here, dad," Mickey informed.

"I know, son," he admitted, slapping his boy on the shoulder, "just wasn't sure if you knew," he laughed.

"We'll be right back," Mickey looked over his shoulder with a smile.

"Oh, we're fine. Go on with your father, dear; he's missed you something awful," Elizabeth shooed him.

"Now then, son," Shanty began, once they were out of earshot, "about this prostitute, . . ."

"Oh, God, . . . Dad, . . . I didn't know she was a prostitute, and please keep your voice down."

"Then you didn't pay her to have sex?"

"No, Dad."

"Oh, . . . well that's good then, . . . but uh, did you, uh, . . . ?" Shanty made a tiny pumping motion with his fist.

"For Christ sake, Dad, is this really the time?" Mickey defended, looking around.

"Easy lad, now I'm the one that has to reassure your mum about this stuff. Tell the man what he needs to know," he insisted.

Mickey took a deep breath to compose himself, then looked at his father and nodded.

"And she gave it to you for free?" Shanty snickered guiltily. Mickey only pursed his lips impatiently.

"Oh, well done, lad; she was one sexy lass. Saw her on the telly," he continued.

"On the telly? Back home?" Mickey queried. "So Mum knows?"

"Oh son, everyone with a telly knows, I'm afraid. It's alright, lad, . . . everyone at the Anchor was quite impressed, in actual fact."

"Oh God, make it stop," Mickey rubbed his face and turned away.

"Now hold on, son. One more thing," Shanty turned him back around.

"What? What?!" Mickey prompted impatiently.

"You, uh, . . . you did use a condom, eh lad?" Shanty raised his brow. Another slow breath. "Yes."

"Right then. No harm, no foul, eh," Shanty clapped his hands together. "Now what are we drinkin'?"

"Anything."

Mickey was mindful the whole evening about Nivi's absence. He knew she wouldn't come, but hoped so all the same. But the evening was still very pleasant. Too pleasant not to enjoy on account of her not being there. His mum and dad, Abbey and Jeffrey, here in America to see him. The daydream he'd had about this moment before he even left England had nothing on the reality. And although nothing was said, Mickey quietly hoped to himself when he noticed that Abbey hadn't had anything to drink.

The Doyles were a hit with all the other players and their families, charmed by the reserved charisma of Elizabeth, delighted by the unabashed joy of Shanty. Mama Sellers, Elizabeth, and Abbey talked long after the players had been sent off to bed. Mickey would find out much later that Shanty and Mr. Kenney sat in the lounge together until nearly 2:00am, finishing a bottle of $500 scotch.

The players were still talking about how much fun 'Papa Doyle' was on the bus to the walk through the following day.

"Hey, Ringo, how come yo' daddy gots a different accent from you?" Vaughn asked.

"Oh, right. Still a ring o' the Isle in 'em, eh," Mickey answered.

"A hm a the wha?" Dillon prompted, looking confused.

"A ring of the Isle, DC. The Island. Dad came from Ireland over thirty years ago and still sounds like a Dubliner," he explained.

"Wouldn't it wear off after that long," Branch supposed.

"Not if you don't want it to," Mickey answered simply, then snickered to himself, recalling how offended he had been when Abbey had accused him of sounding American a month or so before. He had consciously preserved his own accent ever since.

After their walk through, the players watched a set of ominous rain clouds roll in. The forecast had called for light rain in the evening, sunny for the rest of the weekend. But the drizzle started late afternoon, intensifying in the evening, and it would not stop until early Monday morning. Mickey double-checked that his 'boot bag' contained all the lengths of cleats that he might want, then was lulled to sleep by the patter of the rain, his window cracked to let the sound massage his psyche.

Superbowl Sunday.

Chatter came from the usual suspects during the pregame, with Vaughn characteristically pumping up his teammates.

"Whassup, hogs? O-Line ready to roll? Lookin' big y'all! Lookin' hungry. Let's move some folks out there," he bobbed his head. The whole front-five nodded.

"Show-time, Theo," from Dillon, "air and ground attacks both ready to go!" Branch smiled, looking focused and ready as the two athletes touched fists.

Some players were quieter than usual, others more rambunctious, but all were steeped in the adrenaline of a championship game. Concerted efforts were made to stay as even as possible, but it's a losing battle in the tsunami of Superbowl hype. The best that they could hope for was some early success to bolster confidence and calm their nerves.

Light rain made the whole stadium glisten, contributing to the bright, surrealism of the event. But the field seemed to be draining well, in spite of the downpour, the well-irrigated natural turf accommodating the flow.

Both teams introduced their defenses, a statement about what they felt their success would hinge on. But both offenses were peppered with game breakers. One of them stood deep after the Steelers won the toss. DeMarco Sands would try to give his team early momentum on the return.

The Giants' kicker drove the opening kick-off to Sands at the 4-yard line. Sands blasted out of the blocks like a sprinter, paused, waiting for the wedge to penetrate the cover team, then lowered his head trying to salvage what yards he could when the wedge collapsed. He was dragged down at the 21-yard line.

First down. Branch handed off to Dillon who exploded off the heels of Hollweg into a hole that sealed quickly. Gain of two. Second down bore no fruit as a hitch to wide receiver, Zack Jones, skipped short, Branch trying to pull it back after he saw the quick jump of the New York corner. Mickey took a couple of easy punts into his net, getting comfortable with his footing.

Third down, Branch dropped into the pocket looking downfield for Sands. Around the corner on his blindside came the Giants' free safety, unblocked on the blitz, planting his helmet in the middle of Branch's back and jarring the ball free. Giants defensive end, Cornelius Carr scooped it up and rambled into the endzone to the roar of the New York supporters.

Branch rolled onto his back and stayed down, to the horror of the Steeler bench. Wild thought for a moment that he would be forced to hobble out and take the reigns, but Branch slowly got to his feet and shuffled to the sideline, seeming only to have been winded. Convert is good. 7-0 New York.

The two defenses dominated the remainder of the first quarter, chasing the offenses from the field with airtight proficiency. Dillon was never given a chance to get his thick hindquarters rumbling. And Branch searched in vain for open receivers, finding none. But Vaughn and the Steeler front four were equally stifling, with Vaughn drawing the double team on nearly every play, but making plays anyway. New York's quarterback, UCLA standout Blake Ramsey, launched a sixty yard bomb to McElroy, but Bo Townsend tapped it away easily, running stride for stride with the Giant's dangerous deep threat.

Mickey was winning the battle of the punters, comfortable in his toothy soccer boots. He stepped onto the field yet again and stood at his own 40. The snap was perfect, in spite of the wet ball, and he stroked another bomb deep into New York territory.

McElroy fielded the ball deftly over his shoulder and hustled upfield, trying to catch up with the return that had been set up. Mickey shuffled sideways, playing the angle of the return man. His heart pounded in his chest as he saw McElroy emerge through the cover team, his knees driving powerfully.

Keep him to the outside, force him to the sideline, Mickey heard coach Jardine in his head. He took the angle and moved his feet as quickly as they would go, forcing the speedy return man to the sideline. McElroy froze him with a head fake and cut back, but Mickey managed to wrap his arms around him and spun him around, on the strength of his adrenaline. With the added shove of JD Coleman in pursuit, McElroy was thrown deep into the Steeler bench, then jumped up in anger. He thrust both hands to the mask of Mickey, knocking him back, before a protective Vaughn Sellers clothes lined the volatile return man flat on his back.

McElroy and Sellers received offsetting major penalties once the two sides were separated, but the game was quickly taking on the feel of a street fight. A fired up Vaughn singlehandedly stuffed two running attempts up the gut, then hurried Ramsey to a throw that went well over the head of his intended target. Vaughn liked the 'street fight' just fine.

Branch and the sputtering Steeler offense then went to work. If the stubborn Giant defense was only going to give them inches, then inches would have to do. Short, ball control passes to Jefferson, Jones, and Sands gave Branch confidence that he could thread the needle, and the legs of Dillon Carmichael started to roll. The offense slowly chiseled their way downfield, before stalling just inside the New York thirty. Out came Mickey for his first attempt on the wet field. It would come from 45 yards out.

He trusted in the mental quiet of his routine, broken only momentarily by the loud chant of 'Ringo', the nickname that had stuck with the Steeler nation. He smiled in spite of himself, then split the uprights surely. 7-3 Giants.

But Blake Ramsey and the Giant offense answered with a fine-tuned two-minute drill, striking twice to McElroy for gains of 18 and 24 yards, offset with bullets to two other New York targets. They lined up on the Steeler 20 with 30 seconds still to play in the half. Ramsey dropped into the pocket, his offensive line holding the ferocious Pittsburgh pass rush at bay. McElroy curled neatly into a seam in the defense and Ramsey fired a rocket low and through the seam. But the lightning feet of Manny Bunch tore up the soaking turf as he scrambled to the open receiver, diving, and picking the heavy pass out of the air. Interception. He stayed down in the endzone. The Steelers regained possession.

Deep in their end, with 20 seconds to play, the Steelers erred on the side on caution. Branch took a knee to end the half. Still 7-3 for the NFC Champs.

"Four point game y'all, and we just gettin' started," Vaughn reassured as he toweled off his wet head in the locker room.

"Nice recovery, Theo," Hollweg credited. "You're finding your rhythm, baby; I can feel it," Hollweg pumped up the young field general.

"Great leg, Ringo!" Dillon chimed from nearby. A dry Justin Merritt, who had watched the half from under his poncho, patted Mickey on the knee, sitting next to him quietly.

"Threw that McElroy punk down nice too, baby! I liked that shit!" Percy Dawkins approved.

"Probably saved a score too," Coleman further praised.

The mood in the room was decidedly upbeat, despite the small deficit. They knew they would have their hands full, but they were starting to feel the momentum shifting. They eagerly awaited the start of the next half, like horses in the chute. Whether it was the vibe in the room or his damp uniform or both, Mickey shivered, drinking up the electricity. He would get to take that energy out on the ball to start the second half.

Again the speedy McElroy lined up in his own end zone, wagging his head side to side confidently. Mickey again drove the ball into the end zone, and yet again the Giants standout elected to run it out. JD Coleman broke through the wedge and met McElroy head on. The impact seemed to freeze everyone for a moment before it registered that the elusive McElroy had spun off the collision and bolted back upfield. Three critical blocks at the head of the spear, and Mickey saw the same daylight that McElroy did, from the other side of the hole.

Mickey knew instinctively that if he waited for McElroy to come to him then McElroy would simply run around him, exploiting the speed mismatch. So he scrambled to fill the hole before it could split wide open. For an instant, he looked like a miniature Percy Dawkins, squaring up with the ball carrier. Mickey drove his shoulders into McElroy who dropped his head, coming at Mickey with a head of steam. Mickey felt a piercing pain in his shoulder as McElroy drove through him. The hole quickly filled and McElroy was brought down by a gang of tacklers.

McElroy popped up and stepped over the injured kicker, trash-talking him as he did. "Stay down, bitch."

Coleman was in McElroy's face immediately, triggering yet another scrum around the provocative receiver. Meanwhile, Mickey still lay on the field, his legs moving side to side. The trainers hustled to his side to assess the damage.

A few minutes later, they helped an uncomfortable Mickey Doyle to his feet and walked him off the field, helping him to support his left arm. Butch Jardine took a heavy, troubled breath, then turned to Justin Merritt and Davey Carle, who sat together in the rain at the end of the bench.

"Start movin' around a bit, fellas. You're on."

After walking out to greet Mickey and console him, Coach Baker walked past Merritt and stopped, looking him in the eyes and saying, "You'll win this thing for us if you get the chance. I know you will." Justin nodded in acknowledgement, then started his mini sideline warm-up.

Mickey wore a look of despair on his face, laced with agony, both physical and emotional. That he would not be able to help his team for the balance of the game tormented him, but he gathered himself, cut the examination short, and walked over to Justin and Davey, who converged on him in concern. Mickey put on his bravest face and addressed both of them at once.

"Hey lads, you taught me everything I know. Bring it home," he instructed with the closest he could come to a smile.

"You got it, baby," back from Justin, "and hey, . . . gutsiest play I ever saw by a kicker, bro."

"True dat," Carle agreed, in colloquial that he couldn't really pull off.

"Thanks, mate," Mickey replied before having to catch his breath when another wave of pain hit him and nearly turned his stomach.

On the field, the Giants seemed inspired by McElroy's thunderous hit. Their hulking runner, Cole "Train" Weathers was gaining momentum, his 260 lbs. becoming harder and harder to stop as the footing deteriorated. New York started to munch their way into Steeler territory unspectacularly, on the weight of Weathers and his unheralded offensive line. They moved like a glacier deep into the red zone, before Weathers caught a flare in the flats and literally walked into the end zone. 14-3 Giants.

Meanwhile, in the locker room, Doc Maitland managed to get Mickey's shoulder pads off before ripping a hole in his shirt, cleaning a spot on his skin, and freezing the injured area with a needle.

"Pretty sure your collarbone's broken, Mickey, but this will do the trick until the painkillers take hold."

"Thanks, Doc."

Maitland carefully wrapped a sling around Mickey to support his arm, then gently pulled a poncho over his head.

"Go on, son. Go cheer on 'the lads'," Maitland said with a smile. Mickey returned the smile and walked back down the corridor and back onto the field. He returned to the cheers of the crowd and a bit a jeering from a few boisterous New York supporters, which he easily ignored.

Branch and the Steeler offense faced 3rd and 8 from their own 23.

"Come on TB, lead the way mate! Find a way!" Mickey called from the otherwise quiet Steeler bench.

He looked around at his teammates and prodded them along. "Come on lads! We're not finished yet. Chins up!"

"Yeah, baby," Vaughn responded, dropping his oxygen mask and getting up off the bench. "Come on, O! Showtime, y'all!"

Branch caught the shotgun snap and took a couple of steps back. Despite lots of time to throw, the Giants secondary covered the receivers like a blanket. The pocket collapsed, and the Giants' rush converged like a pack of lions on Branch. But Branch ducked under one defender, shook off a tackle, and straight-armed yet another as his agile feet carried him out of harm's way and into open field. His running room closed up quickly and he was met aggressively by all-pro linebacker, Matt Bix, before spinning and grinding forward, close to the first down marker.

All the Steelers players, their fans, and the continental Steeler nation (including a small faithful in the city of Liverpool) held their collective breath while the chains were brought out. As they expired, they were simultaneously inspired by the ray of hope, as the officials signaled for a first down.

Mickey led the cheering loudly on the sideline, swimming in a fog of adrenaline and narcotics. And the offense responded. As Weathers had, Dillon was now wearing down the Giant defense, smashing violently into and over any defender in his path. Five yards up the gut. Eight yards on the pitch. Four more off-tackle. A twelve yard curl to Jefferson. An eight yard slant to Sands. The Steelers slugged their way into New York territory.

On first down, Branch faked to Carmichael and bootlegged out, looking downfield. He rifled a pass to Sands deep downfield, then hopped on the spot holding his helmet as it appeared the ball would sail over his target. But the fifth gear of DeMarco Sands kicked in, and his outstretched hands deftly corralled the wet ball. He high-stepped into the end zone to the deafening roar of the crowd and launched himself up to the first row where a throng of Steeler supporters, adorned with Steeler jerseys and wet, runny black and gold face paint, hugged and patted him before he dropped down onto the field to be mobbed by his teammates. Mickey jumped around wildly on the sideline, high-fiving everyone within a ten yard radius with his good arm. Merritt easily converted, stepping back into his role. 14-10 Giants.

But the tide swung slowly and uncomfortably again, as Weathers and the New York offense picked up where they left off, chewing up hard yardage against the tired but determined Steeler defense. But now the quarterback, Ramsey, was finding little gaps in the secondary and pecked like a vulture with five and ten yards strikes. The Steeler defense would bend but not break, and they forced the Giants to 4th down, just outside the 10-yard line. The Giants' kicker punched the short field goal through. 17-10 New York.

Theo Branch had a hint of Ricky Wild in his step as he stepped confidently under the center to start the drive. He knew the New York defense was also growing tired and barked signals assertively and changed the play at the line, detecting an overload to one side. Dillon took the pitch and accelerated around the outside, picking up 9 before flattening the Giants' strong safety on his way out of bounds. Twelve yards to Sands on the sideline. Another 14 to Jones on a crossing route.

Then on first down, Carmichael and Branch collided in the backfield, so Branch turned up the hole where Carmichael was supposed to go. He was met immediately by two New York linebackers, twisting his back to them. Coach Baker's heart nearly stopped as he watched Branch shovel the ball in traffic to Carmichael who motored to the sideline and around the corner, outrunning the angle and speeding into the Giants' end. The pursuant defenders pushed and tugged at the straight arm of Carmichael but he held them at bay, refusing to go down until he was finally shoved out inside the 10-yard line.

On first down, Branch exploited a panting Giant defense with a torpedo to Sands in the corner of the end zone. Sands flipped the ball to the official then raised his hands to the heavens, beckoning the rain on his face theatrically, fueling the frenzy of the crowd.

Branch smiled sheepishly at Coach Baker, who didn't fight too hard to conceal his own smile.

"You're Goddam lucky that worked, Theo."

Merritt converts again. 17-all.

Now all eyes turned to the clock as the Giants' offense took the field after a short return by McElroy. Under three minutes remained. Sellers looked to the crowd pumping his massive arms in the air, urging them to get louder. They obliged. On first down, Sellers again beat the double team and stuffed the run to his side. On second down, the defense strung out Weathers' carry to the outside and dragged him down with no gain. 3rd and 11.

Ramsey dropped into the pocket, his O-line buying him lots of time to throw. He pumped to the sideline, then aired the ball out, deep down field. McElroy had half a step on Townsend that he closed as the slightly underthrown ball came down. Townsend's arm came down hard on the arms of McElroy as the ball arrived, knocking it safely out of play. An incensed Corey McElroy pleaded vehemently to the official, then relented when he saw the flag thrown, nodding and clapping in the face of Townsend. Baker sprinted towards the nearest official, restrained by one of his assistants, enraged by the call. The crowd groaned as they watched what appeared to be perfect timing on Bo Townsend's part. But the call was not reviewable, and the Giants had a first down at the Steelers' 22-yard line.

The Pittsburgh defense again pinned their ears back and stuffed the Giants on first and second down. The whole stadium watched the clock tick down to the two-minute warning. Ramsey jogged to the sideline to confer with his offensive coordinator and Coach Holden. They would no doubt keep the ball on the ground and in the middle of the field to set their kicker up for a 37-yard attempt, minus whatever yards they gained on the play. But 37 yards was far from automatic, especially on this soaking turf. So Manny Bunch pleaded emphatically for his unit to 'play it honest', staying ready for anything that might be thrown at them.

Ramsey took the snap, took a two-step drop and fired a pass to McElroy on the slant. Townsend got a great jump and tried to make a play on the ball. McElroy somehow got both hands on it, but bobbled it momentarily, and had a loose grip on the ball. Townsend ripped his hand down hard through McElroy's arms and wrestled the ball from him. McElroy dragged him down before again pleading his case with the referee for an interference call. But this time there were no flags. Bo Townsend was redeemed. The Steeler offense would take over from their own 15 with 1:50 to play.

Mickey's freezing had long since worn off, but he was nearly oblivious to the pain, drunk on the adrenaline of his team's surge. His voice was starting to fail him, as he had been abusing it for the whole half of play. But he carried on anyway.

Carmichael and fullback, Jack Baum, put their pass block hats on. If they were to get Merritt a shot. It would be through the air. Branch threw incomplete to Jones, then hit Sands for twenty in the middle of the field, the clock continuing to run. Incomplete to Jefferson, then 14 to Jones on the sideline. As the clock ticked down inside of a minute, Branch looked downfield then dumped off to Baum, who raced for 11 more before being dragged down in bounds.

Baker used one of their remaining timeouts with 34 seconds on the clock. The ball sat on the Giants' 40, well out of Merritt's range. And the steady downpour mocked them, daring an attempt from any distance. Merritt continued to kick into his net, Mickey pinning with his good arm, peppering Merritt with affirmation.

"Nice stroke, mate"; "Money"; "Automatic, mate".

Branch dropped back in the pocket, pumped downfield, then scurried through a small opening in the pass rush and downfield. A crushing block by Jones coming back bought him a little more space and he kept his feet going, the crowd of blockers pushing the pile forward. The gain was 16 yards. Carmichael carried up the gut for no gain, but the clock ran down to 6 seconds and Baker used their last timeout.

Merritt and the field goal team came onto the field. Merritt set up, his routine very similar to Mickey's. The attempt would come from 41 yards out. Both teams lined up. Merritt nodded coolly to Branch. Predictably, the Giants used their last timeout in an attempt to ice Merritt. He walked calmly to the huddle and continued to play his kick in his head, his breathing deep and slow to manage his nerves.

They lined up again. Branch handled the low snap skillfully and pinned it. Merritt knew the moment he stroked it. He sprinted to the sideline to his kicking partner, Mickey, who wrapped his one arm around him as time expired and the kick split the uprights. The Steelers had won the Superbowl.

Mickey was lifted off the ground by a delirious Vaughn Sellers. He nearly passed out from the pain as his unstable shoulder was shaken, then fell into his friend's arms and wrapped his right arm around his massive teammate.

"We did it, Ringo! We did it! We Superbowl champs, baby! We mufuggin' Superbowl champs!" Vaughn shouted hysterically, looking to the sky and closing his eyes. Mickey started to well up when he saw tears squeeze from the closed eyes of his dear friend, though he was probably already close to tears from the pain of Vaughn's hug.

"We did it, mate," Mickey agreed. "You were brilliant, mate. Absolutely brilliant," he commended.

"Nah, *we* was brilliant, dog! All of us was brilliant!" Vaughn corrected.

Whether it was the mix of Percocet and alcohol, I don't know, but I was quiet and reflective for most of the celebration. I had never felt so happy in my life. The interesting thing was, in the end, my role was a familiar one: moral support from the sideline. But curiously, this time it didn't matter. It didn't matter a fig what part I had played. All that mattered was that I felt a part of something very special, something much larger than myself. The joy in the faces of my teammates filled up and nourished my soul completely. It was about us, an entity that I became indistinguishable from on this day.

Me dad and I sat into the wee hours with Killackey, and a raucous group of Steeler supporters who had actually **bussed** to the game, completely bloody hammered for the whole weekend. What was most remarkable was that they were all as happy as I was, as we were. The Steeler faithful live and die by their team. A good portion of the hope, exhilaration, and heartbreak that they experience in their lives hinges on the successes and failures or their team. At a distance, it looks a bit pathological, I'll admit. But on that night, I was simply honoured to be a part of it.

Inevitably, my evening ended with intense vomiting, the retching of which further inflamed my injured shoulder. And I woke to complete agony, as both the booze and the drugs had worn off completely. It was in the cold sweat of the morning that it hit me how much I wished I could have shared it with Nivi. She had gone to the game after all, but Abbey decided not to fill me in on their limited conversation until the celebration was over.

I was admittedly put off when I realized that I had somehow ended up on the floor, while two unconscious naked women were wrapped around a snoring Dillon Carmichael in **my** bed. Ah, piss it. He was me mate.

12

Wherever you go, go with all your heart.
~ Confucius

Despite my parents' urging, I decided to stay in Pittsburgh until the end of March. That way I could be treated by the team physicians and physios and make sure my shoulder healed completely. There also was the question of what team management would decide about the following season. If there were discussions to be had, I preferred that they be in person, not over the phone.

I wasn't holding out much hope about Nivi. I hadn't heard from her and hadn't tried to reach her, per her request. Abbey had sat next to her at the game for four hours. She said that Nivi had been perfectly nice to her and said she'd heard a lot about her, but whenever Abbey had tried nonchalantly to talk about me, Nivi had not engaged. Abbey did say that she was visibly upset when I got hurt, but that seemed like a flimsy foundation for hope.

Most importantly, I was determined to see through at least one critical step with Mama and her family: the three-month follow-up. She'd had a chest CT the day before and Dr. Mason would discuss the findings with the radiologist and see us in his clinic.

It should not have surprised me, but it was Nivi who greeted us and saw us into the examining room. She was kind and professional, and didn't seem the least bit uncomfortable around me, which I took to mean she'd come to her own peace with the whole thing. For that much, I was glad.

Then the relief. Both Dr. Mason and Nivi cautioned us that it was still early, but the news was as good as it could be. Her CT was clean. No sign of cancer anywhere. And her blood work corroborated that finding. Three months out, Mama appeared to be cancer-free.

Again the whole room seemed to exhale. Mama, Papa Sellers, Vaughn and I were all smiles. Both doctors seemed genuinely thrilled to deliver the tentatively *good news, like we'd fed their most basic reason for getting into medicine in the first place. Nivi gave Mama a big hug, without the slightest bit of awkwardness about the doctor-patient boundary. She was highly invested. Mama was very much her friend too. It warmed me to see it.*

"Well then, I'm taking the lot of you to lunch. Where to, Mama?" Mickey announced with a clap. "Anywhere you want to go."

"Oh how about just some place close, like the *Panera* down the hill," Mama suggested, not wanting to be fussed over.

"Doctors, can we buy you a bite since we're dining nearby?" Mickey took a chance.

"Thanks, Mickey, but we've got a pretty full clinic," Mason declined politely for both of them.

"Of course. Thought I'd ask all the same," Mickey conceded. "Right then, let's let the good doctors get back to it," he moved the group along.

As they were making their way slowly and happily down the hall, Mickey heard Nivi's voice behind them.

"Mickey," she called. He dared not hope, but his heart jumped all the same.

"We'll meet you down there, dog," Vaughn said with a wink.

"Yes?", Mickey answered as he turned to Nivi. "Don't worry, I won't come back and bother you over your tuna sandwich again," he joked nervously. Nivi's laugh revealed a nervous tension of her own. She crossed her arms and leaned against the wall, then looked him in the eyes.

"I was wondering if you'd like to go to a baseball game," she suggested warmly.

"Well now, hold on, . . . you just . . . had better know in advance what I do for a living," the kidder in him again held trump.

"Oh, and what's that?" she laughed, going along.

"Um, . . . I kick a ball," he said modestly.

"Oh, really, . . . sounds complicated," she teased.

"Horribly sometimes, . . . but mostly not at all."

"How's your shoulder?" she asked sympathetically.

"Almost better. Thanks for coming to the game," he offered.

"Well I wasn't about to miss that, was I? The ladies here would never forgive me." Then she grew serious, "Mickey, I knew I'd see you in a couple of months, so I had time to think, time to reflect," she started, looking down shyly.

"And?" Mickey prompted cautiously.

"And, . . . you were right. Since I've known you, you've been a perfect gentleman, a perfect friend, . . . minus that one little secret that was aired around the globe," she tacked on playfully.

"Well, . . . thank you," he accepted that much.

"And there are reasons why that was such a sore spot for me, . . . which I can tell you in time, . . . but I'd like to have another go, . . . if you're planning on sticking around," she qualified.

"That's fantastic, Nivi," he began excitedly, "but um . . . well, that's not entirely in my control, as you probably know."

"I know, but part of it is," she reminded.

"Right," he said quietly, reflecting.

"Well, you'd better catch up with the Sellers," she said to close, knowing that she'd said her part, respecting his need to digest it. She stepped in close to him and kissed him softly on the lips, then held his hand with both of hers. "If you call me, . . . I'll answer," she concluded.

"Lovely," he smiled, "then I will."

Mickey walked into Ross Killackey's office slowly.

"Ringo," Killackey greeted warmly.

"Rosco," Mickey barked back playfully.

"Have a seat, buddy," Ross insisted, gesturing towards the chair opposite his. Though his father had suggested he play his cards close to his chest, Mickey had been completely transparent with Killackey. What Mickey had decided was that his reasons for wanting to stay in the US were rooted in the relationships he'd formed, not in a particular desire to remain in the NFL. So if he was not going to be in Pittsburgh, he did not want to start the whole process again. He would return to Liverpool.

Across the Atlantic, bad news had come, with a huge silver lining for Mickey. Harold Sheffield had sustained a career-ending knee injury. But he was immediately offered the coaching job with the U20 club team and had accepted. No sooner had he accepted, than he called Mickey to ask if he would take the venture on with him. It was a great fit, one that tugged hard at Mickey.

"So here's the scenario, Mick," Killackey began, "Green Bay is interested in Justin to the pitch of a first rounder," he explained, "which would help us a lot if we get the kid we're after, and it helps us with the cap if we could sign you for less than what he was making." Killackey turned a contract offer on his desk for Mickey to see: 1.6 million dollars per season, plus bonuses, for three years. "But I need to know, . . . if I pull the trigger on the Justin thing, will you sign?"

"Mickey sat on a plane bound for London, with a connection to Liverpool. He seemed very content, and sat staring at the empty window seat beside him.

"Oh, you're back," he said to Nivi, who returned from the lavatory, and he got up to let her in to her seat.

"So what exactly does a Godfather do?" Mickey started. "Vaughn and I watched all three movies and they didn't help a bit," he joked.

"Oh, perfect," she laughed, "Coppola flicks and prostitutes," she teased, "lovely foundation."

"Tweet. Offside," Mickey defended himself.

"Sorry, love. Couldn't resist. I *know* you understand," she added with a kiss.

"So we're staying with Abbey and Jeffrey, Christening is tomorrow, then we're on our own for the rest of the week?" she checked.

"Well, not exactly. I'll have to fit a spot o' training in there somewhere, and of course, my whole family is dying to meet you."

"Whole family," Nivi repeated. "Smashing," she added sarcastically.

"Oh they're not that bad," Mickey insisted. "Then it's you and me in London for two full days," he promised.

"That I like," Nivi affirmed, not really dreading the rest.

"Then I've got a week back in the 'Burgh to tune up for camp," Mickey added, already preparing himself for the coming season.

Funny thing, life. About the time you figure out who you want to be, what you think you want, and where you think your home is, you get a good shake that teaches you that you were that person already, you had it all along, and that home, as they say, is where the heart is.

And for now, my heart is with Vaughn Sellers, the behemoth that almost killed me on Day 1, then let me into his life and that of his remarkable family. To Dillon Carmichael, who blesses us all everyday with his spontaneous joy, his humour, and who is already excited about the new Penguins season, though I'm sworn not to say so. To Manny Bunch, who opened his mind to me, and eventually his heart. And to the lovely Nivedita Sahay, the Indian-born, British-educated, US resident surgeon that makes me feel at home wherever I am. Who for now doesn't realize that she's far too good for me. But perhaps by the time she figures it out, she'll be past letting go.

Some blokes can't run that fast. But in the end, perhaps it changes them in ways that allow them to find themselves, and to find true happiness.